To Con a Gentleman

SARAH ADAMS

To Chris,
my love and inspiration.

This book wouldn't be here without you.

Chapter One

London, 1815

It was time to go, but Rose couldn't leave yet. She stood there facing her rented flat of two weeks that only a few days earlier she had thought was dingy. Now that it was time to leave the place she couldn't help but think it was quaint and charming and homey and other words that people used when they wanted to make a place sound more wonderful than it was. But honestly, it was just small and musty.

Sunlight slipped in through the single window, illuminating the heavy clouds of dust in the air. Even if the light had not attested to the apartment's age and outdated mode, the smell certainly did. No amount of beating the curtains or airing the place out seemed to cure it of its heavy scent of neglect. And yet, here she stood, unwilling to look away from the place she had temporarily called home.

Why must she put herself through this after every job? It would be easier to just turn around and walk away without looking back. Instead, her feet felt cemented to the floor, keeping her from moving on. She felt an odd tug of emotion from somewhere deep within her she didn't like, couldn't name, and really just wished it would go away. She had been feeling it more and more lately. It made her feel incapable of not taking the last few moments in every rented room or apartment to look around and imagine—for just one fleeting moment—what it would be like if she stayed.

Time stretched for a moment as she stood still and allowed herself to imagine a different outcome. She pictured herself unpacking her worn valise and placing her few dresses into the oak wardrobe in the corner. She would trade out the dust in the empty vase on the table for a bundle of colorful flowers and try her best to remember to refill the water when it looked low. When friends came over for a dinner party, they would all comment on the beauty and vibrancy of her flowers and insist on learning the secret to their longevity. Or would they? Rose didn't know exactly what close friends discussed at dinner parties because she had never allowed herself to have friends. And as for loved ones, well…Papa had been gone thirteen years now. All of this dreaming was really a useless waste of time.

She wouldn't stay. She never did. Rose would continue to live her life the way she always had and the way she preferred it — alone.

The door behind her flew open and slammed into the wall, causing the dusty vase to teeter on the entry table. She lunged and caught the vase just as Uncle Felix rumbled into the room, tripping over Rose's valise and practically trampling the poor old piece of luggage.

So, maybe she wasn't completely alone.

"Blast!" he said leaning over his increasingly round stomach to pick up her valise.

Rose pursed her lips together to hold off the smile tugging at her mouth. The man had become quite clumsy in his old age, though he would likely give her a fine trimming if he knew she had ever thought of him as old. But this incident alone only solidified Rose's decision to keep him on the planning side of their operation rather than join her on the performance side.

"Rosie girl, I don't suppose you have a bit of that good Burgundy left that we swiped from the Pinkerton's ball, do you?"

"I would," she said, letting her gaze rest heavily on his round wrinkled face, "if you hadn't drunk it all the very night I brought it home. But no, I don't suppose you would remember that, seeing as how you were drunk as a wheelbarrow."

"Aye! I remember now—" Somehow his Scottish brogue always intensified when he smiled. "You can hardly blame a man for enjoying a fine drink."

"No, but I can blame you for singing those Scottish drinking songs at the top of your lungs throughout the night. I'm not sure if you or I had a worse headache the next day." The fact that in the eleven years she'd worked with the man, the worst thing he had ever done when in his cups was sing loud tavern songs spoke volumes of his character. Well, that and the time he'd thrown his boots in a pond. Wading up to her knees to fetch them had been rather annoying. Annoying and cold.

His thick brows pulled together. "If we don't have anything to drink, what are we doing kicking our heels in here?"

"Nothing." Too sharp. Really, had she never lied before? She forced her shoulders to relax. "I was only…taking a moment to make sure I hadn't left anything behind." She was not about to tell him about her girlish ritual.

"There'll be time enough for moments once we've stuck our spoons in the wall," he said. "We've a large sum of money to take, my girl!" The man really should learn to lower his voice. They were going to get caught one of these days.

"And yet—you seemed to have enough time to spare a moment for a drink," she said with a smirk.

He matched her smile and doubled it. "Aye. But, Rosie girl, if ever I've taught you anything it's that there's always time for a drink." He winked. "Have your look-about moment while I take your bag out to the hackney. But be quick about it. We've a lot to discuss."

"Fine." Rose shooed him out of the room, eager to be alone again, and listened as he left the room, chuckling his usual infectious laugh as he did.

Sometimes she caught herself thinking it was too bad the man wasn't really her uncle. But as quickly as she thought it, she pushed it away. No matter how much she liked him, she would never let herself grow attached to him or anyone else. Having someone to love meant having someone to lose. She didn't care to have that happen again.

Rose picked up her single remaining piece of luggage and shut the door behind her as she went outside to join Uncle Felix in the hackney. The December air bit at her face and hands and she tugged her wool coat more firmly around her. A curse slipped from her lips and hung as a cloud in front of her. Winter had never been her friend. Every gust of frigid wind reminded her of those miserable years as a little girl sleeping alone in a damp alley and wondering if that would be the night her toes were going to fall off as that other urchin's did. She pushed those memories away and hurried toward the hackney.

But just then, something down the street caught her eye. A man—a familiar man—crossing the street. Rose knew that tall, skinny frame anywhere. It was the Bow Street runner that had been trying to catch her for years. Rose had never worried too much about the boyish-looking law officer because, in the past, she had always stayed one step ahead of him.

Although Uncle Felix tried to hide it from her, she knew that he had accomplices all over town that kept him informed about the runner's movements. He had no idea that Rose had asked those same people to tell her the information first. And they always did, allowing her to anticipate the runner's moves almost before he made them. But she had not anticipated this particular movement, and he felt too close. Alarmingly close.

Before he had a chance to see her, Rose jumped up into the hackney with Uncle Felix and shut the door. Part of her wanted to worry about finding the runner so unexpectedly close to them. But what good was worrying? It never helped anything. Decisive action was what had kept her alive all this time. So she decided to be more careful going forward and sat down on the bench.

She blew out a puff of air and attempted to shake the cold from her fingers.

"If you'd stop giving all your blasted gloves away your fingers would likely stay warm," he said as if he had just presented her with a revolutionary idea. Rose tried not to find it endearing when Uncle Felix accidentally allowed his protectiveness to show despite her years of censure anytime he tried to coddle her.

"Where am I off to now?" Rose asked, pushing past his comment and focusing on what really mattered—the next job.

The hackney lurched into motion and began bobbing over the familiar cobblestone streets. Uncle Felix's smile broadened enough to reveal the gap in his teeth which never failed to remind Rose of the time he ran straight into a street lamp while outrunning the watch. "We've got a big one this time. I'd say it's big enough that you'd finally be able to hang up your bonnet somewhere if it was agreeable to you."

Rose cringed. "And why the devil would I want that? I can't think of anything less agreeable." No. She would never do that. Her life was fine how it was.

Uncle Felix fixed his eyes on her a little too intense for her comfort. "You never wish you'd chosen a different path all those years ago? Taken up life in service instead of learning under an old fool like me?" Rose watched Uncle Felix look down at his clasped hands and fidget his thumbs round and round. What was this insecurity? The man really must be getting old.

"Not for a minute," she said, meaning every word. "Do you regret teaching me everything you did?" She wasn't sure she wanted to hear the answer. It wasn't that she needed his approval. But the thought of hearing him say that he regretted the years he'd spent with her stung a little.

"Regret is a fickle mistress, Rosie. I'll never regret teaching that grubby little urchin the means to look after herself," he said. "But sometimes I regret that I didn't teach you to do it differently, in a way that didn't require so much risk. Perhaps then you would feel more inclined to shackle your leg to a good fellow." His grin went lopsided. "Maybe even a gentry cove who could treat you right and proper."

Oh. Was that all?

Rose adjusted her posture and smoothed out the thick blue fabric of her skirt. "Well, I rarely ever do what's right and I find being 'proper' deucedly dull. Can we quit being missish and get on with it?"

"You know, Rosie," he continued, his eyes still looking as if they held a sermon within their depths. "You rig yourself up in all that armor, but I suspect that underneath it there's a woman wanting to be loved and cared for."

She tried but couldn't resist the urge to grimace. "Keep talking to me about what I want, Uncle Felix, and you will likely find yourself with a hole blown through you." He knew her ways. And he knew that she was perfectly serious about the pistol she kept strapped to her leg at all times. It was most likely why he laughed a full hearty laugh.

"Alright, you don't have to warn me twice! I'll quit prosing and tell you what we've got."

"Please do," she said, feeling more inclined to jump out of the moving carriage than endure one more second of personal conversation.

Uncle Felix leaned down and picked up a small bag that looked to have come from a fancy milliner's shop off Bond Street. Whatever was inside that bag, Rose would not let herself become attached to—no matter how much she liked it. Discarding the finery after a job was a necessity. She could not risk being identified by the objects after a job was finished.

He sat the bag in his lap and pulled out a light blue bonnet with a touch too many ruffles for her taste, along with a pillow. So. It was that kind of job, was it? She had, unfortunately, pulled it off enough times to recognize the costume. Dread settled over her.

"Which unlucky gentleman is about to find himself with an increasing mistress?" said Rose.

That dangerous glint entered Uncle Felix's eyes—the same one that had helped them scam wealthy gentlemen out of thousands of pounds over the years. "That would be the Earl of Newburry."

Rose's body stiffened. "Lord Newburry?"

Although she had never personally seen the disreputable earl in person, she knew everything about him. Actually, anyone with ears in most of England knew who the imbecile was. The notorious libertine was known for his extravagant tastes and a fortune to match them. If the rumors were right, the man possessed an income of ten thousand pounds each year.

Lord Newburry—her nose crinkled even thinking the name—was

just the sort of entitled aristocrat who felt himself at liberty to call a housemaid into his bedchamber in the dead of night for reasons that had nothing to do with housework. Unfortunately, too many young women felt the need to obey their master's orders out of fear of losing their post without pay or reference.

That was one particular reason Rose decided to hold the strings to her own life instead of entering service. And even though hers was not the noblest profession, it kept her stomach full and her body untouched. She made her own rules and would be dashed before willingly handing herself over to another's untrustworthy authority.

She narrowed her eyes at Uncle Felix. "I've been hoping to get my hands on that devil's fortune for years. Why now?"

The hackney bumped and jolted, making Uncle Felix's full smiling cheeks vibrate. "Because I've finally got the perfect reason to pay the rakeshame a visit." But the far too eager twinkle in his eyes gave Rose a little pause. "Didn't even have to dig around for information with the usual gossips. The tip came from my own flesh and blood."

"Brutus?" It wasn't difficult to figure out since Rose knew that Brutus was Uncle Felix's only living relation. And although usually Uncle Felix had nothing pleasant to say about his starched-up, know-better-than-anyone-else, butler of a brother—his words not hers—it would seem that the man's tip was good enough for him to claim kinship again.

"Happened a few months ago. Seems our mighty lordship went for a visit to old Grantham's estate and took a fancy to one of the chambermaids. The girl found herself in the family way a few weeks later and was kicked out without a reference." Poor girl. Why was it always the servants who were left to pay the devil for a gentleman's indiscretions?

"And I'm to play the part of this chambermaid?" she asked, already knowing the answer and not at all relishing the idea.

"Right! And you won't take less than two thousand pounds to keep this business quiet. Play your hand right and we will walk away from this one with plump pockets." He patted the pockets of his waistcoat as proof of where he would stuff the banknotes.

But something tugged inside her. She didn't feel good about profiting from another woman's misfortune. The pregnant young maid was most likely scared, alone, and penniless. Those feelings were all too familiar to her. "I'm assuming the girl has not already approached Lord Newburry herself about the matter?"

Uncle Felix shook his head. "Was too scared of word getting out and her never being able to work again after the baby is born. Brutus says she's gone to hide it out at a tenant's farm as long as they'll have her. If you ask me, I say the girl's daft to not go bleed the earl dry herself!"

"Well, I didn't ask you," she gave him a reprimanding look. "And I dare say the girl is too afraid to face him." Most females had not grown up as self-sufficient as she had.

Uncle Felix eyed her for a long moment, searching her face for something. And then, he cringed. "Oh Lud, there's the look. Devil take it, Rosie, you aren't gonna give our money to the girl are you?"

She smiled. "Of course I am. No, don't give me that look. She ought to have a cut of the haul since it's her story we are using."

He eyed her from beneath heavy, suspicious lids. "How much do you intend to give her?" Excitement did not touch his voice.

"I think it's only right that she gets half of the cut since she'll be the one with a child to support."

He agreed, but only after a dramatic sigh of long-suffering. Rose knew that inwardly, he was just as content to give the money to the girl as she was. It's probably why they were the poorest and yet most successful criminals in England.

Rose took the blue bonnet and plopped it on her head. "So what's my story?" She fumbled with the ribbons of the ugliest bonnet she had ever beheld before tying it under her chin. When this job was over, she was revoking Uncle Felix's purchasing privileges.

"Your name is Daphney Bellows," he said. "Lord Newburry took a liking to you at a house party about three months ago. The real Daphney didn't spend much time with the earl outside of that night so you don't need to bog yourself down with the details of her life. Just state the facts. Threaten to release a scandal and get out of there as quick as you can with the rhino." If Rose hadn't grown up on the streets, she likely would never understand that the man was talking about money. But really, street slang was her first language. It was more difficult for her to speak as a gently bred lady than a thief.

"No wig this time?" she asked, not that she was brokenhearted to go without one. The dashed things were itchy.

He shook his head. "You got lucky this time. The girl has your coloring. Just toss that little pillow under your dress and that should be enough." Rose had pulled this scheme enough to know that these disgusting sorts of men never really remembered what their ladybirds looked like, especially when she was just a lowly maid. Keep her eyes down and feign the nervousness she didn't feel. It was too easy.

Rose and Uncle Felix spent the rest of the drive talking strategy and where they would meet up after she had the money in hand. And there was no doubt she would have the money in hand. With a solid backstory and an earl that would be eager to stifle yet another scandal, she was sure that he would be eager to toss her the blunt and send her out of his house as quickly as possible.

Uncle Felix let out a low whistle as the hackney drew up to Lord Newburry's large house in Grosvenor Square. Rose knew this house well. It was, in her opinion, the most beautiful house in that elite part of town. More than disappointing to realize that it belonged to such a coxcomb. "A fine ken, that one!" he said eyeing the three-story home with lifted brows.

"Too bad a fine gentleman does not own it."

"Aye! But if he were some stand-up fellow, you'd never let us con him out of his coins. So I say it's a good thing he's an ugly customer."

She lifted a brow. "I'm not so sure that Miss Bellows would share your sentiment."

Uncle Felix looked away as Rose quickly stuffed the small pillow under her dress and managed quite impressively to squeeze the thing under her stays. She looked down and assessed that it was an accurate size baby bump for a woman who would only just begin to show. Perfect.

Uncle Felix gave her his usual good luck wink before she stepped out of the carriage and watched him ride off in the hackney. The two kept very little contact while she was on a job. Everything was safer and easier when she worked alone. Once she was finished with Lord Newburry, she would hire another hackney and meet Uncle Felix at Hopewood Orphanage. Rose tried to disregard the feeling of warmth that the thought gave her, but it was useless. It had been far too long since she'd been able to visit the children and she was eager to know how her little urchins were getting on. But for now, she needed to keep her mind on the situation before her.

Rose took in a deep fortifying breath, patted the small pistol strapped to her thigh for good luck, and mentally recited what she needed to know back to herself. She gripped the handles of her leather valise and started up the massive front staircase. The wind whipped at her silly bonnet so forcefully that she had to put her hand on her head to keep it from flying away. She noted her own slow and steady breaths as her half-boots clicked over the front stone steps.

At one time, her breaths would have been fast and her chest would have felt tight. But not anymore. Not today. Nerves and sensibilities had fled her long ago. She cleared her throat and squared her shoulders at the imposing black door before reaching for the brass knocker and placing three solid raps.

Chapter Two

"Oliver, why the devil do you insist on plaguing me at this ridiculous hour?" asked Carver, giving his friend a look he hoped was intimidating.

Unfortunately, Oliver was his oldest friend and now seemed immune to the look.

Oliver just smiled the trademark smile that had won him the nickname of *Charming* amongst the debutantes of the *ton*. "I think the word you were looking for was *visiting*."

"No," said Carver. "A visit sounds far more pleasant than you showing up in my bedchamber at eight o'clock in the morning to tell me you're going out of town. You act more like a deuced wife every day, Olly."

Since they were rarely ever apart, the running joke amongst their friends and family was that he and Oliver more closely resembled an old married couple than friends. It was sadly true.

Oliver smirked. "Someone has to do the job."

"I don't think I like the idea of you being the one to fill it." Carver finally sat up and tossed his feet out of bed.

It would be wonderful if Oliver showing up in his bedchamber before noon was a rare occurrence. But it wasn't. Ever since they had met at Eton—a boarding school for boys—ten years prior, the blasted man had been showing up in his bedchamber before Carver had the opportunity to open his eyes. How he managed to slip past his butler, Jeffers, Carver would never know.

Carver motioned toward the servant's bell hanging on the wall. "Pull the cord, will you?"

Oliver put his hand over his heart and feigned a deeply remorseful expression that was too put-on to be sincere. "I hope you're not getting up on my account! I'll only be here another minute." Doubtful.

Oliver could talk more than a girl freshly launched from the school-room. Carver rarely minded, unless it was eight o'clock in the morning and he had the devil of a headache and a body that felt as if it had been trampled by a herd of cattle as he did just then.

Oliver's eyes fell to Carver's torso, and he winced, sucking in air through his teeth in the sound of a hiss. "Blast, man. Your rib looks broken."

Carver looked down at his bare chest. He had been too exhausted from his fight the night before to do anything other than shed his shirt and fall into bed. Exhaustion was good. When he was exhausted, he slept. And when he slept, he was given a break from his memories. Although, more than not those same memories found their way into his dreams.

He tenderly touched his ribs. Severely bruised but thankfully not broken. He made a quick assessment of the rest of his body: bruised ribs, a cut above his right eyebrow, swollen and torn knuckles, and at least a dozen other minor injuries; but otherwise not terrible. It had been the best match he'd fought all year. Jackson was right when he warned that it would be Carver's most difficult fight so far. He had almost lost. *Almost*, he thought with a cocky smile.

But then he stood up and felt very much like a crumpled piece of paper unraveling and some of his smugness left him. "Not broken. But very nearly," said Carver. "Brooks was a better boxer than I'd given him credit for."

Carver had been boxing nearly every day for the past three years and never once had he fought anyone who had displayed to such advantage as Mr. Brooks. Jackson—the owner of Gentleman Jackson's Boxing Saloon—said he was sure he would make a champion out of Brooks. Which is the same thing he had been telling Carver since he walked into his boxing academy his first year living in London. But unfortunately for Carver, it would never be able to be anything other than a hobby—and a distraction. He was the oldest as well as the only son of his father—The Duke of Dalton—and as such was his father's heir. Nobility could not be professional boxers. Or, so he was told by his tender-hearted mother in attempts to keep him from showing up with cuts and bruises all over his body.

Oliver shook his head slowly while eyeing the offending rib again. "Blast. I can't believe I missed it. Heard you fought your best fight yet."

Carver took a shirt from his wardrobe and gingerly pulled it over his head, noting that everything on him hurt. "You could have seen it for yourself if you would stop trying to be a Bond Street beau." He tossed a smirk at his socialite friend.

Oliver returned the smirk but added a hint of mockery to it as well as a squint. "You know very well that I would have rather been at the fight than at the ball, but I had already given my word to Lady Summers that I would dance attendance on her dowdy niece."

"And how did that go?"

Oliver shuddered. "Took me half the night just to draw a smile from the stone-faced girl."

Poor Oliver. Or—no. The man did it to himself with his overly engaging manners and freely given smile. Those two things alone made him not only a favorite of every young lady in London, but every matron who needed their daughter, granddaughter, or niece to feel special and noticed during her come out. That was one reason why Carver refused to accompany Oliver to any society events. The thought of preening society misses fawning at his feet gave him the irrational urge to go lock his door.

And besides, no other woman would ever compare to—

"It wouldn't kill you to attend a ball or two yourself, Kenny." Oliver had made that nickname for him when they were still just young bucks, saying that his title of Kensworth sounded much too old for him. Oliver shortened the title and from that day on called him by the name of Kenny.

"Probably not, but I'd rather not risk it."

They both walked into the parlor adjoining his bedchamber and sat in the chairs by the fire.

Oliver settled into the leather chair, making it creak as he stretched his legs toward the fire and crossed his ankles. "But you know you're quickly gaining the title of *eccentric recluse*, don't you? It's about time for you to step back out into society a little." Carver didn't like where this was going.

"Miss dancing with me, my dear? I should warn you, I won't waltz with you anymore." He raised his hands and wiggled his fingers. "Your hands travel too much."

Oliver's eyes narrowed, but he was clearly trying not to smile. "Be serious."

"Why? So you can read me a lecture?" said Carver. "No, I thank you." He had no desire to hear whatever Olly was going to say next. And he had a pretty good idea of what that next thing was going to be. "Now, besides informing me of your travels, what was so deucedly important that you felt the need to wake me?"

"Well...actually," Oliver looked a little shy which was odd. "It kills me to ask, but...I need to borrow some money."

Carver looked down and inspected the swollen and scabbing cracks on his knuckles, not feeling the need to ask any questions. Oliver was more like a brother to Carver than a friend. He would give him any amount of money he needed. "Just tell Jeffers the amount and he'll give it to you on your way out."

"Thank you." Oliver smiled at Carver with an almost challenging sort of look. A look that said he was prepared to defend whatever his reason was for needing the money. But Carver just looked at his friend with a grin. They looked at each other like that for a minute before Oliver's smile dropped along with his shoulders and he broke. "Don't you want to know what it's for?"

"If I say no will you go away and leave me alone?"

Oliver just smiled even broader. "I'm in love."

Carver barely suppressed his groan. Was it possible for Oliver to go a week without 'falling in love?'

"I believe you can expect to wish me happy before long," said Oliver with a notable amount of pride in his voice. It was the same pride Carver had heard the last five times his friend had entered his bedchamber saying almost the same thing. The time to wish him happy would never actually come.

"Famous," said Carver. "I'll go ahead and do it now so you can take yourself off."

"I can see you don't believe me," said Oliver, not looking offended in the least. "But I swear it's real this time. I've never met another woman like her. She's perfect."

Not true. The only perfect woman to ever walk the earth died three years ago.

Carver heard the door to his bedroom open and knew that Brandon, his valet, must have entered. He stood and stretched the ache from his arms as he prepared himself mentally for the task of listening to a story that he had no desire to hear. But the sooner he heard the story the sooner he could go down to breakfast.

"Alright," said Carver. "Tell me about this woman."

Brandon entered the room with Carver's wardrobe draped over his arm and then began to help him dress without ever saying a word.

Oliver leaned over to rest his elbow on his knees, watching as Carver stepped into a pant leg of his breeches. "She's perfect."

"Yes, you've said that already."

"Well, she is." Oliver took on a far off expression as if the woman's portrait was being painted onto the wall. "She has the most captivating eyes I've ever seen. They are brown yet gold, yet somehow red. I swear I could get lost in the stories they tell."

Carver turned his back to Oliver under the pretense of allowing Brandon to help him shrug into his jacket. But really, it was so that he could roll his eyes. *Get lost in the stories they tell.* How stupid. Eyes were eyes. They could be beautiful but they did not tell stories. Oliver was becoming too much of a romantic.

15

"And just how did you meet this woman with storytelling eyes?"

"I can hear the condescension in your tone, but I'm choosing to ignore it," said Oliver, making the corners of Carver's mouth twitch up. "I met her at an informal ball the other night. The poor girl was driven to distraction." Sensitive females never failed to annoy Carver. But they seemed to be just Oliver's type.

"She snuck out of her uncle's house to attend a card party a few nights before the ball," said Oliver. "There were a few high flyers at the table that took advantage of the fact that she was a green girl and—well…she lost a good bit of money."

Carver lifted his chin for Brandon to begin arranging the cravat around his neck. "She told you all of this in the ballroom?"

"Of course not." Oliver leaned back in his seat again. "She told me *outside* of the ballroom in the gardens where I found her crying." Oh, yes. A much better place to share personal information with a stranger. "Kitty—that's her name—didn't have enough pin money to cover the debts she had accumulated, and she was worried that her uncle—who is something of a brute apparently—would send her to work at a girl's school if he found out about her misstep."

"How dreadful for our poor Kitty," said Carver while stepping into one of his boots.

Oliver leveled him a glare. "I know you think this is funny, but you should have seen the poor beauty. She couldn't even enjoy the ball because she was terrified it would be her last."

Never having to attend another ball actually sounded rather nice. But he and Oliver were different in that way. They were both tall and broad and generally considered good looking, but Oliver enjoyed spinning ladies around the ballroom whereas Carver much preferred Cribb's Parlor and bare-knuckle fighting until at least some part of him was bleeding.

"Very well, I can see why you felt compelled to help her. How much did the girl set you back?"

There was a long pause before Oliver finally responded with, "Five hundred pounds."

Carver's eyebrows shot up to his hairline. "Kitty's eyes must tell some fantastic stories."

Oliver ignored his barb and stood up. "I know it's a lot. But believe me, she's worth it. She's going to Bath for the month to visit a friend, but I plan on offering for her the moment she returns."

"After only spending one evening together?" asked Carver.

"One evening is all I needed to see that she's perfect for me in every way."

Again, Carver suppressed a groan.

If he thought for one moment that Oliver would ever end up actually going through with offering for the girl, he would have lectured him on the dangers of proposing to a woman he hardly knew. But it was Oliver. The man had been in love more times than Carver could keep track of. But they never lasted. Eventually, Oliver would come to his senses and begin the pursuit of some other pretty female.

"Well then, I wish you happy," Carver said untruthfully while assessing his newly tied cravat and slate blue jacket in the mirror.

As one who belonged to the sporting corinthian set, dark blue was possibly the most extravagant color that he would ever allow his valet to dress him in. Poor Brandon. The man insisted that Carver had *the shoulders and calves of a Greek god* and should allow himself to be dressed as such. But since dressing the part of a mythological deity apparently consisted of flamboyant colors, skin-tight pantaloons, and a dozen glittering fobs, Carver chose to continue his look of a mere mortal.

"You're leaving for Dalton Park today, are you not?" asked Oliver, steering the conversation in a direction that Carver wasn't sure he wanted it to go.

"I am. And you leave for your hunting trip today?" Were other friends so in tune with each other's schedules as he and Oliver were?

"Just as soon as I leave here. Will you be alright going home without me?" Oliver said with a twisted smile.

"As remarkable as it sounds, I believe I'll manage."

"Will you, though?" Disheartening that he felt the need to ask again.

"Yes, believe it or not, darling, I am fairly sufficient on my own."

Oliver did not even register the sardonic pet name Carver called him. His face grew more serious. "What I meant was, will you be alright *traveling* to Dalton Park without me? I know you haven't been able to make the journey since—,"

Carver cut him off. "I'll be fine, Oliver." But really he wasn't sure himself.

Would he actually make it all the way home this year without turning back after reaching the halfway point? He would not even be going if it wasn't for the ball his mother was throwing in honor of his father's birthday. And he couldn't avoid the place forever, could he? Probably not, considering he was to inherit it one day. No, he needed to go home. He just wished the memories didn't live there along with his family.

"Are you sure you don't need me to come with you? I was already planning on attending the ball, but if you need me to travel with you I can cancel my hunting trip."

Carver chuckled, hoping that if he seemed light-hearted and unaffected, Oliver would drop the subject. "Thank you, but that won't be necessary. I've already hired a nursemaid to hold my hand in your absence."

Oliver's green eyes narrowed, clearly unimpressed—as well as undeterred—by Carver's attempt to lighten the mood. "It's your first time home in three years, Kenny. It's okay to be a little unnerved by it."

Carver dismissed his valet, not wishing for his servant to overhear such a private conversation. Because if he knew Oliver, he would not drop the subject before they had explored every part of it.

"I'm not unnerved, Oliver. I'm completely fine." *Completely fine.* He was, wasn't he? He had gotten on with his life.

"Completely fine?" Oliver tipped a taunting brow and crossed his arms. "Then say her name."

That was too far. Carver's jaws clenched and his nostrils flared as he took in a deep breath. "Drop it, Oliver. If you push this topic, I'll hit you. And you know it."

"See. You're not fine." Oliver's brows pulled together. "It's time to move on and get some closure, Kenny. Maybe if you finally visit her grave while you're—,"

"I *have* moved on," Carver snapped through his teeth while curling his toes into his boots to keep himself from crossing the room and throwing his fist into Oliver's nose.

"Really? Then why is it you haven't come up to scratch with one of the dozens of ladies that want to marry you?"

"Not that itchy?"

"Stop," Oliver said, adjusting in his seat. "You're the biggest catch on the marriage mart. Too good looking for your own good. Titled. Wealthy. And could marry almost any woman you wanted in London. And yet, you will hardly even look at another woman since—"

"Don't," Carver said, deciding it was the last warning he would give his friend.

"You need to be able to say her name."

"What I *need* is for you to drop it or get out of my bedchamber." The skin on his knuckles stung as he tightened his hands into fists.

For a moment Oliver looked like he was going to press the subject further. Unfortunately, Oliver was never afraid of coming to cuffs with him. But then Oliver let out a deep sigh of relent and looked away.

"Fine. I'll drop it. But think about what I said." And then the entire atmosphere of the room lightened as Oliver's face shifted into a lopsided grin. "After all, I know what I'm talking about. I'm very wise and almost a married man."

Carver shook his head and walked to open his bedchamber door, eager to be done with the conversation and on with his day. "Don't forget to tell Jeffers how much you need on the way out."

"Thanks. I'll pay you back," said Oliver standing from his chair and walking toward the open door.

Carver just waved him off and smirked. "Don't bother. Consider it a wedding gift."

Even though in that moment he ached to fight the man, he was happy to be able to help him in any way he could. Even if it was for such a stupid reason as giving his money to a woman he barely knew and would likely never see again.

"Try not to miss me too much," Oliver said with a grin while walking through the door.

"My pillow will be soaked through with tears until we are reunited." He heard Oliver laugh on his way to the stairs.

An hour later, after Carver had finished his breakfast and was on the way to his study, he heard three raps at the front door. He stopped and waited for Jeffers to attend to the knock, but after a glance around the foyer, he realized that none of his staff had been present to hear it—most likely because everyone was in a frenzy trying to close up the house and pack for his trip home. He rolled his shoulders and quickly adjusted the cuffs of his jacket before going to open the door himself.

Chapter Three

R ose contemplated placing a fourth knock on the door, but before she had a chance, it flew open. Startled, she took a step back. She hadn't anticipated the door opening so quickly or finding a gigantic handsome gentleman on the other side. Although she ought to have expected it since she knew that Lord Newburry was widely considered to cut an attractive figure. Rakes were very rarely ugly.

She was, however, most taken by surprise that the door was answered not by a butler, but instead by his lordship himself. She blinked at the mountainous earl and realized an absurd amount of time had passed while she stood there gaping at the man. Realizing she was, in fact, the one who had called upon him, she wished she could summon one word to speak, but none came. She had, quite frankly, forgotten why she was there in the first place. Had she ever been so terrible at a job so quickly before?

Lord Newburry's cool grey eyes swept over and then behind her before speaking, reminding Rose of her purpose there.

"And to what do I owe the honor?" he said, one dark brow lifted making him look haughty and pretentious.

The sound of his deep voice jolted her back to the present. She shook her head—instantly wished she hadn't—and then dropped a curtsy.

Get yourself together, you ninny!

"I beg your pardon, my lord. I was hoping for a private audience with your lordship."

He hesitated a moment but then stepped aside, emphasizing just how much his shoulders had filled the doorway before, and gestured for her to come in.

She forced her mind to focus before flashing him the meek smile of a nervous maid and then stepped across the massive threshold into a lavish foyer and noted the four-tiered crystal chandelier, porcelain vases, and decadent tapestries on the walls. The room practically dripped with money. Maybe she should try to squeeze a little more out of him.

She re-focused her attention on the earl several steps away. But goodness he was big. He had the broad shoulders of an athlete and she imagined that there was not a single man in all of London that could approach his height.

Based on the gossip, Rose had always assumed Lord Newburry to be more of a dandified tulip rather than the sporting corinthian that he appeared to be. Just looking at him made her feel like her throat was closing and she needed to clear it for air.

But he was a cad, and she needed to get herself together.

She clasped her hands together just below her fake belly bump, allowing the shape to show through her skirts. The next step was to introduce herself and try to recall to his memory to an event that had not actually taken place—at least, not with her. She was hoping he wouldn't remember that. In truth, she was sure he wouldn't.

His steely eyes slid from hers to the small fake belly bump. His brows pulled together, and he smirked. "Why do I have the devilish suspicion that you have not visited to remark on the state of the weather?"

"No, my lord," she looked coyly down to her stomach. "I have not. In fact, Lord Newburry, I have—,"

But he cut her off. "Pardon?" he said, tilting his head toward her as if to hear her better. Was the man hard of hearing or just rude?

She took a cleansing breath and re-adjusted on her feet to start again. "I was only agreeing that, no, I have not come to remark on the weather." She breathed. "In truth, my lord, this visit is of a more sensitive nature."

She could see him open his mouth to argue, but she did not allow him to interrupt again. He had already set her off balance once that day and she could not let it happen again. It was important that she remained in control.

"I don't believe I need to remind you of the...*attentions* you paid me a few months ago at Lord Grantham's estate." She continued to look at her stomach as she was sure Daphney Bellows would. Maids very rarely made eye contact with those they were serving, or anyone above their rank.

"Actually, I *do* need for you to remind me."

She glanced up and saw that he had the audacity to look amused. He shook his head slightly and shrugged his shoulders with the slightest of confused smiles. "Who are you and what attentions have I paid you?"

Her eyes widened in fake shock. Inwardly, she was pleased he didn't remember. Pleased and revolted. It was a tedious business she was in.

"I was a chambermaid at Lord Grantham's house when you came to stay. And you...well...you—" He continued to look just as amused as before with his eyebrows pulled together and a teasing grin on his mouth. She wanted to slap him. "Good heavens, must I really say it out loud, my lord?" She forced a tremble into her voice.

"I wish you would," he said.

"You..." her eyes bounced back and forth from the green rug to his grey eyes, "You made love to me, my lord!" she finally said, willing a blush into her cheeks.

His brows shot up. "Did I, now?" Blast the man! He looked as if he were witnessing an amusing scene from a play rather than listening to a scared maid he had compromised.

Well…the face of a woman who was impersonating the maid he had compromised.

"Y-yes." She shot her eyes back down. "Surely you remember me?" *Be pitiful.* She peeked up from under her lashes.

He laughed. Actually laughed. "No. But you remember me of course?"

"Of course, I do! I would never be able to forget you or the attentions you wrongly paid me."

"Is that so?" he was still smiling.

Rose balled her hands into fists at her sides. So help her, she was going to slap that smug look right off his face.

"Yes," she said with a little too much force in her tone. Rose took a slow breath in through her nose. "As you can see, my lord, I am now increasing and unfortunately out of the job, thanks to you." Too much again. Why was she having such a difficult time staying in character with this man?

"And I—," he placed his hand on his chest, "*Lord Newburry*—am the lucky father?"

"I know you are, my lord. There simply isn't—," Rose was interrupted yet again, but this time by several footmen who began marching through the foyer carrying trunks and boxes.

Lord Newburry lifted his chin to look at her over the parade of boxes and luggage. "Continue, my dear."

Rose flexed the muscles in her legs and tried to speak over the noise without actually yelling. "I was saying, that there simply is no one else that could be the f-father, my lord. Without a doubt, the situation I find myself in came about because of my unfortunate encounter with you." She tried to be firm and yet meek, balancing her own backbone with Daphney's fragile sensibilities.

The steady stream of footmen and maids continued their work of carrying luggage through the foyer and out the door. A footman removed the knocker from the door, and two maids began covering furniture in the little parlor across the hall. Were they closing up the house? Rose tried to catch a glimpse of the earl in between the line of servants. This was not going well at all.

The earl spoke loudly and without shame across the foyer. "I see! So, to make sure I have this straight, *I* am the man who has stolen your virtue?"

Goodness! She wouldn't have to try hard to feign embarrassment that time. Did the man have no scruples about speaking of such sensitive matters in a remarkably busy room? And even worse—he was not cowering or showing the least bit of remorse.

"You're certain it wasn't anyone else?" he said.

"I am quite certain it was you, my lord!" Rose's voice raised to an octave that made even her cringe. Servants continued to bustle about, completing their tasks. She felt discomposed by the commotion, and more importantly, the earl seemed to be distracted by it as well. She could feel what little power she had slipping. "My lord, might there be a more private place we can talk?"

"Darling, you needn't worry over the discretion of my staff. I assure you they have far more important things to care about than the loss of your virtue."

Ardent hatred began to take root. At least other gentlemen that she had scammed similarly had had the good grace to be fearful, sometimes even remorseful, and were always eager to pay what duty owed.

This man, however, didn't give a dash.

"Even so—I would feel more comfortable speaking with you in private."

"Would you?" There was that amused tone again. "Well, I am afraid that you've caught me as I'm going out. Ah, Jeffers!" he said, turning away from her to address the butler who had just entered the room. "Please see that my mother's crystal vase is safely packed. The woman will have my neck if it arrives in pieces."

Was that it? Had he dismissed her so quickly? Her pride prickled. Rose had never been so patently unsuccessful before. Clearly, she was going to need to display a bit more of her backbone.

She waited—unable to keep her foot from tapping beneath her dress—as the earl addressed a maid, the housekeeper, and two footmen before he turned on his heels and walked right out of the house without excuse or apology. Rose's foot stilled as she blinked at the front door.

Had he really just left? Had he forgotten she was there? Never before had she been treated as such an afterthought. A nuisance, yes. Hated, absolutely. Ogled, often. Completely ignored, never.

Rose lifted her chin in the air, tightened her bonnet's strings under her chin and marched after him. She had never failed at a job, and she did not intend for this to be the first.

Chapter Four

"**M**y lord!" Rose called out while taking the outside stairs in quick succession. He paused, one boot perched on the bottom stair of the enclosed carriage, and turned his eyes to her. "I'm afraid that I must demand a private audience with you!"

He smirked. "Are you still here? I thought you had left."

Her jaw and fists tightened in unison. "*You* were the one who left, my lord! You may think that because you are titled and wealthy, you are not held to the same morals as everyone else, but believe me when I tell you that I will not be fobbed off no matter your station."

A bit too much. But at least it changed the expression on his face from one that was amused and unfeeling to one that seemed as if he were really looking at her for the first time. His eyes roamed her face as if searching for something. She saw a flicker of something in his eyes that she could not name. Before she had time to figure out what it was, it was gone, and he smiled, almost mischievously. She didn't trust it.

"Very well, get in," he said, extending his hand to assist her up into his waiting carriage.

Rose looked from the empty carriage back to the earl who was easily twice her size, and now that she could observe his face more closely, in possession of a menacing-looking cut above his right eyebrow. "In… your carriage, my lord?"

"Yes, where else would we talk? I told you I was—"

"Going out. Yes, you need not repeat yourself."

He smirked and extended his large, calloused hand once again.

She didn't love the idea of getting into an enclosed carriage alone with such a notorious rake, but seeing as it was the only way to have a private conversation with him, she took his hand and stepped into the carriage. She swallowed against a lump forming in her throat and placed her valise on the seat beside her. Everything would be fine. And if he did not behave, there was a pistol on her thigh reminding her that she could take control of the situation at any moment.

Although she had never actually been forced to shoot anyone, Rose knew she was a fine shot. Along with the lessons of pick-pocketing and conning, Uncle Felix had insisted from her first day under his tutelage that she learn how to handle a pistol. And thanks to his thorough instruction, Rose could shoot a playing card out of a man's hand from twenty-five paces away without so much as grazing a single finger.

Lord Newburry stepped into the carriage, making the whole thing shift from his weight, and sat on the bench facing her. His legs were so long that even without intention their knees were almost brushing. She shifted a little closer to the door.

A footman shut the door, allowing Rose to experience firsthand what it felt like to be a bird shut inside a cage with a hungry cat. No matter. She could handle herself. And at least it was a very well sprung cage. The warm brick at her feet, a luxury she would have, at other times appreciated, only added to the perspiration pooling in her palms.

She looked up and was startled to find him staring at her with a soft smile and lifted brow. "Alright, my dear. You have my attention." Why did those words make her want to squirm? And why did she have to find the horrible man so blasted attractive? It was inconvenient and getting in the way. She would do well to picture him with long nose hairs and awful brown teeth.

Blast.

28

It didn't work. Her rebellious mind instead took the time set aside for imagining the man as an ogre to notice instead that he had a very strong jawline and maybe even a dimple if he smiled fully. All of these observations only served to make the carriage feel smaller. Maybe the air beside the door would feel a little cooler. Rose scooted an inch to the right and then stopped short when her seat made an uncomfortable sort of noise. One that sounded far too much like a bodily function.

No, no, no, no, no.

Her eyes widened and flashed to the obnoxious earl who was clearly trying to school his amusement, his smile breaking through pursed lips.

She flushed for real this time. "Surely I do not need to tell you, my lord, that it was the seat that created that unfortunate noise?"

"Oh, certainly." But he cleared his throat into his hand to cover up his chuckling.

She narrowed her eyes. "It was the seat," she said enunciating every syllable and sounding more like a defensive child than a grown woman.

"Mmhmm." The overblown look of agreement that he gave her made Rose want to dissolve into the carriage bench.

He didn't believe her. Or was he simply teasing her? She crossed her hands over her torso and tipped a brow. "It was the seat. And I will make the noise again to prove my innocence." Oh, no. Had she really just offered to recreate the sound of flatulence to remove his suspicions that she was an idiot? And why—*oh, why?!*—would the seat not make the sound again? How many times could she scoot back and forth on that seat before he thought her a madwoman and had her shipped off to bedlam?

Thoroughly put out with the now silent seat, Rose huffed and crossed her hands primly in her lap. She raised her eyes, reluctantly, to meet the earl's. His eyebrows were lifted in a devilish grin. This job was going wonderfully.

If Rose ever wanted to see that two thousand pounds, she needed to regain some control. And quick. "Well, my lord. First, I'm not surprised that you do not remember me," *But you certainly will after this carriage ride.* "It's why I was nervous to come in the first place. You see…the night you—er…summoned me, you had been drinking rather heavily."

He grimaced but his eyes danced. "That couldn't have been very pleasant." She fought to resist a smile. Probably because her sense of the ridiculous was already heightened from the seat noises. Certainly not because the awful man had wit.

"I'm not here to discuss the pleasantries of our encounter, Lord Newburry."

"Then what are you here to discuss?" Was his face simply frozen into that lazy smirk?

"To speak plainly, my lord, I am here for compensation."

He nodded. "Naturally." Was he enjoying this?

After her idiotic attempt to recreate the embarrassing noise made when she scooted across the seat, Rose was struggling to maintain both her control and her dignity. She wanted to slap herself for being so bird-witted.

"As I said before, I have been released from my post due to this pregnancy without recommendation and I feel that it is only right to be compensated since I will very likely not be able to regain employment until after the child is born. If at all." Was her language too polite? In all of her irritation, she had completely forgotten to resort back to the vulgar tongue. Apparently, there would be no end to her mistakes that day.

"Seems fair. How much compensation, my dear?"

"If you would be willing to give me enough money to live on, I wouldn't trouble you again and no one would need to know that the child is yours." Rose made sure to phrase it in such a way that he could hear the threat in her statement.

There. She had regained a little ground.

"And out of curiosity, just how much would it take for you to continue living?"

Again, she found herself biting her cheeks to keep from laughing. She was realizing that it was possible to both hate someone and find them funny at the same time.

"Two thousand pounds?" she unleashed her puppy eyes.

His eyebrows shot up and a low chuckle pushed through his broad chest. "Goodness, woman! Keeping you alive is not going to be cheap, is it? What if I just want to keep you barely breathing? Would that save me a thousand pounds or so?"

Her lips twitched, but she kept herself in hand. "Perhaps you might ask your butler what the going cost of living is, my Lord."

"So she does have claws. I thought so." His smile grew wide and somehow more handsome. Infuriating.

"Beg your pardon. That was impertinent," said Rose, forcing herself to slip back into character. A maid would never have spoken so freely to an earl as she had a moment ago.

"No, don't apologize," he said, settling back comfortably in his seat. "I like you far better with a bit of pluck."

A strange sparkle entered his eyes. Was a sparkle good or bad? She honestly could not tell how this job was going anymore. She felt as if she had jumped into the ocean but had forgotten how to swim.

"What's your name?" he said. "No, don't frown at me. You said it yourself, I do not remember you because I was foxed." She wished he was less funny.

"My name is Daphney Bellows, my lord."

"Middle name?"

Her brows pulled together. "You wish to know my middle name?"

"Of course," he said. "How else am I going to convey when I am cross with you? A middle name adds a certain amount of threat, do you not agree?" Threat? What was that supposed to imply? She got the feeling that he was teasing her but she wasn't sure whether she should be angry about it, or laugh. Really, she should get out of the carriage. Something was afoot but she couldn't quite grasp what.

She proceeded, gauging his expressions carefully, looking for some hint of where he was going with this conversation. "I do not intend to make you cross during this drive."

He shrugged his big shoulders. "Why should that matter? We are bound to be cross with one another at some point."

"But why?" Were they even having the same conversation?

Lord Newburry leaned forward in his seat and spoke low as if he were about to tell an exciting story. "Daphney, have you never been around children before? The little things can pit one parent against another in an instant." Maybe he was drunk? That was the only reason she could think of to make sense of his ridiculous ramblings and unaffected manners.

"Forgive me, my lord, but—"

"Carver." He interrupted, yet again throwing her off balance. She was beginning to feel dizzy. Talking circles around a person, until they couldn't remember what they were discussing, was usually *her* tactic.

"Beg your pardon?" she asked.

"Call me Carver."

"I think that would be improper."

He grinned and sat back again. "So would pushing a lady from a moving carriage, but I can't promise I won't do it if you keep calling me by that title."

Rose gave up and fell back heavily against her seat. "I don't—" her shoulders rose and fell and she shook her head a little, "I can't even remember what we were talking about."

"Your middle name," he graciously reminded.

Rose gaped at the man thinking that maybe if she stared at him long enough he would make sense. Finally, she said, "Ingrid," without really thinking.

"Ingrid? *Daphney Ingrid Bellows,*" he said the name slowly as if contemplating it. "I like it. Has a nice rhythm to it."

Drunk. That had to be it. What she still couldn't decide was whether to hate the man or like him. Perhaps if he were uglier the decision would be easier. But instead, her eyes just kept wandering to where his jacket stretched across his shoulders. Is this what it felt like to be cast under a spell? She needed to get out of the carriage—now.

"I'm sorry, my lo—Carver," she corrected, not willing to find out if the earl would actually toss her from the carriage. "But—there is still the matter of my compensation." Bluntness was the only tactic remaining in her arsenal.

"There will be no compensation," he said.

"None?" she asked, but not truly surprised at his refusal. This whole job had been an utter disaster. The sooner she could get away from this odd, confusing, good-looking earl the better.

"None," he said again, but with a growing intensity in his eyes that made Rose's stomach turn over. "I'm going to marry you."

Chapter Five

"Are you ill?" Carver asked the minx sitting across from him. "You look as though you might cast up your accounts. But I understand that's normal for women in your condition." She looked utterly stunned. It was difficult not to laugh.

Clearly, marriage was not part of the scam she was trying to pull off. And he had known it was a scam almost from the moment he met her.

Carver knew the woman was correct in her assessment of Lord Newburry's character: he would likely never remember the face of a maid he had pursued, drunk or not. But he was just as certain that a maid who had fallen prey to Newburry's advances would not forget the face of her pursuer. Which left him with the inevitable conclusion that this woman had never before met Newburry and was betting on his nefarious reputation to pull her through whatever ruse she was running.

Perhaps she would have managed to scam the man of his money if she had gone to the right door—which was actually two down from his. He wished she had. Lord Newburry was the worst sort of man and it would have been satisfying to see him taken in by this woman.

At first, Carver had been eager to write her off. But then she had shown that one bit of backbone before he had stepped into the carriage. That pluck was strangely compelling, and only intensified every minute they shared in the carriage. The more they sparred, the more he realized that she was not at all what she seemed. It was like watching a flame try to hide beneath a sheet of fabric. The more she spoke, the more the flame threatened to engulf the fabric. And for reasons he couldn't identify, Carver desperately wanted to see it set fire.

"But—surely you don't want to marry me?" said Daphney—if that was even her real name—in that same meek voice he knew was put on. She was right. He didn't want to marry her. And in the end, he wouldn't. Carver just wanted to see how far he could push her little shenanigan and hopefully remain entertained enough during the long journey to avoid dwelling on the pain that would meet him at home.

"Who truly wishes to be married?" he said, taking on the personality he knew belonged to Lord Newburry. "But alas, I am a gentleman trying to turn over a new leaf. As such, the honorable thing to do would be to marry you as soon as possible."

"How convenient you choose now to turn over a new leaf," she mumbled, barely audible. The poor vixen looked ready to throttle him for messing up her plans.

He had to inspect his knuckles to keep from laughing. "What was that? I couldn't hear you."

Quick as that she pulled back on her shy maid facade. He had seen enough of her fire to know it was only a mask. Could he be dealing with a professional thief? He liked that idea. "Of course, I appreciate you wishing to do right by me, but don't you think a marriage between an earl and a pregnant maid might cause a bit of a scandal?"

"As the notorious earl?" He shrugged it off. "Hardly. I dare say everyone will find it a dead bore. Marrying a proper lady would be much more surprising."

He smiled to himself as he watched her struggle to calculate a way out of the mess. For some reason, it was clear that she did not take to the idea of being married to him. Perhaps she was already married? Why did he hope she wasn't? But he did know the pregnancy was fake. At some point during her humorous seat-scooting performance, the pillow under her dress had dislodged and moved precariously to the side of her abdomen.

"Could it be that you do not want to accept my offer, Miss Bellows?" Carver knew that she could not, in her right mind, deny him without looking strongly suspicious. Only a madwoman would not accept the hand of an earl. Especially when supposedly carrying his child.

Her eyes flashed to his. Goodness, they were beautiful. So much lurked beneath their amber surface. He remembered Oliver's romantic notion of eyes telling a story and felt a little bad about ever thinking the man was daft.

"Oh, of course I do!" said Miss Bellows, holding his eye contact. "I'm only shocked. I had not expected something so…generous of you." Oh, he heard the way her teeth tightened over those last few words.

He smiled. "Remarkable, aren't I?"

Carver watched her purse her lips and flare her nostrils, biting back a remark. He wished she wouldn't.

"Just right, sir." Her eyes bounced around the carriage. Was she looking for a way out? Perhaps she would cave sooner than he expected. Oddly, that disappointed him a little.

He leaned forward and took her hand in his. Those bewitching brownish-gold eyes looked back at him, wide and full. Carver realized he had never seen such an eye color before. They looked exactly like brandy. "My dear, I can see that you are apprehensive. Come sit by me and I can soothe your nerves." He had to clench his teeth together to refrain from laughing when her eyes widened at the innuendo.

Clearly, she thought him every bit the rakeshame that Lord Newburry was.

Her lovely pale pink lips formed a tense smile as she pulled her hand away from his. "Apprehensive? Oh no, not a bit! I'm only trying to understand what all of this means. I just—I cannot imagine that you would truly be happy married to me. I'm afraid that you are acting rashly and, if given more time to think about it, would prefer to simply provide for my financial needs and be free of any responsibility." She would like that, wouldn't she? But that was definitely not going to happen.

He moved her valise to the ground. Why *did* she have a valise with her? Convenient—he'd say that much. Carver then moved to her bench and sat so their shoulders were touching. He wasn't actually going to do anything untoward. But she didn't have to know that.

He took her hand in his once again, this time taken surprised by how nicely her hand felt in his. And was it her that smelled so wonderful? It was soft and airy, but also warm and comforting. She smelled like vanilla.

Keep your head straight, man. "Let us get to know each other better, shall we?" He could hear her sharp intake of breath.

"I think we know each other plenty." She laid her free hand on the skewed baby bump, and as he felt her body stiffen beside him, he had to hold back a grin.

Out of the corner of his eye, he could see her discretely pull her cloak around her stomach.

"I would disagree," he said. "I believe there is still much I have to learn about you."

How long would it take for the woman to cry pax? He reached out and touched her chin, tilting her face up to look at him. Unfortunately, the moment her eyes locked with his, he completely forgot that he was acting. The air felt too thick to breathe and his heart pounded against his chest. His eyes slid to her bow-shaped lips. She did not turn away or even show any hesitation. In fact, her lips parted slightly. He leaned in only a breath away before realization took hold of his senses. What the devil was he doing? He wasn't actually going to kiss her, was he?

Yes. *No!* That was not part of the plan.

Daphney seemed to have the same thought. She looked down as he scooted away from her. And of course, the bench made that horrible squelching sound again. Perfect. Heat rushed up his neck as he waited for the 'I told you so' look that Miss Bellows was sure to give him. Instead, her face was pale and almost concerned. Maybe he had taken the act a little too far.

"You know, I think I am feeling a little unwell after all." She adjusted her posture until her arm was pressed against the wall by the door. "Could you have your coachman stop the carriage and let me out here? I think I just need some fresh air."

He smiled, both relieved that perhaps she hadn't heard his embarrassing noise and because he knew full well that she was hoping to find a way to escape without having to admit to her scam. He knocked on the wall of the carriage and it pulled to a stop.

Daphney looked at Carver with a pleased smile, maybe a touch smug, before the footman opened the door and let down the stairs. Apparently, this was the part where she would get out and plan to never see him again. "I'm terribly sorry to leave you in the middle of our discussion, but I think a walk is just the thing to help my queasiness. I'll send a note around to your house with directions to where I may be reached so that we can settle all the details of our engagement." Mmhmm.

He smiled and nodded mutely while handing the woman her valise. The footman reached out and helped Daphney from the carriage. Carver stayed where he was, holding a smile on his face. He didn't need to look out of the carriage to know what she would find. Or rather, wouldn't find. If his estimations were correct they were about a half-hour outside of London and exactly in the middle of nowhere.

Carver picked a piece of fuzz off of his jacket. *She'll be back in 3...2...*

"Where the devil have you taken me, Carver?" There was that spark again. She sprang back up into the carriage with all the agility of a woman not with child. But the bump was centered again, so that was something.

"We are currently on our way to visit my family at Dalton Park." He stiffened.

Dalton. Had he accidentally given himself away with the slip of the family title? As the first son of a duke, Carver held his father's courtesy title, Earl of Kensworth, until he succeeded his father and would take over the dukedom. If Daphney knew anything about the peerage, she would know that the Earl of Newburry had already succeeded his

38

father and inherited the earldom. Did Daphney know that Dalton Park belonged to a duke?

He watched her face closely and was relieved to see that she didn't seem to understand the significance. For once, Carver was thankful that titles among the peerage were vastly complicated and hard to keep track of.

"Where is Dalton Park?" Her voice rattled with restrained anger.

"In Kent. About a six-hour journey so we really ought to be getting back on the road."

Her eyes widened. "Kent! Oh, for heaven's sake, I am not going with you to Kent! I must insist that you turn back now and kindly set me down in London." Gone was the meek little maid that had been sitting across from him earlier. Her gorgeous eyes flashed fire.

It was very difficult for him to keep his amusement from showing. "Afraid not. I'm already running late as it is. My family is expecting me in time for dinner and I don't want to disappoint them." That much was true.

Those eyes just blinked at him as if unable or unwilling to understand what he was telling her. "You will not take me back to London?"

"I will not."

She moved to sit on the edge of the bench and looked around the carriage, at a loss for how to proceed. It was clear that whoever she was; she was unaccustomed to her demands not being heeded. She found her fire again and faced him with a sharp movement. "Did you not think it pertinent to tell me that we would be leaving town before I entered your carriage?"

He shrugged. "You didn't ask."

"I didn't think I needed to!" The woman was maddeningly beautiful when in a passion. "What kind of gentleman sweeps a female into his carriage, then carries her out of town without her consent?" she asked.

"Romantic isn't it?"

Her eyes narrowed. "It's abduction."

He couldn't help but smile. It *was* abduction. "Either way, I believe you are stuck with me, darling."

"Oh!" He thought he could see steam coming out of her ears. "Do not *darling* me one more time. It's insufferable."

"Only half an hour together and we already sound like a married couple of many years. I'd say that's a good sign." Her eyes were strangling him.

The footman re-appeared at the open door of the carriage. "Shall we continue, my lord?"

Carver looked to Daphney. "What will it be, my dear?" Knowing she hated the endearment made it all the more enticing to use. He could live with her feeling a little annoyed.

For a moment, she looked as if she might get out of the carriage. But then a crack of thunder sounded and was followed by large glorious drops of rain. She rolled her eyes, sat back in her seat, and folded her arms, looking very much like a pouty child. "Oh, for goodness' sake. Let's go! I certainly cannot get out here now."

He nodded to the footman who shut the door and in the next moment the carriage leapt into motion again.

Carver suddenly filled with the realization that he was bringing a woman home. To meet his family. Unfortunately, he had not considered the consequences of detaining her in his carriage for so long, but it was too late to turn back now. He would just have to play it off as if she were really his betrothed until she decided to confess. Of course, he could tell Miss Bellows that he knew she was scamming him right then and there. He could drop her at the nearest posting house and arrange to have her sent back to London and his family would never need to know a thing about it. But what fun would that be? His family could forgive him later.

Daphney eyed him with tight lips. "What is your middle name, Carver?"

He chuckled, knowing full well why she wished to know it. "Timothy."

This time it was Daphney who leaned forward in her seat. She leveled him a glare with such icy undertones it threatened to freeze all of England. She spoke with a slow, ominous cadence. "Carver Timothy Newburry—,"

"Ashburn," he corrected. "Ashburn is my surname. Newburry is just a title." Not even his title.

She sat back with a defeated huff and folded her arms. "Well. That quite takes the wind out of my sails, doesn't it?"

"Don't give up now," he said with a smile. "I was very much enjoying that icy glare."

"You're not supposed to enjoy it," she said. "It's supposed to scare you."

He shrugged. "Perhaps I enjoy being scared?"

She rolled her eyes again. Why did he seem to enjoy her so much? He would do well to remember that the woman was trying to con him. That should really bother him more than it did.

Chapter Six

R ose was angry. She was angry because she had somehow been outsmarted by the womanizing earl sitting across from her. The fact that she couldn't seem to keep herself from liking him only intensified her anger. She should hate his sarcastic devil-may-care attitude. Instead, she was drawn to his lazy smile and the way he constantly looked at ease no matter how much she tried to ruffle his feathers.

For some reason, she was finding it difficult to view him as the disgusting pig that his reputation implied. There was something about him that was almost...kind. But then again, rakes didn't get women to warm their beds with a gruff, off-putting demeanor.

She had never before lost control of a situation. And yet, here she was, sitting in an earl's carriage, betrothed, and on her way to spend a week with his family. It was maddening. More than once, she considered pulling her pistol out and threatening him to turn the carriage around. Even then, she assumed he would simply grin and say something witty that would make her want to laugh. He was too easy going.

It would serve him right to get shot.

Rose pulled up the shade on the window and looked out. The low winter sun danced across the expansive hills and farmland. In any other situation, she would have enjoyed the sight immensely. As it was, she was cursing every inch because it took her further away from the safety of London. The safety of solitude.

"Oh, come on," said Carver with a playful grin. "You can't still be vexed with me. You've tortured me enough this last half-hour with your silence. This is no way to begin a betrothal."

She leveled a glare at him. "*Abduction* is no way to begin a betrothal and yet here we are."

He smiled fully—making the dimple she suspected a reality. "Touché! But in my defense, I had no way of knowing that you would be so opposed to spending a week at my family seat." A week? "Most women would jump at the chance. And it will give us plenty of time to get to know one another before we marry." Of all the absurd!

Was he truly planning to marry her? Rose didn't think so. She had studied him quietly that past half-hour and had decided this must have been some sort of game for the earl. But she was good at games and certainly was not going to be the one to show her cards first. For now, she would continue the ruse and play along, at least until she got to Dalton Park and could make her escape.

"I just don't like to be surprised, that's all. It makes me feel…"

"Surprised?" he said with a tipped brow. Blast him. "No use hiding it. I can clearly see you are trying not to smile." Did he miss nothing? Rose had a sinking feeling that she had finally met her most well-matched opponent. Would he uncover the truth of her identity? Turn her in? She refused to allow herself to grow nervous. And yet, every time his gaze settled on her, her heart raced.

"I am trying not to smile because I do not feel like smiling. And I think it very ungentlemanly of you to force me into it."

He chuckled a little. "And just how am I forcing you to smile?"

"Well, you don't exactly leave me any choice when you continue to say things I find funny."

He smiled and raised both of his brows, somehow looking boyish and more genuine than she'd seen him look so far. "You find me funny?"

"Only a little," she said, adjusting skirts that really didn't need adjusting.

"Poor thing. That took a great deal for you to admit, didn't it?" *Do not smile. Do not smile.* "Why else are you cross with me? Have I not done exactly as you secretly wished? You cannot honestly say that you would have preferred to have been paid off rather than enter into marriage with a wealthy earl. You'll be much more comfortable this way."

Doubtful.

Rose knew that she would be much less comfortable as a married woman than a self-sufficient thief. And although he was turning out to be much kinder than she had anticipated, he was still a cad.

"Is there perhaps someone else you care for? Someone who will be deprived of your affections if we married?" he asked when she didn't respond to the first question.

She shook her head. "I have no one else to care about." The honest words flew into the air before she could think better about it. And now there they were, staring and taunting her for making yet another mistake.

His brows lifted. "No one? Not even family?"

She swallowed and quickly tried to invent a new story. But for some reason, when his eyes were settled so intently on her, she had a hard time thinking straight. "I do not have any living family. And life in service hardly provides enough time to develop any relationships." Or the life of a criminal.

"That sounds lonely." *Lonely.* That unwelcome word buried itself deep in her chest without permission. Is that what she had been feeling lately? She forced her gaze back out the window, unwilling to give in to the weakness she had begun to feel over the past few weeks.

When she didn't answer after a few minutes, he spoke again. "Well, you won't have time to be lonely this week. My rather enormous and doting family will be all too eager to monopolize your time." *Enormous family.*

Rose wasn't sure she was comfortable with that thought. No, actually, she knew she wasn't. Even when her family was still living, it had only ever been her and Papa. She swallowed at the familiar lump that formed in her throat. How was it possible to still miss someone after so much time?

She was well aware that it wasn't just Papa that she missed, but her life that died along with him. The day before he was taken from her, she had been cared for, comforted, safe, and happy. The very next day, she had been left orphaned, penniless, homeless, and scared. She had learned quickly to take care of herself. To close off her heart in attempt to protect herself from ever feeling the pain and vulnerability she felt the day her sweet Papa died. And it worked. If she kept people at arm's length, she never grew attached. And if she never grew attached, she never had to feel the sting of loss again.

"I cannot imagine that your family will be pleased to see me show up unannounced at their doorstep," said Rose, pulling her thoughts away from her past. She didn't know much about polite society, but she did know that they were often very stuffy about propriety and protocol.

He smiled. "You don't know my family." After a pause, he added, "Besides, it's been three years since I've been home. They will just be pleased that I finally managed to make the trip in its entirety this time." That was an interesting confession. And one that he looked to instantly regret admitting just as much as she had regretted her words a moment ago.

"Three years seems like a long time to stay away. What's been keeping you from returning?" Rose asked and then noticed Carver's face harden. "Forgive me, it's no business of mine." Could it be another scandal with yet another maid? She hoped not, for the maid's sake. Not because she had begun to like the man in any way.

He surprised her by continuing the topic. "Do you have any memories you'd rather never re-live?" And again, the air in the carriage felt too thick and suffocating. She looked him in the eyes but didn't dare speak. Her emotions felt too close to the surface. And she was always careful to never let them reach the top. So instead, she just looked to him and gave a brief nod.

"I do as well. And they all live in that house." Rose could almost feel his anguish. It was the oddest sensation. She barely knew this man, and yet, she was beginning to feel a tether to him that she couldn't explain. It was not good. Not good at all.

She watched as he harshly rubbed his hands over his face and then back through his hair. When his hands fell back to his side, Rose noticed a streak of blood running down his face.

"Your cut is bleeding," she said motioning toward the wound above his eyebrow. It must have been fresh to have bled so easily.

Carver dabbed the cut with his finger and then looked down at the blood as if to verify she was telling the truth and not just playing some sort of prank on him. "Blast," he said.

"Do you have a handkerchief? Hurry—it's about to drip on your jacket," she said looking around for something to put on it but coming up empty. He pulled a linen from his jacket pocket and dabbed around his forehead to find the cut. It was miserable to watch. Could he not feel where the wound was? Was he purposely trying to annoy her? If so, it was working.

"Here," she said impatiently while scooting over to his bench and taking the linen from his hand. She placed it on his cut and applied pressure.

It was when she smelled the cool clean scent of his shaving soap that she realized just how close she had sat to him. An odd warmth surged through her. When she looked down at his eyes, she saw that there was a deep crease between his brows and again he looked as if he were searching her face for something important. It was most uncomfortable to be looked at like that. Somehow she felt as if he were seeing into her very thoughts.

She cleared her throat. "Hold it there for a few minutes," and shifted away but not back to her own seat. Why? Now it would look odd if she decided to move across the carriage after sitting for several seconds in that spot.

"Has the sight of my blood offended your sensibilities?" he said, eyeing her with a playful look.

She chuckled and felt herself relax a little. "Perhaps it would have, had I any sensibilities to offend."

He smiled inquisitively. "Blood doesn't make you squeamish?"

"Not a bit." She looked again to the cut he was dabbing with the handkerchief. "Do you box often?"

His brows lowered. "How did you know that I box?"

It was her job to know. She was constantly reading people and their body language for clues on how they were feeling, what they would do next, and how to interact with them. "You have that cut above your eye, and I'm assuming from the way you wince and bend to the right every time we hit a bump, you have something of a bruised rib. At first, I thought that you'd taken a toss from your horse, but then I noticed your swollen red knuckles and realized that you must have been in a fight recently." She decided not to mention that his muscular physique also lent itself to her conclusion.

He smiled, a touch smug. "Last night, in fact."

"Did you win?"

A bigger smile. "I did. But it was a near-run thing."

"Is your rib broken?" Not that she cared. It was just a long journey, and she needed to make conversation. Better to talk about him than herself.

"I don't think so." A mischievous twinkle entered his grey eyes. "Do you want to assess it for yourself?"

She narrowed her eyes and resisted the blush she felt sweeping over her skin. Who knew ears could feel like they were on fire? "No. I do not. And if you're not careful, you will find yourself with a matching bruised rib on the other side." But the more he said things like that, the more she had the feeling he was teasing her rather than flirting or trying to seduce her. Something was not adding up about Lord Newburry. Most rakes exuded villainous airs. Carver did not. What game was he playing?

He held up his hands in surrender. "I'll be good, Daphney." Never had a name felt less like her own.

Rose looked back out the window for a time and allowed a comfortable silence to blanket the carriage. When she finally glanced sideways at him, she noticed that he was staring at her middle. She covered it with her hand and hoped to God it wasn't crooked again. He blinked and looked away. Was he suspicious? Or simply curious at the idea of a pregnancy? Either way, she did not want to risk him detecting that she was only warming a pillow under her dress instead of a baby.

"How many siblings do you have?" she asked, trying to turn his thoughts away from the non-existent child.

"Three sisters and a brother-in-law." Goodness. So many women. She would have thought that coming from a family of women would have taught him to treat the opposite sex with more respect. And yet, she hadn't actually experienced his disrespect firsthand. Something felt odd about that.

"Are you the oldest?"

He shook his head. "I have an older sister, Mary. She is married and has a little girl of her own. And then two sisters beneath me. Elizabeth and Kate."

"And will they all be at Dalton Park?" She needed to gain as much information as she could before being thrust into the undoubtedly awkward situation that was to come.

"Oh, yes. And believe when I say it will be nothing short of chaos the entire time. My family is…unconventional, to say the least."

"And yet you speak of it with fondness."

He smiled and leaned back against the bench. "That's because I'm very fond of them." He looked at her. "Did you ever know your family?"

There was no way she was going to dive into that topic with this man—or any man. "Is Dalton Park much further?"

His brow twitched, but he smiled. "I can take a hint. I won't ask you about your family anymore."

"Thank you," she replied.

Over the remainder of the journey, Carver told Rose everything that she needed to know about his family. They talked about what they would tell his family regarding their sensitive relationship and decided to not disclose her (fake) condition. Rose hated that she would have to embroil Carver's family in her ruse but she didn't seem to have a choice. She simply needed to get through dinner and wait for nightfall before escaping.

It was more than a little disappointing that she had not been able to secure the money but there was nothing for it. She had failed. It only stung because she knew that there were exactly fifteen children, three women, and one pregnant maid counting on that money, not to mention Uncle Felix.

She would simply have to find another way. She always did.

Chapter Seven

"Would you like to go in now or do you wish to continue reenacting a statue?" Carver's voice cut through Rose's moment of shock.

With a slack jaw, she continued to stare up at the monstrosity looming above her. "I don't know quite what I was expecting of your family's seat but a castle certainly was not it." Rose gestured toward the enormous home before her.

"What? This little cottage?" he said looking up at the stately three-story brownstone home. "Trust me, the longer you live here, the smaller it feels." That comment somehow missed the mark of his usual playfulness.

Carver took Rose's arm in his and led her up the massive front staircase. She refused to acknowledge the flutter in her stomach at his touch. Why did he have to smell so blasted good?

The massive oak entry doors opened, revealing an aged but kind looking butler. "My lord!" The man looked genuinely pleased. "It is a pleasure to have you back at Dalton Park." Did his eyes look misty or was she imagining it?

"I couldn't take another day without seeing your handsome old face, Henley," Carver said while patting the butler on the shoulder. She would never have expected that a man like Lord Newburry would be affectionate toward his serving staff. Well, affectionate in a familial way that is.

She grimaced, thinking of this man she had begun to like—only the very tiniest bit—taking advantage of a helpless young maid.

"Henley, this is Miss Bellows—but don't get any ideas. I've already snagged her for myself." Carver looked to her and winked, making her stomach jump oddly.

Henley bowed with a smile. "A pleasure, Miss Bellows. If you will excuse me but a moment, I will ask your mother in which room she would have me place Miss Bellows."

"Never mind, that. Put her in the gold room," said Carver.

Henley flashed the earl a look of hesitation. Carver smiled a smile that Rose was sure would turn everyone he knew into pudding in his hands. "I will deal with my mother."

"Yes, my lord," said Henley before bowing and instructing a footman dressed in fine red livery to have Rose's bag placed in the gold chamber.

"I believe we have a bit of time to change and wash up before dinner. I'll show you to your room."

She hesitated a moment. "Should you?"

He tossed her an amused frown even as he began to lead her up the wide wooden staircase. "What do you mean?"

"I'm not sure it's quite the thing for you to be showing me to my bedchamber."

He chuckled. "My dear, I believe the very nature of our relationship is *not quite the thing*. Walking you to your door is the least of my worries." Technically, he was right. But when viewed in the light of the truth, their relationship was really quite innocent. Well, as innocent as conning a notorious libertine out of his money could be.

They reached the second floor landing and Carver gestured down the long hallway to the right. The house became more breathtaking by the minute. Large, regal paintings hung in perfectly measured intervals along the walls opposite enormous windows overlooking the vast park grounds of the estate. The walls were all papered in various cool-toned shades with lovely detailed floral patterns. Even the wood trim lining the top and bottom of the walls was ornately carved, demonstrating the care taken with every detail. Rose found herself wishing that she could stay a day or two to explore the beautiful castle and grounds. But that simply couldn't happen. She would leave as soon as darkness descended.

They continued to walk down the hallway in silence. Even if Carver hadn't mentioned that there had been painful memories keeping him away from his family home, she could feel it in the tension radiating stronger and stronger from his body with every increasing step. From the corner of her eyes, she could see his jaw flex and the muscle in his arm tighten.

What had happened within these walls to pull such a strong reaction from him? For a moment, Rose forgot that she completely hated the man and everything he stood for. Her feelings felt tender and her instinct told her to comfort him.

She squashed those feelings. Feelings and attachments were not what she needed.

They stopped and Carver gestured with his head to the door in front of them. "Your bedchamber, my dear."

"Why did you have me placed in the gold room?" It was curious to her that Carver should care about her accommodations. She only hoped it wasn't for improper reasons, like proximity to his bedchamber.

He smirked with mischief in his eyes. "I hoped you'd ask that." He stepped a little closer. "I chose this room because the golden paper on the walls will accentuate the golden flecks in your eyes."

Rose tried to contain it but couldn't. A laugh sputtered from her mouth. "Heavens!" she said, a chuckle still running through her voice. "Did you choose this room just to be able to use that line?"

He looked down at her, a grin twisting on his face. Again, it felt like a glimpse at the real man behind the rakish mask. "I hoped for it. Did it work in my favor?"

She crinkled her nose. "Not in the least! Besides, my eyes are not golden. They are more like…" she paused to find the right description.

"Like a glass of good brandy." His tone was no longer fake. Or sultry. It was soft and sincere in a way that told Rose he had already given the idea a good bit of thought.

She studied him for a moment, trying to figure out whether he was being genuine or just flirtatious. When all she found was a look of sincere admiration in his eyes, she blinked and looked away. "I was going to say mud, but your assessment is certainly more poetic." She forced a chuckle that sounded stupid even to her and then hazarded a glance back up at him.

She shouldn't have. His eyes caught hers and held them in his gaze. Rose felt her heart quicken from his nearness, much like it had when he had almost kissed her in the carriage. He looked into her eyes for what felt like a ridiculous amount of time—but in reality; it was probably only a few seconds. He didn't smile. He just looked. What was he looking for when he did that? Rose could have sworn he wanted to say something, but held it back. Was he having second thoughts about the engagement? Was he trying to remember her face? Would he realize that she was not telling the truth?

She willed herself to look at the floor to regain a bit of her composure. She needed to get a better grip on herself. This man was nothing more than a target.

Then his calloused fingers slipped under her chin and tipped it up again. "You should know that your eyes are beautiful and do not share the least resemblance to mud." Hang the man, he was good. Is this how all rakes made women feel? She began to see how they earned their reputations.

Breathing felt more difficult as her heart threatened to burst from her chest. He looked down at her lips and against her better judgment; she looked at his. He leaned down toward her face and she sucked in a quick breath.

But before his lips had the chance to meet hers, she heard the click of the latch on the door behind her. Her head swung back to see that he had only leaned down to reach the doorknob. He straightened up with an amused smirk on his mouth. "I was just opening the door for you." Oh, she hated him!

Heat clawed up her neck and face and she took a fumbling step backward into the bedchamber. "Of course…I knew that," she snapped. But she knew he didn't believe her.

"Dinner is at seven, my dear. Don't be late." He smiled smugly, bowed, and then turned on his heels and started back down the hallway. "I'll have a maid sent to your room to help you dress," he called back without turning around then disappeared down another corridor.

Rose slipped into her room, shut the door, leaned against it and slid to the ground. "Rose, you idiot," she whispered into her hands. "You are not actually marrying him!"

And she didn't want to, either—despite what her pounding heart was saying. She knew her heart could never be trusted when it came to real life. Emotions and attachment to people only lead to pain, heartbreak, and vulnerability in the end. Those were things Rose never desired to feel again. She preferred to be in control of her life at all times. The only way to truly do that was to remain as unattached to people around her as possible.

She had to leave. As soon as the family retired to bed, she would make for the stables. Carver would undoubtedly be relieved when he realized that she had bolted. A rake could never truly be happy about the idea of settling down. And besides, she didn't think for one second that he truly wanted to marry her. Most likely, he had just been feeling an odd and fleeting sense of honor and would completely regret the whole thing in the morning. Or even more likely…he would recognize that it was a scam and turn the tables on her.

Either way, I won't be here to find out.

Rose untied her deuced ugly bonnet and tossed the horrid thing to the floor, glancing around the room for the first time. She stood up and walked over to the lovely four-poster bed. She ran her fingers across the luxurious bed linens as she admired the heavy drapery lining the windows and fresh flowers on the bedside table. It was the dead of winter. How on earth did they manage to have such a lovely spray of flowers?

The walls were not covered in the heavy gold-colored paper she had been imagining. Instead, it was creamy with a metallic gold floral design that wrapped the room like vines. It was light and beautiful. Rose couldn't imagine a more lovely room.

An involuntary and completely ridiculous smile hovered over her lips as she thought of Carver's horrid flirt. It was a bad line. But the one that followed…

Well. It had her darting to the looking glass and observing her eyes. *A glass of good brandy.* She didn't see anything so captivating. Brown. They were brown. And while assessing her features, she noticed a few additional flaws.

She placed a finger on either side of her brows and tugged upward trying to smooth out the new small lines she found around her eyes. When had she developed those? And all those freckles? Was that a grey hair? It was stupid of her to be surprised. She might be playing the part of a young housemaid, but the harsh reality was that she actually carried twenty-three years in her dish.

Rose had always looked young for her age, often able to play the part of a blushing young debutante without fear. But with a sinking feeling, she realized the day was quickly approaching when she would no longer be convincing in such a role. Her career would have to change, as her roles would change. And she was quickly exiting her marriageability window.

Stop. You don't want to be married.

She couldn't help but picture herself standing next to the unfairly handsome Carver Ashburn, Earl of Newburry. She was too dowdy and plain for him. It was a very good thing that she didn't give a dash for the rake. And that she would be leaving in a few hours.

Chapter Eight

C arver walked to his bedchamber feeling a touch odd, with a vague suspicion that he had made a mistake by bringing Daphney—or so she said was her name—to his home.

Originally, he had assumed she would be a needed diversion from the memories that lived in these halls. He could spend a few days teasing the minx before he confronted her on her scam. But something had shifted during the carriage ride that he couldn't quite identify. And just a moment ago outside her room—what had that been? He had nearly kissed her...again. And not as a tease, but from a very real desire.

He couldn't seem to shake the strong feelings tugging him toward her. Those eyes of hers felt like a beacon. They promised him a new life away from his pain, memories, and loneliness. But that was absurd. She was some sort of thief; he was certain of it. He couldn't be falling for a thief—beautiful or not.

He stopped just outside the door of his bedchamber. Entirely too many memories lived inside that room. Opening it would mean opening himself back up to the same pain and heartbreak he had felt the day she died. It was where he had written sweet letters to her, dreamed of their future, and in the end, mourned her death. A death that had come far too suddenly for such a lovely young lady, and a death that was partly his fault. If only he hadn't come home late, it never would have happened, and she would still be his.

Willing himself to finally open the door, Carver stepped into his room and froze. Instead of facing a flood of memories, he found his mother sitting in a chair beside the fire reading a book. His three sisters were gathered on his bed, looking precisely the same way they had when he was still living at home. His heart ached to see them all in this familiar scene again. It had been too long.

He whistled low. "Who's the unfortunate sap that's found himself in the suds with you beautiful ladies?"

Their eyes all snapped to him. "You!" they said in unison with that look that only females could achieve.

He raised his eyebrows, and a smile pulled at his lips. "Surely I'm not in trouble with you, love?" said Carver, walking over to lay a kiss on his mother's cheek. It was amazing how she never seemed to age. Her hair was still almost as golden-blonde as Elizabeth's, but with a few streaks of grey threaded throughout.

"Oh! Do not flatter me, you wicked boy," said the duchess, looking at him from under her thick lashes, precisely as she had when he was a boy and she was about to scold him for putting pepper in his governess' tea. "You know what you have done."

Carver made a theatrical show of innocence. "I? Done something wrong? That doesn't sound like me." No matter that it had been three years since he had been home, he felt as if he could pick right back up with his family just as he had before he left. Of course, he had seen them every year when they had come to Town for the Season, but somehow it was different back at home. In town, they all had appearances to keep up and frequent calls to make. At home, they were simply family. No airs. No prying eyes.

Mary, his older sister and the one who most closely resembled him, spoke up. "Oh, Mother, that's far too vague for a man who is constantly in one scrape or another." She cast a pointed look to the cut above his eyebrow as if the injury alone proved her point. "Allow me to make it clear, brother. You brought home a lady of whom none of us have ever heard, and informed Henley that she is your intended."

"Oh, that," he said, smiling.

"Do you not deny it?" asked his mother, eyes narrowed.

"I could...but then it would be devilishly awkward when she walks into dinner tonight."

The duchess stood and swatted him on the arm in her usual way. "How could you be so unfeeling as to not write to your mother that you were engaged?"

"And miss seeing your face when you found out? Absolutely not." Outwardly, he was joking. Inwardly, he was cringing at the realization that he was going to be in a world of trouble with his family when they learned the truth. He was beginning to wonder if they even needed to know the truth. Maybe he could work something out with Daphney after she finally decided to come clean? Perhaps they could stage a fight and he could return her to London without his family becoming suspicious.

"Carver, I am told that you two arrived in the same carriage and without a chaperone. That was most improper."

He shrugged a shoulder. "I suppose I'll just have to marry her then." He took in his mother's expression and added, "No need to release your maternal wrath, Mother. I was a perfect gentleman to Daphney." But then he thought back on the ride and that almost kiss. "Well...most of the time I was." He smirked and his mother narrowed her eyes into slits.

"Carver, this is not a joke," said Mary. "We all know how significant this is for you. I didn't even realize that you had been thinking of courting again."

He and Mary had always been the closest out of all of his siblings. They had an odd way of knowing exactly what the other was thinking. He hoped that she couldn't see what he was thinking just then.

Had Carver actually been planning on marrying Daphney, it would have most certainly been a significant moment. But he wasn't. He was just using her to divert his attention, as she was using him to fill her pockets. Surely that made what he was doing more honorable? His family would forgive him. If he thought it enough, would it become true?

He addressed Mary's statement with as much truth as he could. "I wasn't thinking of courting, but Daphney simply…showed up at my door. All it took was one look and my heart wanted her right away." He had only said that last bit to make his case more convincing. But he tensed a little when he realized that some part of that statement rang true. Did he want Daphney? No. Stupid. He didn't even know who she was.

Carver's two youngest sisters sighed and pretended to swoon at his words. He narrowed his eyes and waved them off. "Enough of that. How is our dear Robert?" Carver asked Mary. "Still disgustingly in love with you?"

"I prefer *devastatingly*," she said with a twinkle.

Mary and Robert had been married four and a half years, but from the little bit he had seen of them, they still acted every bit the newlywed couple. He was able to see Robert, an earl as well, when parliament was in session. But ever since having her first child a little more than three years ago, she had rarely left their house in the country. Carver had visited them there a few times, but he knew it was not enough.

"What is your lady-love like, Carver?" said Kate, the baby of the family and by far the most romantic. How was it possible that she was already eighteen years old? "Did you meet in a ballroom?" she asked with fluttering eyes.

It was then that Carver realized how inappropriate Daphney's made-up tale would be for his sisters' innocent ears. Hearing such a vulgar tale of their brother seducing a maid would be a little more than shocking—not to mention untrue—and not an image he was willing to put in their minds.

"Actually, yes. That's exactly where we met." He would give Daphney the revised edition of her story later.

"Is she a beauty?" asked Elizabeth, the sister that was just under Carver in age and getting ready for her first season in London.

To most, twenty would seem a touch old to experience her first

Season, but the duke and duchess saw wisdom in waiting until their daughters were more mature to handle the London ballrooms. Carver, for one, was thankful for their prudence. He was not at all ready to see his baby sisters parade around the marriage mart, being courted by hordes of maggots who would never deserve them.

His mind flashed to images of men like Lord Newburry pursuing Elizabeth and his hands involuntarily flexed.

The women all continued to bubble over with questions about Daphney. Well, all except for Mary. She was eyeing him with a narrowed gaze as he answered the questions any doting fiancé would be happy to field. How was it possible that she already knew something was amiss?

Before he knew it, a half-hour had passed while they laughed and recalled tales from the past few years. He had seen his sisters in town when his parents had come for a stay, but it had never felt like this much of a reunion. The beautiful young women they had grown into both astounded and frightened him. Especially Elizabeth. She had far outgrown the slightly plump little girl he had left behind three years ago when he moved to London. Elizabeth now held the sort of looks he knew London would deem Incomparable.

"Alright, my darlings, I must kick you out or else I'll be late for dinner and Daphney will think I have already jilted her."

Before fully leaving the room, Kate paused with a dreamy look. "*Daphney*. I like that name. Do you think she will mind if I call her by her given name?" But was it her given name? The thought was beginning to eat at Carver. For some odd reason, he felt the name was not at all right for her.

"I don't think she will mind."

The rest of the girls continued to file out of the room, each one pausing to hug him.

Mary, however, stopped short of the door. Her light grey eyes pierced him with an intense look. It never ceased to amaze him how similar his eyes were to hers. Is this what it felt like to be on the receiving end of one of his glares?

"You took long enough coming home." She knew exactly why

Carver hadn't been home. And as the closest to her in birth and relationship, he knew his absence had been hard on her. Truth be told, it had been hard on him as well.

He took her hand and squeezed it. "I know. I'm sorry."

Mary's eyes darted away as they began to pool with tears. Goodness, the woman never cried! She must have missed him more than he realized. "Oh Mary, don't cry," he said, pulling her into his chest.

"Don't flatter yourself," she said with a small chuckle. "It's this baby making me cry, not your ugly face."

He pulled her away by the shoulders to look at her. "You're expecting again? That's wonderful news, Mary!" This would be number two for his sister. He was particularly fond of his little niece Jane. Being the fun uncle was a role he hadn't expected to enjoy as much as he did. Though he didn't go to visit his niece often enough. He would change that in the future.

Mary smiled but with a distant and almost sad look that he didn't quite understand. "Number two," was all she said.

"And Robert hasn't jumped out of the window yet?" He hoped to bring a lighter smile to his sister's face.

"I boarded them up," she said with a twinkle. It struck him that Mary and Daphney had similar senses of humor. Perhaps Mary would like Daphney after all.

Why the devil do I want Mary to like Daphney?

After everyone had finally made their slow progression out of Carver's room, Brandon, his valet, helped him quickly change for dinner. He pulled on his favorite black dinner jacket and biscuit colored pantaloons, then all but darted from his chamber. He didn't want to spend a minute more than necessary alone in that room of unwanted memories. Or any rooms of that house for that matter. But at least there were other people to distract him in those other rooms.

Speaking of, where was Daphney? If he kept his attention focused on teasing Daphney, he wouldn't think on the fact that his best friend and love of his life would not be at the dinner table, as she often had been when she was alive. Or that she wouldn't wink at him from across the table. And that he wouldn't smell the familiar scent of her lilac perfume when he would steal a kiss before handing her up into her carriage at the end of the night. None of that would happen ever again. Being home again was making something he had refused to acknowledge feel frighteningly real.

Part of him was debating packing his things and riding back to town that night. But then he stopped just a few paces from the stairs when he spotted someone. It was Daphney. The last remaining rays of light were pushing through the windows and bathing her skin in a soft warm glow. What was she doing just standing there? Her gloved hand was poised on the banister but she wasn't moving. He couldn't see her face but her body looked stiff. Not that he was noticing her fine figure. Blast. He must have been noticing it to realize it was fine.

But not again.

He cleared his throat to announce his presence and went to stand beside her. "Pardon me, miss, are you in need of a handsome gentleman to escort you down to dinner?" Playing the part of a flirtatious rake was turning out to be more fun than he had expected.

Daphney turned around and Carver's breath caught in his throat. He hadn't realized how much the bonnet she had worn earlier in the day had hidden her features. The woman's hair was a rich dark brown and swept back into a loose chignon with two soft curls hanging down to rest on her lovely collarbones.

No, don't notice her collarbones.

He forced his eyes back up to her face. The contrast of her dark hair and soft complexion made her eyes startlingly vibrant. She wore a fine but simple cream-colored gown with a light blue satin overlay that made her trim, elegant figure—the figure that he wasn't noticing—even more apparent. This was definitely not a young maid he was looking at. This was a beautiful *woman*.

"That would be lovely. Do you know where I might find one?"

A beautiful, feisty woman. And he was in trouble.

Chapter Nine

R ose had barely set foot in the drawing room on Carver's arm before she was accosted by two blonde, blue-eyed young ladies. Rose knew who they were simply from the brief description that Carver had given of his sisters during their journey that afternoon. But no amount of warning could have prepared her for their energy.

"Daphney!" said the youngest sister of the bunch, taking her by the arm and tearing her away from Carver. "Oh, I hope you don't mind if I call you by your given name! We never stand on ceremony around here, and since we are soon to be sisters, I cannot bear to call you anything different." A touch dramatic. This one must be Lady Kate.

"Of course I don't mind." *Because it's not my name.* "You must be Lady Kate," said Rose, fixing her mouth in a polite smile.

She was now—as Carver had quickly informed her on their way downstairs—his very proper affianced wife. They had not met in his bedchamber, but in a ballroom.

Rose was a highly experienced thief, but even with her advanced skills in lying it was proving difficult to keep all of her stories straight. She was a thief, pretending to be a pregnant maid carrying an earl's child, pretending to be an upstanding gentry miss. She could do it. She could keep it all straight.

Lady Kate's pouty look pulled Rose back to their conversation. "What gave me away?" said Kate. "Has Carver been warning you about us?"

"Not at all. Only regaling me with endearing stories about each of you." And yes, warning.

The other sister smiled and curtsied to Rose, looking much more controlled and refined than her younger sister. She looked to be only a few years Carver's junior and absurdly beautiful. However, despite her refined beauty and elegance, Rose could see a nervousness in her large blue eyes.

Carver walked to stand next to Rose and his sister. "Elizabeth, may I make known to you Miss Daphney Bellows. Daphney, this is my younger sister, Lady Elizabeth."

Lady Elizabeth smiled, revealing her bright white teeth. "I'm so happy to meet you, Daphney! And please do not worry over formal addresses around us. We are just happy that Carver has finally found a lovely lady to make him behave," said Elizabeth. "Carver says that you met during your first ball of the Season? Do tell us the story."

Rose looked back at Carver for approval and found his amused smile again. "Yes, darling, tell them the story." There was a look in his eyes that told Rose he was finding far too much pleasure in her discomfort.

Rose had an amusing idea of her own. "That is partly true. But I believe it was several balls into the season before your brother found the confidence to approach me. He's actually quite shy in London."

She slid her gaze to Carver, whose smile had dimmed and eyes had narrowed. He moved closer to her side. "Daphney, darling, I believe you are remembering it wrong. *You* were the one that seemed quite overwrought by my attentions. I only kept my distance because I was afraid you would fall to a swoon in the ballroom." The man knew how to play the game, did he? Once again, Rose found it difficult not to smile in his presence.

"How romantic!" said Kate with wide adoring eyes.

"Oh yes, I remember now," said Rose, shooting Carver a challenging look. "Only, it was that the scent of your essence was so strong and repulsive that it gave me a headache." She turned her attention back to the sisters who were gazing on them with wide eyes and very clearly soaking up every word. "I dropped him subtle hints, you see, that I absolutely would not dance with him until he changed his scent to something less...flamboyant." Oh, he would hate that last bit.

Rose felt Carver move closer before she looked to confirm it. Something odd always happened to the air when he drew near. It felt warmer and in short supply. He towered over her and his smile made Rose's stomach flutter. "Again, you are remembering it wrong. That was Mr. Covington you are thinking of. A horrible smelling man, you're right." She was biting her lips and wiggling her toes but still afraid that her smile was going to break free.

He stepped even closer. "*You* were so intimidated by my good looks that I could barely get you to come near me," he said with a grin and a mischievous look in his eyes. "But then, when I couldn't bear having to look on your beautiful face from a distance any longer, I took you by the hand without asking—," and then he was taking her hand, "and I lead you out to the dance floor where I held you in my arms for a waltz that scandalized the whole room." Her heart was hammering in her chest while he reenacted their fake memory, actually pulling her to him and placing a hand on her back in the pose of a waltz.

She had to tilt her head up to look in his eyes and the warm look he gave her did nothing to stop the heat rushing through her arms and neck. She swallowed, feeling all too aware that this moment was being watched by two young ladies.

"Oh yes. I do remember now." She was admitting she had been beaten. Only he didn't let her go after the declaration. He was still looking into her eyes in that frightening way. He was too close. Close enough to verify that his scent was not at all flamboyant, but masculine and far too pleasant. And she could see the way his brown wavy hair curled up a little at the nape of his neck, saying that he was probably in need of a haircut. But she didn't want him to cut it. She wanted to reach up and run her fingers through—

"Uncle Carver!" The voice of a small child entered the room and pierced through the moment. Rose breathed again. A little girl with dark brown, bouncing curls and wearing an adorable white nightgown rushed to Carver's side. He let go of Rose and turned to the girl, caught her up in his arms, and threw her into the air.

"My darling! Goodness, how you have grown. What are you now, twenty-five?" It would seem the earl was good with ladies of all ages.

"No, Uncle Carver!" She giggled in his arms. "I'm just three!" She proved the number with her chubby fingers.

He frowned theatrically. "No, certainly that cannot be true. You look like a proper lady!"

"I do know how to curtsy," she stated with pride.

He set her down. "Do you now? Let me see it."

Carver, in his nicely fitted black jacket and tan pantaloons, bowed to the little girl with as much honor as he would have bestowed upon a high society matron. The girl blushed and dropped a clumsy, yet endearing, curtsy.

"Very good, my dear! I'm impressed. You'll be the envy of the *ton*, I am certain."

Rose felt her brow creasing more and more after every interaction she witnessed of Carver with his family. He did not seem like a rake. A charming gentleman, yes, but not a rake. However, he had to be. It was widely known that Lord Newburry was a womanizing libertine. Facts do not lie.

But maybe there was another side to this man. A side that wasn't entirely horrible, and that loved his family and perhaps wanted to be better. Maybe he really did intend to reform his life and do right by Rose and their imaginary child. She felt a pang of remorse. If that was true, should she confess the truth and point him to the woman who truly did need his good intentions?

Carver scooped his niece back up into his arms and gave her all of his attention. The sight of such a tiny, fragile child being held gently in Carver's gigantic frame filled Rose with an odd longing. One she'd never had before.

"Uncle Carver?"

"Yes, love?"

Oh, come on.

"Are you still sad?"

A crease formed between Carver's brows as a nervous smile tugged at his lips. "Sad? How could I be sad when I have such a wonderful bundle in my arms?"

"Mama said you might not come because your heart was sad."

An unmistakable heaviness fell over the room, thick and obtrusive. Carver's mask slipped, and he did look sad. Rose's heart pinched at the sight. What had happened to this man to create such a fierce ache inside of him?

He never looked away from his niece, but still Rose felt the need to avert her gaze, afraid that he would not want her to see such raw, exposed emotion. Elizabeth and Kate's eyes were also downcast. She had done right to look away.

When she glanced back at Carver, she found him looking at her from the corner of his eyes. His face softened as he looked back at his niece and kissed her on the forehead. "Uncle Carver is much happier now, Janie." Because of Rose? Or because of little Jane? Or was he just saying that to soothe his niece's fears? How stupid. Of course he wasn't happier because of Rose.

All attention turned toward the doorway as another lady entered the room, along with a gentleman at her side. "Oh, there you are, Jane! You are supposed to be getting ready for bed." The woman was unmistakably Carver's elder sister. She and Carver shared the exact same shade of light grey eyes and chestnut hair. Lady Hatley—or Mary, as Carver had referred to her during their carriage ride—was also very tall, standing at nearly the same height as her husband, Lord Hatley.

Carver made a show of putting Jane behind his legs. "Jane, you say? That name isn't ringing a bell." The little girl giggled behind his legs. Carver shushed her.

"You wouldn't be teaching my daughter to tell a tale would you?" said Lord Hatley, barely holding back a smile.

"Why shouldn't I? Every lady needs to know how to tell a good tale now and then." He winked at Rose so subtly that only she caught it. It made her heart race.

Surely he was referring to the story they had just concocted a moment ago, and not the fact that she was a con woman running a scam? Her chest tightened with fear that perhaps he knew the truth. But if he knew, why hadn't he said anything?

Never had she felt more mixed up and out of control on a job. Was this man truly a rake? Did he actually intend to marry her? Or was it all a trap? No matter the answer, she had to get out of there.

"Alright, give her up, you rebellious uncle," said Lady Hatley.

"Absolutely not. I haven't had the chance yet to teach her how to cheat at cards or win a duel."

"There is always tomorrow," Lady Hatley said, holding her hand out for her daughter.

Little Jane came out from behind Carver's legs with a pouty lip. "I don't want to go to bed. I want to stay with Uncle Carver." The girl's bottom lip trembled.

"Yes, darling, I know, but—" It was then that Lady Hatley turned around and seemed to notice Rose for the first time. "Oh, you must be Miss Bellows." Her's was not a pleased sort of tone. Rather, largely skeptical.

"I am, my lady." Rose curtsied politely. "And you are Lady Hatley if I am not mistaken."

Her eyebrow twitched up in the exact same way Carver's did. If the lady were a foot taller, she and Carver could be mistaken for twins. "Could it be that my brother has remembered we exist enough to talk about us while he is away?" At first, Rose thought the woman was angry. But then Lady Hatley tossed a smirk at Carver and Rose realized that not only did she share Carver's eye color, but his sarcasm as well.

"Only when something annoying occurs and I'm reminded of you," said Carver with a returning smirk.

Lady Hatley wrinkled her nose at him before turning her attention back to Jane. "Come along, dear. I'll return you to the nursery. You may play with your uncle tomorrow." Lady Hatley gave Rose one more look—an unnerving looking—and then she was gone. Rose got the feeling that not everyone was happy about Carver's sudden engagement.

Don't worry, Lady Hatley. I'll be gone by tomorrow.

"Where is she?" sounded a sudden booming voice from the doors of the drawing room.

The whole room paused as an older gentleman of the same height and stature as Carver jaunted into the room. He paused only briefly to scan the room until his eyes fell on Rose. When he saw her, his hard, unreadable face transformed. His eyes softened and a large, infectious smile bloomed. "My dear, you are even more lovely than we all could have guessed!" The man promptly strode to her and picked up her hand and kissed it lightly.

Carver stepped beside her, once again bringing that warm air with him. "Daphney, this is my father—" He hesitated a moment before clearing his throat and continuing, "His Grace, the Duke of Dalton. Father, may I introduce Miss Daphney Bellows." But all Rose heard was, *the duke.*

The duke? Carver's father was a duke? That meant that Lord Newburry was the heir to a dukedom? Why did she not know that? For some reason that information did not sit well with her. Now that she thought of it, she was almost sure that Lord Newburry's father was dead. She would have to sort that out later...on her way out of here.

"An honor, Your Grace," Rose said with a deep curtsy. Did she do that right?

"No, the honor is all mine, my dear! Any lady that brings my son home is forever in my good graces. Now, when is the happy day?"

"Father—" said Carver, but was interrupted when the duke threw up his hand in Carver's direction.

"Shush boy, I'm not talking to you," he said with a warm smile that contradicted his harsh words. "I'm talking to your lovely Miss Bellows."

Rose couldn't help but smile. "Well, Your Grace. We have not formally set a date as of yet."

He tipped his head to Carver. "Not set a date? Are you daft, son? An engagement to such a lovely girl ought to be finalized as soon as possible."

"Oh, are you talking to *me* now?" said Carver.

The duke suppressed a smile. "That depends. Is it true that you lost your cart race last week to that Ellis boy and those bonesetters he likes to think of as horses?" he asked with one eye narrowed.

Carver's lips pressed into a line, but he couldn't keep the amusement from showing in his eyes. "I was ill that day." The whole room erupted in laughter. Even Carver chuckled a little. "How the devil did you even hear about that?"

The duke tipped a brow. "I am the Duke of Dalton, Carver. I hear everything." Goodness, Rose hoped that statement wasn't true.

A new voice sounded in the room. Carver was not exaggerating when he said his family was enormous.

Rose turned her head to see the most enchanting, regal woman sweep into the room. She stopped at the duke's side and rested a light hand on his arm. "Oh, you all leave my son alone. We do not want to scare him away on his first day home." This was the duchess, then. And also where the youngest sisters received their beautiful blonde hair. "And you must be my newest daughter," said the duchess.

Rose's heart swelled at both the words and the fondness in the duchess' tone. She had often dreamed of what her own mother would have been like had she lived instead of dying in childbirth. Papa had given Rose detailed descriptions of Mother's hair, eyes, and personality. But no matter how hard she tried, Rose could never conjure a fully realized image of her mother. For most of her life, Rose had watched the women around her and wondered if her mother had moved like that one, or worn her hair like this one. And now, Rose found herself wondering if her mother had possessed a voice like the duchess', so beautifully kind.

Carver broke through Rose's reverie by once again performing the polite introductions.

After, the duchess reached out and took Rose's hand. "We are so happy you are here, my darling! I can already see that you and Carver are meant to be." Her beautiful warm smile pulled at Rose's heart. Then the duchess did the unexpected and wrapped Rose in a tight embrace.

For an awkward moment, Rose's arms hung limp at her sides. How long had it been since she had been hugged like that? She didn't have to think long to find the answer. Thirteen years. Papa was the last person who Rose had ever allowed to wrap his arms around her in that comforting way. She hadn't realized how much she had missed it. How secure it made her feel.

Keep them at a distance, Rose.

But Rose knew it was rude not to return the gesture. Not that she would allow herself to enjoy it, but she could at least return the embrace. Rose placed her arms around the duchess and lightly patted her back stiffly. There. She did it.

When the duchess finally released her from the hug, Rose noticed that Carver was staring at her with furrowed brows.

Chapter Ten

N ight had taken its sweet time falling over Dalton Park. Rose sat on the floor, leaning against the foot of her bed simply watching the ticking clock on the mantel. She might be nothing more than a thief, but Rose had studied enough of high society's rules and conducts from previous jobs to know that when in the country, families generally retired earlier for the evening than when they were in town. That's what led Rose to settle on midnight as a suitable time for flight.

She closed her eyes and thought back on dinner as she waited for the shorthand to reach the twelve. The meal had passed rather quickly. Not because it was a light meal, but because Rose found the entire family so amusing that the time flew by effortlessly. Theirs was certainly not a normal family. She was sure of it based on the horribly dull balls and dinner parties she had attended on other jobs.

Rules and propriety clearly had no place at the Dalton table. Everyone had something to say and voiced their opinions loudly, thoroughly, and usually right over another person. The sisters were completely infatuated with their older brother, but their favorite way to show their adoration was by flinging set downs at him—which he readily accepted with a smile and a laugh. Rose was certain that at least one person, if not all, was always laughing through the course of the unfashionable dinner. No one among polite society would have ever expected that this was the way the Duke and Duchess of Dalton conducted their dinners.

Rose learned two important facts about the Ashburn family over the course of the evening: They were fiercely devoted to one another and all used terms of endearment liberally. That last fact made Rose feel a touch silly for ever having been offended when Carver called her *my dear* or *darling*. After realizing that endearments were normal among the family, hearing herself called by them made Rose feel an odd sense of inclusion and acceptance. She felt *wanted* and despite all of her effort; she liked the feeling.

Rose had sat quietly and listened to the family as dessert was being laid on the table. The sisters told Carver a lively story about a shy young buck that had begun calling on Elizabeth. Carver and Lord Hatley both schemed to run any gentleman through who even looked at one of their sisters the wrong way, and the duchess had glanced across the table to the duke with a look of strong love and contentment. Rose ached at the sight. She liked them too much.

Never once, on any of her previous jobs, had she felt any sort of connection with any of her targets. Usually, she hated the pretentious snobs. But here, she could genuinely see herself growing attached. And for that reason alone, she had to go as soon as possible.

The duchess had stood and signaled the end of dinner and the ladies all moved into the music room for after-dinner entertainment, where the gentleman would join them after their drinks. But Rose didn't feel like participating in any of that. She couldn't allow herself to get to know this family any further. Thankfully, Carver made an excuse of fatigue on her behalf, which allowed Rose to retire early to bed. Or as he didn't know—to her escape.

She watched the small hand meet the twelve. It was time to go.

Rose laid her hand on the valise she had never unpacked and noted the odd feeling in her stomach. Not nerves. Certainly not morning sickness. But rather something she hadn't felt in a long time—dread. She didn't want to leave this place. How could she have been so stupid, allowing her heart to long for a life that could never be hers? She had never—not once—made that mistake before.

But she hadn't actually lost her heart to Carver. Had she? The very idea was ridiculous. She knew the man was a womanizing philanderer and a deep gambler. But he was also remarkably funny, loving to his family, and achingly tender at times. Each side of his personality seemed to be at war with the other. In the end, which was the real Carver? There was a sadness in the depths of his eyes that didn't match the rakish mask he wore.

But then again, there was the fact that he didn't even bat an eyelash when she had declared herself his increasing mistress. Could a gentleman who was truly loving and tender really have acted so dishonorably to a young woman? Truly more concerning, if he couldn't even remember that she was not a mistress of his, that would have meant there had been enough to cause confusion.

Had he looked at all of them the way he looked at her? Thinking about that almost-kiss made the hairs on Rose's neck stand up and her stomach twist in odd, unfamiliar knots.

She finally stood up from the floor, smoothed the fabric of her plain green skirt, and picked up her bag. Out of habit, she moved to the door and began to turn around and allow herself her usual moment of reflection. But this particular time was somehow different from all the others. It felt wrong and too difficult to leave. Goodness, what was happening to her? Maybe she ought to take a little break from criminal work when she returned to London.

Rose hurried through the door and closed it quietly behind her. She glanced briefly in either direction, taking note of her surroundings. Everything was dark and still. She had blown out the candle inside her room instead of carrying it with her so that no one would see the light and grow suspicious.

The air in the hallway was cool, giving her a taste of the cold winter night waiting outside. Treading as lightly as possible across the rugs, she moved through the hallways, barely hearing the muted steps of her boots. After passing down several blackened corridors and two flights of stairs, Rose was confident that no one in the family remained awake. Even the servants had all retired downstairs. That made her escape far easier.

Making it to the first floor landing, Rose paused one last time to listen for sounds of movement in the house. Nothing. All was still. She tiptoed toward the door. When she and Carver had first arrived at Dalton Park, she had been careful to take note of where the stables were situated on the estate.

All she needed to do was make it out of the front entrance and turn to the right, walking roughly forty paces to the stables where she would hopefully find a suitable horse to saddle. Her years of experience had made her a fine judge of horses and she'd yet to come across one that she couldn't ride.

Rose made it out of the house and down the front stairs without a hitch. The air felt especially cold that night and the wind bit at her fingers. Maybe Uncle Felix was right about keeping at least one pair of gloves. But she'd never admit it to him.

Rose pulled her wool cloak more tightly around her as she approached the dark stables. Her heart began to thud harder in her chest in anticipation of leaving. Riding in such cold weather would not be pleasing by any means, but she knew she could manage it.

Chapter Eleven

C arver silently stared into the roaring fire in his father's study. The flames danced and rolled inside the grate, but all he could see was her beautiful face. "Come back to me, Claire," he whispered into the empty room.

No answer. No sounds other than the cracking and popping of the fire. His cravat felt tight and stifling. A quick adjustment and the linen was off, easing his suffocation only slightly. He always felt like he couldn't breathe at night. Alone in the dark, there was nothing to stop his mind from teasing him with what life could have been like had she lived. No matter what he did, pain wrapped around him, squeezing and pressing the life out of him.

He leaned back in the leather chair and it creaked under his movement. He looked down and swirled his glass of untouched brandy. That, however, *did* distract him with thoughts of another beautiful face. With a sinking feeling, he realized that he might never be able to look at the drink again without thinking of Daphney and her haunting eyes.

Wonderful. Now his mind was obsessing about *two* women he couldn't have. But only one of those women could he think on without pain, so he let his mind wander, attempting to puzzle her out.

Dinner with Daphney had been a disaster. But only because she had been enchanting—and that was not what he needed. How could he have been so stupid to bring a woman like her home to his family?

No one had acted as he had anticipated. Each of his sisters had taken to Daphney like a new fashionable bonnet. And Daphney seemed to fit perfectly among his family—his slightly eccentric and not at all normal family. They had all laughed and jested and poked fun at each other in their usual way, and Daphney had not only watched but joined in at times.

However, none of that mattered. She had to go. The woman was a liar, feasting on that lie at the expense of his family. But then an unwelcome thought popped into his head. Was *he* actually the liar? Daphney had not even wanted to come to Dalton Park in the first place. What had seemed like an amusing diversion was starting to become a real fix.

"By the way you are staring that drink down, I'd say you are expecting it to grow legs and run away," said Robert, standing in the door of the study.

Carver looked toward his smirking brother-in-law. "A man never can be too careful about his drink."

"May I join you?" asked Robert, walking to the adjacent empty seat.

Carver gestured for him to sit. Robert sat down and leaned back heavily, jutting his booted legs out toward the fire and crossing his ankles. "What's keeping you up?" asked Robert.

The same thing that keeps me up every other night.

Carver hadn't actually tried to sleep yet that night, but he didn't have to try to know with certainty that sleep would not find him in his old room. Too many memories were in there. Really, they lived in almost every inch of that house. But his room was the only place where he was left alone long enough to dwell on them. The silence would be too loud. This room, however—his father's private study—did not hold a single memory of *her*.

But he didn't say any of that. He never said anything about any of it.

77

"Perhaps if you drank the brandy instead of just looking at it you might feel more inclined to talk about whatever is bothering you."

Carver smirked. "Probably a little too much. I've been told I talk a lot when I'm foxed."

"You do." Robert pulled his snuff box from his waistcoat. He flicked it open and took a pinch of snuff. "You turn into a flittering schoolroom miss after two drinks."

Carver laughed, knowing that unfortunately, Robert was correct. "True. But I'm not even sure that brandy will help tonight. A cup is only so deep." He grimaced and looked up from his glass. "Sorry, I didn't mean to become so profound."

Carver tossed back the contents of the glass and felt the familiar burn. He cleared his throat against the sensation and set down his empty glass. "What is it that's keeping you from your bed?"

Robert's mouth flattened into a line. "A very pregnant and unhappy wife."

Carver tried not to laugh. "And what have you done to anger my sister this time? Or do I want to know?"

"I made the mistake of commenting on her growing figure."

Carver winced. "Bad form, my man! Even I know a comment like that will land you sleeping in the stables."

"And you are also not married yet," said Robert. "You will quickly find that when faced with a wife, everything you thought you knew goes out the window. Up is down. Left is right. None of it makes sense. If I comment on her lovely growing midsection, she kicks me out. If I do not comment on it, she accuses me of finding her utterly repulsive...and kicks me out. It all ends with me sleeping in my dressing room."

Carver could very well picture it. Mary was fiery and opinionated even when she wasn't with child. He had to admit it was possibly his favorite character trait of hers. Daphney had a fiery temperament at times as well. *Ugh.* Why could he not seem to go five minutes before his thoughts turned back to the woman?

Carver stood up and walked toward the beverage cart. "It seems to me you are the one in need of a drink."

"Or three," said Robert, rubbing his face.

Despite Robert's sour mood, Carver knew his brother-in-law was still very much in love with Mary. What the man needed was to vent, and that suited Carver's mood perfectly. Robert could talk and Carver could focus all of his attention on helping his brother-in-law. Conveniently, it would also keep his thoughts away from Daphney and Claire.

Carver filled a glass and handed it to Robert before filling another for himself and retaking his seat by the fire. "Are you happy about the child?" Why not jump right in?

Robert's expression turned serious. "Of course. Just worried."

"Worried for your marriage?" asked Carver. "I'm sure you and Mary will pull through."

Robert shook his head. "No, no. Our marriage is fine. A good fight now and again only makes for a sweeter make up."

Carver grimaced. "I'll thank you to never say anything like that to me again." Maybe this wasn't a conversation he could have after all.

Robert didn't laugh or lighten a bit. His face only grew more somber. He rubbed the back of his neck, his anguish showing in the lines of his face. Carver hadn't realize until that moment how much Robert had aged since he'd last seen him. The man was already a good ten years older than Mary, but he had never looked his forty years of age until tonight when the glow of the fire highlighted the lines between his brows and patches of grey on the sides of his black hair.

"She lost a baby a few months ago, you know?" No. He didn't know that.

"I'm sorry," Carver offered the weak words, not really knowing what else to say. "I had no idea." Why didn't he know that?

"No one knows what caused it...not even the doctor. One day she was healthy and the next..." He didn't finish that statement, just rubbed his fingers over his brow. "Anyway, she was terribly ill after she lost the baby. Whether it was from an actual ailment or despair, I'll never know. I'd never seen her so sick before." He paused, deep creases settling between his eyes. "I was honestly scared for her life."

79

Carver leaned forward and rested his arms on his knees. "Why did no one write to me?"

"I wanted to but Mary wouldn't let me." Robert gave him a pointed look. "She's been worried about you and afraid to add to your burdens."

His burdens? That was ridiculous. Mary could never be a burden to him. Especially when she was needing comfort. She should have told him. He would have been there for her.

"Why the devil does she think I'm so fragile?"

"Because you are," said Robert.

"What about me is fragile? Clearly, she didn't see my fight with Brooks last night or she wouldn't be worried in the least."

"She's not worried about you physically, you idiot," said Robert. "It's your mental state she's concerned about."

His mental state was just fine. He was getting through the days well enough.

Another stinging gulp of brandy rushed down Carver's throat.

"Her fears are unfounded." He could feel his anger rising but tried to push it back down. Boxing had helped with that problem when he was in London. But at home, he'd have to find another way to help the tension. "I'm perfectly fine." The words sounded weak even to him.

Robert narrowed his all too knowing eyes. "Really? Because you haven't been home in three years. That does not sound like a man who is doing well to me."

"I'm home now." He opened his hands, indicating his very presence.

"And you're also sitting up late in your father's study instead of going to your own chamber." Robert eyed him closely. "Why is that?" Robert continued without waiting for an answer. "I think you still haven't faced your grief. You ran away after she died and have been avoiding it ever since."

Carver dropped his eyes away and clenched his teeth together. He attempted a calming breath through his nose. "How did we get on this topic? I thought we were talking about you and Mary." Carver let the warning hang heavy in the air as he attempted to soothe the tension at the back of his neck.

Robert did not waver. "It doesn't help, does it? Burying yourself under alcohol and boxing. She still finds you at the end of the day, doesn't she?" If Carver leveled the man, would Mary forgive him? "You're not fooling any of us, Carver. You're hurting. And that's normal."

Carver's eyes snapped back to Robert. "If I wanted a recounting of my life, I would have asked for it." Each word fell out sharp and clipped.

Robert's gaze intensified as he leaned forward. "You can mill me down when I'm done if you'd like, but right now you're bloody well going to listen because I love my wife and my wife is worried about you."

It would seem Oliver wasn't the only one immune to Carver's threatening look.

Robert continued, "You think staying away is going to help you heal, but it's not. It's time and passed for you to mourn Claire's death and allow yourself to truly grieve. Quit running from it."

Carver's whole body stiffened at the sound of her name, just like it always did.

Robert seemed to notice his discomfort, and some of his rigid demeanor softened, along with his tone. "And the fact that you still can't say her name after three years tells me that you've also not accepted the fact she is gone."

How could he have not accepted it? The evidence was everywhere. Nothing smelled like lilac. Her bubbling, infectious laughter no longer floated down the halls. And yet...he still looked for it. Did that mean he hadn't accepted it after all?

Still, his anger boiled that Robert would insert his opinion where it wasn't wanted. "What do you know about loss, Robert? Your wife is safely tucked in bed upstairs, while the woman I love is buried under the ground." But hearing the words out loud made him instantly regret them.

"What do I know of loss?" Robert's voice was weak. "Six months ago I had to stand beside my wife and bury our stillborn child. Not only do I mourn the loss of our child, but I mourn the dreams we carried for her future." He paused and met Carver's eyes. "Yes, the baby was a girl, and I am faced every day with the pain of not getting to hold her in my arms. The pain of finding my wife weeping when she thinks I'm not watching." Carver wanted to look away, but Robert's eyes held his. "I know loss, Carver. And I also know that running away and never talking about it is not going to help me heal. And for Mary's sake, I have to pursue healing."

Carver wished the flames of the fire would open up and swallow him. "I'm sorry, Robert. I shouldn't have said what I did. It was thoughtless."

"Yes, it was…but frankly, Carver, you've been a little thoughtless and selfish for a few years now. Everyone's just been too afraid of hurting you more to tell you they needed you."

What? How on earth could he have been acting selfishly? He hadn't even been around them enough to act selfishly.

Oh.

"Now that you are home, be home. Be there for your sisters. Maybe even go visit Claire's family. I know they would like to see you."

He could certainly be there for his sisters, but there was no way he was ready to go to see Claire's family. Would they even want to see him since he was the reason Claire wasn't alive anymore?

One thing was clear, his sisters did need him. He had been gone too long. Rectifying that should be his first priority. And in order to do that, he needed to get rid of Daphney. Why did that thought not sit well with him?

He knew nothing about the woman other than the fact that she was lying about everything she had told him. So why in heaven's name did he feel so drawn to her? It didn't matter now. Robert was right that he had been using his town endeavors to avoid his pain—Miss Bellows being one of those endeavors. She needed to go so that he could focus on his family.

Carver stood from his seat and looked Robert in the eyes. "I'm truly sorry for the loss of your daughter, Robert. You're a good

TO CON A GENTLEMAN

husband to my sister and an excellent father to Jane. They're lucky to have you." He smiled. "A touch prosy but also a bloody good brother-in-law. I can't do everything you said, but I did hear you."

And almost punched you.

Robert stood up and put his hand on Carver's shoulder. "One step at a time, Kensworth. Start by going to your room and going to bed."

Going to his bedchamber was probably meant to be the simplest of the tasks ahead of him, but was actually a significant obstacle. Mary and Robert hadn't been there that day. His brother-in-law had no way of knowing that inside those walls, his father had told him about Claire's accident and death. And he remembered all too well what it felt like to retch on the floor as the weight of his father's words consumed him.

But Carver just nodded and began to walk toward the door.

Robert spoke again before Carver had left the room. "Oh, and Kensworth! For goodness' sake, whatever arrangement you have with Miss Bellows, do not call it off until after the ball and you are back in London." Carver froze. "The doctor said these first few months of Mary's pregnancy are the most fragile. She needs to stay stress free."

He turned sharply on his heels and faced Robert. "What do you know about Miss Bellows?"

Robert smiled indulgently, smoothing some of the lines Carver had noticed earlier. "Nothing. But I've played cards with you enough to know when you're bluffing on a bad hand."

"Confound you, Robert, I'm devilishly good at cards," said Carver, smiling.

Robert just laughed. "But not as good as I am. I don't know what sort of wool you're trying to pull over everyone's eyes, nor do I wish to. In fact, I'll insist that you not tell me."

Carver's shoulders sunk. He needed to tell someone. "You're not even a little curious?"

"Of course I am. But I also couldn't keep a secret from your sister even if my life was hanging in the balance. And I have a feeling that whatever is going on with Miss Bellows needs to be kept in confidence. I'll not have anything disturbing Mary's peace this week."

Carver shoved a hand through his hair and groaned. "You have no idea what a fix you're putting me in." How the devil was he supposed to keep her around a full week? And did that mean he had to tell her the truth? For some reason, he felt bad about the idea of stringing her along further. Even if she was a scheming thief.

"No, you got yourself in whatever fix this is all on your own," said Robert. "But I give you my word that I'll help you out of it just as soon as we are past the duke's birthday ball and Mary is safely back home."

Was he insane? Carver couldn't keep Daphney around to attend his father's ball, full of family and friends. And besides, he needed her to go back to London. He was starting to not entirely trust himself to not develop feelings for the woman. Those eyes called to him with every look.

"Could I not just say that she was called home on some urgent business?"

"No."

"Why not?"

"Because Mary will know. She will smell a secret and then will rip and tear at me until I tell her everything I know. She's bloody good at extracting information. And the doctor was very clear that Mary should avoid any added stress during these early tender weeks. As wary as she is about Miss Bellows, seeing you engaged to a woman who makes your eyes sparkle has gone a long way to alleviate her anxieties."

His eyes sparkled? Not the most masculine reflection.

Robert added, "I want to do everything I can to make sure this pregnancy goes as smoothly for Mary as possible. Even if that means shackling your leg to poor Miss Bellows."

Carver's eyes widened. "You're not going to actually make me marry Daphney, are you?"

"I didn't realize your voice could get that high. But no—of course not. Just get through the ball and wait until my family and I return home. Then you can write to her that the engagement didn't work out." Robert's eyes held a threat. "But not until we are further along in the pregnancy." He was far more successful with the threatening look than Carver had ever been.

Carver wasn't entirely sure about the plan. He had to admit, the idea of Daphney staying a little longer oddly relieved him. But if he was going to keep the beautiful scammer around, he was going to do it on his terms, and that meant he first needed to find out who the devil she was.

"At the risk of sounding like a petulant child, you won't tell my father, will you?"

If he knew his father at all, the moment he learned of Carver's subterfuge, he would procure a special license within the day. Criminal or not, he would expect Carver to have treated Daphney with more respect. And...perhaps he should have.

"As long as you get through this week without any more shenanigans, I'll keep your secret," said Robert before pausing and drawing his brows together as if he suddenly became aware of something. "Carver—should I be concerned on Miss Bellows' behalf? She doesn't exactly have anyone here to protect her."

Carver fought the scoff threatening to burst from his mouth. "You needn't worry over that. Miss Bellows is quite safe with me. And more than that...I have a strong feeling that she can take care of herself."

Chapter Twelve

After pushing open one of the large double doors leading inside the stable, Rose began to wonder if she had been foolish to not bring a candle.

Once inside the stables, the heavy smell of horse and hay filled her senses, but she could not so much as see the hand in front of her face. There had to be a lantern somewhere nearby. She stood still for a moment waiting until her eyes had adjusted to the darkness—then hopefully she would be able to see enough to find a lantern. Saddling a horse in the dark in an unfamiliar place would be difficult, but not impossible. She knew because she had done it at least a dozen times, if not more.

When Uncle Felix had found her all those years ago, one of the first scams he had her run was as a new stable boy. She had already been pretending to be a boy the first two years after Papa died. And then she met Uncle Felix and started learning everything about scamming and stealing from him. Somehow he knew she wasn't a boy right away—but still, he found it impressive that no one else had detected her femininity during those two years. Since it was so easy to get her hired on as a stable boy in wealthy households, Uncle Felix included it in a few of their scams.

She and Uncle Felix made their way around England targeting the stables of the most well-known whips, where Rose would enter pretending to be the newest hire, and leave during the night on the back of the stable's finest horse. Uncle Felix would sell the horses off to another nobleman in another county before word of their crime ever had time to reach them. It was a lucrative scam, and one that Rose enjoyed probably a little too much.

The familiar sound of horses rustling in their stalls met Rose's ear. She couldn't help but wonder which of these horses was Carver's? A pang of guilt pinched her. Would he forgive her if she stole his horse? What was she thinking? Of course he wouldn't. The man would be livid. Or maybe she was wrong, and he would actually be relieved she had taken herself off and released him from his obligation.

But then Rose heard a larger rustling noise, one coming from behind her, and she froze in place. Before she had time to fully process the observation, someone had seized her from behind and clapped a strong large hand over her mouth.

Involuntary panic gripped her chest, but she managed to not release a scream into the calloused hand restraining her. Years of training had taught Rose to quickly push past fear and move to action.

She noted that whoever was holding her was easily twice her size and capable of committing significant harm, but he was not restraining her arms. Poor choice. Instinct took over and in one fluid motion, Rose flicked up her skirts, withdrew her pistol from its holster on her thigh, and pressed it firmly to the man's temple behind her. He dropped his hand from her mouth but did not release his hold around her waist.

"Move and I'll kill you," Rose said with a chilling calm that conveyed her intent.

She was not exactly in the most commanding of positions, and she knew that the man could likely bat the pistol down easily enough. But she figured if she exuded enough confidence, he would not risk the movement.

For one tense moment no one said anything. She heard her own fast breath and felt the rapid pounding of the man's heart against her back.

Good. Let him worry a touch.

Then a slight breeze pushed through the stables and swept a familiar and welcome scent under Rose's nose—*masculine and cool.*

～

Was that? Oh, yes—the feeling of cold steel against his temple was most definitely the barrel of a pistol. Considering her alarmingly quick and precise drawing of the weapon, it was clear that the woman had been in a similar situation a time or two. Whether that made him feel better or worse, he wasn't sure.

She had said not to move, but she hadn't mentioned anything about talking.

"I haven't come to hurt you, Daphney."

She did not lower the weapon an inch, or even seem surprised to hear his voice. "Why are you here, then?" She sounded perfectly calm but the slight tremble in her shoulders told him she wasn't completely carefree.

"To talk to you," he said. "And find out exactly who you are and why you're pretending to be my mistress."

He heard her push out a heavy breath. Was she relieved he knew the truth?

"How long have you known?" she asked.

"Are you going to shoot me if I say the whole time?"

The gun lowered, and she squirmed against his arm. "For goodness' sake! Let me go," she said, sounding more annoyed than actually upset.

He reluctantly let go of her waist, belatedly realizing he was still holding her. Under different circumstances, he would have vastly enjoyed getting to hold her in such a way. Actually, who was he kidding? He had enjoyed it even with a gun to his head.

She spun around and took a step backward, leveling the gun at his chest. "How did you know I wasn't telling the truth?" Her eyes were narrowed. The woman looked fierce even in the darkness. It made his skin prickle as she held him in her gaze.

"For starters, I do not have any mistresses. And also…" he smiled,

"I'm not Lord Newburry. But if you had knocked on the door two down from mine, you would have found him. I am Carver Ashburn, Earl of *Kensworth* and heir to the Duke of Dalton."

He had the enjoyment of watching her mouth fall open at some point during that speech. But she quickly shut it and took an irritated breath in through her perfect nose.

"I'm going to kill the old fool," she said through her teeth.

"Lord Newburry?"

"Uncle Felix," said Rose, looking far away in thought.

"You told me you don't have any living family. Or was that just part of your lie?"

She shook her head, still distant in thought as she tried to pull all the pieces together. "That was the truth. I don't have any family. He's my…accomplice."

Accomplice? So she really was some kind of professional thief. He knew it.

"And by the way he handled this job, it seems my accomplice is in need of retirement." She raised her gun and gently tapped the barrel of the dashed thing against her mouth, deep in thought.

Never had he seen anyone—man or woman—handle a weapon with such easy assurance and authority. The woman was…a lunatic. A beautiful, captivating lunatic. And the fact that he was going to ask her to stay said a lot about his own sanity.

Daphney leveled the gun at him again. "Why did you propose to me and bring me along if you knew I wasn't telling the truth?" She was only a slip of a woman, but goodness did she have a commanding presence, especially now that she was being completely herself. She was unbridled but in complete control. He liked her that way.

Carver smirked, feeling oddly playful for a man staring down the barrel of a gun. "Amusement?"

"I've been lying professionally for most of my life, Carver. Which means I have also become quite proficient in recognizing them." She shot him a pointed look.

"Have you been—" he waved in the air gesturing toward her gun, "doing whatever this is most of your life?"

"A wonderful deflection, but not good enough. Why did you bring me here? Was this a trap and you mean to turn me over to the magistrate?"

He laughed, hoping it would set her at ease and also get him out of having to tell her the whole truth. And also maybe get her to lower that weapon. "No—on both accounts. I never had any intentions of trapping you or turning you over to the magistrate. If you will remember, you are the one holding the gun, not me. And by the way, have you made up your mind on shooting me yet? If not, would you mind terribly to put it away?"

She smirked and cocked her head. "Do I make you uncomfortable? Afraid that a woman doesn't know how to handle a pistol?"

"I'm terribly uncomfortable, in fact. But only because I'm a little too certain that you *do* know how to handle it and I'd rather not have a hole blown through my favorite jacket if it can be avoided."

Her lips twitched, but she didn't give in to the temptation to fully smile. It was going to take work, but he was feeling a new determination to make that woman fully smile.

She held up a finger and moved it in a circle telling him to turn around.

He quirked a brow. "You mean to have me turn my back on a woman with a pistol in her hand? No, I thank you."

"Well then, we are at a dagger draw, my lord. I'm certainly not going to put the thing away with your top lights gawking at me." She sighed deeply and rolled her eyes when he simply blinked at her. "I can see that you have not put two and two together yet. The holster is on my leg. Now either respectfully turn around so I may replace it or say goodbye to your fetching jacket."

He smiled. "Fetching?"

"Oh, turn around!"

Carver obeyed with a smile and turned around so she could do whatever it was she needed to do to replace the gun. The fact that the pistol lived under her skirts made the speed at which she was able to retrieve it, all the more impressive. Did she find herself in those types of situations often? Had she shot anyone before? He had an endless supply of questions for the rogue.

"Alright, you may turn around." And he did, only to find her slowly backing toward the door. "I'll offer a quick thanks for not turning me in and be on my way."

She was leaving? Not only was it extremely cold outside, but it was completely dark. It wasn't safe for her to travel through the night.

She picked up her valise and turned around to leave. She really was going to leave. He could have sworn she had been feeling the same attractions that he had been experiencing. Apparently, it was only a part of her act. An unfortunate blow to his pride.

Watching her walk away made his insides churn painfully. Not only did he need for her to stay so that he could fulfill his promise to Robert, but...no. He didn't let himself explore that thought any further. He needed her to stay to fulfill his promise. That was it.

As she reached for the door, Carver frantically searched his mind for anything he could say to get her to stop. "You were going to leave without saying goodbye first?" Great. Now he was going to play the part of a love-sick fool too.

She froze. She didn't look back but turned her head a little to the side so that the moonlight fell over her right cheekbone. "I never say goodbye to my targets."

Targets. How flattering.

"What about friends?" he asked.

There was a long pause. He felt as if there was a tether pulling him toward her. How could he cut it?

He had no reason to care for her, every reason to hate her and mistrust her, but unfortunately, all he felt was lighter when she was near. It was difficult to put into words. There was just simply a connection. A draw. A strong force that grabbed him anytime she looked at him. He shouldn't be feeling this way. He already had too many feelings to balance.

Chapter Thirteen

"I don't have friends." Her voice sounded softer than it had before as it carried through the stables and settled heavily on Carver.

He resisted a groan. Why did he want to make her feel better?

"I would have to disagree with that statement," he said.

She turned around to face him. The blue rays of the moon swept across her face from the open door. Sadness reflected in her eyes— some deep fear or longing pulling him to her with even more force. "You don't know me. You know absolutely nothing about me." She shook her head. "We are not friends."

Surely she felt the force pulling them together? It was so strong.

He took a step closer, the sound of hay crunching under his boots, but stopped when he saw her posture tense. Was she fearful of him? "Who are you then, Daphney? And we'll have the truth this time, if you will."

The skin between her brows crinkled. He felt the urge to run his thumb across her worry lines and erase them. "Why should I tell you that? You led me to believe you were Lord Newburry and then basically laughed at me by throwing a proposal into the bargain. Why should I trust anything you say or do?"

He dared a step closer, a smile hovering on his lips. "Because, *Miss Innocence*," her scowl cracked a little, "if you do not tell me the truth, and do decide to run away into the night, you will never receive your one thousand pounds."

Oh, idiot! What are you doing?

Her brows lifted. "My what?" At least now he had her attention.

Although it wasn't the smartest idea to employ a thief, he had to get her to stay—for Mary and Robert's sake. Definitely not because he was attracted to her. Or because when he was close to her he felt the air twist and tangle between them.

"I need you to stay until I return to London after the ball my mother is throwing for my father. If you do, I'll give you the one thousand pounds as payment."

This time it was she who stepped toward him, her look skeptical. Three more steps and he would be close enough to hold her hand. Smell her warm vanilla scent.

Stop it.

"Why?" she asked. "What reason do you have to keep me here?"

He cleared his throat and his mind. "That's for me to worry about. Not you."

He was in control of this transaction, not Daphney—or whoever she was. If he was going to have her stay, he was going to be the one in charge. There would be rules and he would be the one to set them.

"Very well." She shrugged as if nothing in the world mattered and made for the door with determined strides. "I don't take any jobs without knowing all of the details."

"Wait!" he said a touch too loud before his mind had time to tell him to stop making a blasted fool of himself. "It's because of Mary." Again, his mouth hadn't listened to his mind. So much for staying in control.

Daphney turned around slowly. "What does our pretend engagement have to do with your sister?"

He waved for her to move closer toward him as he walked to a work table where he knew there would be a lantern. She didn't budge.

Of course not. *This* version of the woman was nothing but stubborn and more than a little infuriating.

An annoyed breath escaped his lungs as he went to the work table himself and lit the lantern. It took an embarrassing amount of self-sacrifice to lay down his pride and walk to where the woman was standing with folded arms and a raised mocking brow.

"How does my staying affect Lady Hatley?" asked Daphney, once he had stopped in front of her, lantern in hand. Her face was glowing, warm and lovely from the light of the flame.

"First, I want to know your name."

Hesitancy marked her face. "Why do you suspect Daphney is not my name?" Because…it just didn't feel right. But he couldn't say that.

"Well, I get the feeling that you are a rather experienced criminal and as such I imagine you are not so daft as to give me your real name."

She smirked. What did he have to do to get that woman to really smile? "You're right, of course, but will unfortunately have to settle with Daphney because I never reveal my given name."

"That hardly seems fair. I went so far as to tell you my middle name. Also—out of all the fake names you could have chosen, why *Ingrid*?" He made a show of disgust.

Her mouth opened, and she released an offended puff of breath. "You said you liked that name."

"You're not the only one who lied."

She crossed her arms mimicking his pose. "Now I am certainly not going to tell you. Suppose my middle name was the only part of my persona I did not lie about." An eyebrow quirked up. She looked exactly like Mary had when they were children, demanding to know where Carver had buried her favorite doll.

"Is that really your middle name?"

She smiled slightly and shook her head. "No. Now, tell me what's wrong with Lady Hatley."

Clearly, he wasn't going to be able to get the woman to stay without a bit more information. He rubbed at the headache growing in his temples. How could a woman be both so appealing and so very obnoxious at the same time?

"After dinner tonight, Robert—Mary's husband—informed me that about six months ago Mary miscarried a pregnancy. I didn't know about it because...well, she didn't tell me." His chest tightened at the thought of his sister hurting and him so far away. "Anyway—as we learned tonight, she is with child again. The doctor has been very clear that she is not to endure any stress during these early months. I would imagine that finding out the depth of our situation is likely to cause my worrywart of a sister a great deal of stress. I had planned to end this shenanigan tonight and send you back to London, but after all that Robert told me...well, I need you to stay so that I can protect my sister."

He finally stopped to take a breath and noticed that Daphney's expression had changed. She was quiet and still. Her golden amber eyes hooked him with a tenderness—a depth that reached into him and soothed his pain.

"What about after the ball? Will she be through her difficult months?" Was she asking because she was worried for Mary, or fearful that they would have to extend their betrothal if Mary wasn't yet out of danger?

"We will go back to London the day after the ball and there you will be given your promised money, and your freedom. I'll write to Mary after a month or so and tell her that we ended the engagement due to a mutual disagreement with the match."

Daphney bit her lips together deep in thought as she cast her eyes to the ground. What was it about the arrangement that was giving her the most pause? Was it having to pretend to remain engaged to him that bothered her? Most women would jump at the chance. Even if it was only to fake an engagement for a week. But here was Daphney, a woman unlike any he'd ever known before, clearly wrestling with the idea.

After the span of five full breaths, her eyes snapped to him with such shocking directness that he nearly took a step back. "Two thousand," she stated.

He resisted the urge to laugh at her audacity. "This is not a negotiation. One thousand pounds is all you will get."

"Two or I won't do it." The warm glow of the lantern flickered across her skin, her freckles, her mouth and eyes, making those haunting eyes and soft features all the more alluring. It was hardly fair. She had the advantage, and they both knew it.

He sighed in defeat. "Very well, you ruthless woman. Two thousand it is."

She looked up at him, a frown once again on her face. "You need to agree to a few things before I commit to the job." *The job.* How ridiculous. He supposed that was what he got for bringing the blasted woman to his house in the first place. "First, I am not a light skirt or a brimstone. I expect to be treated with the same respect you would show a lady."

"A lowering reflection that you felt the need to state that, but yes I give you my word that I will not compromise you in any way."

"Good. And second, the less you know about who I really am the better. It will make interacting with your family much easier and less confusing for you...and me." If she hadn't added that last bit he might not have agreed.

"Fair enough."

"Third. You absolutely cannot develop a tendré for me. Everything between us will be a ruse and nothing more. At the end of this job, I will leave and we will not have contact again."

Well, that was it. Even if he had just admitted to himself a moment ago that he felt a strange attraction for that woman, her presumptive words made him determined to not feel it again. "I'll try to refrain from flinging myself off of a bridge from heartbreak."

"Alright, then." She sighed deeply as if resigning herself to some great trial. "I'll stay." She added firmly, "But *only* because of the two thousand pounds and the situation with Lady Hatley. Not at all because I desire to spend any more time in your company."

"Wonderful," he said, a sardonic tone lacing his words. "Now that you've unburdened yourself of those sentiments we can move on."

She bit her lips but couldn't completely keep from hiding the smile. "I apologize. I can be rather blunt at times."

"You make me long for the meek little maid who showed up at my doorstep afraid to make eye contact."

Her smile twisted in a way that made his heart speed up. "Do you really? I think she would have been a dead bore to you." She would have. He could never long for a meek, shy woman. Claire had certainly never been either of those things.

Claire. He forced his thoughts to keep moving. "You're probably right." He gestured toward the stable doors. "Shall we go inside now? It's getting late and there will be time to discuss the rest in the morning." And he needed to get some space.

She agreed and then looked shocked when he picked up her valise. Was she not used to a gentleman helping her? He hadn't meant it as some grand gesture but the way her eyes brimmed with surprise and appreciation made him feel like a hero rather than an ordinary gentleman performing an ordinary task.

"So, tell me then, Daphney Ingrid Bellows..." Every inch of him was aware of how close she was as they progressed across the lawn toward the house. Her arm brushed against his and he had to grip the handles of the luggage tighter to keep himself from reaching for her hand. So much for not feeling any more attraction to her. "What were you doing out here in the stables before I caught you?"

The wind whistled through the night air and somewhere in the distance an owl hooted, but all he could think about was that rueful smile she was giving him and how her mischievous eyes were twinkling. "Stealing your horse," she said.

By herself? "And you think you would have been able to manage it?"

Daphney blinked a few times. "What do you mean by *manage it*?"

He chuckled. "No—put your sword away. I only meant that you would have had to saddle the beast in the dark as well as mount it all on your own. That would have been a difficult feat for anyone to accomplish."

Her hand touched her cheek. "Good heavens, I might have even been forced to ride it!"

He couldn't help his laugh. "You mock but the truth is that I do not know a woman who could saddle her own horse without assistance—let alone a horse she had never ridden before."

"Well," she glanced up at him and he almost felt his heart stop. The most beautiful and genuine smile beamed from her face. "You do now."

"Prove it," he said.

Chapter Fourteen

Carver awoke the next morning feeling certain that he had only fallen asleep little more than an hour before. All night his thoughts had pulled and warred with each other between memories of Claire and thoughts of Daphney. Had he made a mistake asking Daphney to stay? And what would Claire have thought about the situation? When he was away from Daphney, he could see clearly. She had no place in his home among his family. But when he was with her...his insides melted and he felt as if peace and happiness were something physical he could reach out and hold. It had been so long since he had felt that way. And that made him feel guilty. It wasn't fair to Claire for him to continue his life as if she had never been.

A ray of golden light broke through the gap between the drapes and reminded him that he needed to get up. Despite how much Carver's body protested waking, he knew that Daphney would be up soon, if she wasn't already, and they had an arrangement for the morning. Last night, they had decided they would go for a morning ride, and that Daphney would saddle her own horse. When he had made the challenge, she had looked at him as if he were completely insane. Not insane for having suggested she saddle her horse, but insane for thinking that anyone else had ever done it for her.

Daphney was so different from any woman he had ever known. Whether he liked it or not, she captivated him. It was both thrilling and dreadful. She was unpredictable. Unreadable. She didn't demurely flutter her lashes when he looked at her, and she certainly didn't back down from a fight. She stirred feelings inside him that he wasn't at all ready to feel.

Willing himself to get out of bed, he sat up straight, stretched his arms, and rolled his neck. A surge of pain through his middle reminded him that his ribs were still significantly bruised. He looked down and ran a hand over the tender black and blue area. Painful, but healing.

The quiet of the room began to overwhelm him. There was no cravat around his neck but still, he was suffocating. For once, he missed the early morning distraction of Oliver. He needed to get out of this room. Out of this house. He rang for his valet and quickly dressed in buckskin breeches and a riding jacket before going downstairs to the breakfast room. The air in his lungs felt like thick cement as he passed by reminders of Claire. They were everywhere. In every corner, every hallway, every room. As his best friend and childhood neighbor, she had spent almost as many days in that house as he had. Memories lurked and twisted in the air around him but he forced his gaze straight and his mind to the present.

He finally made it to the breakfast room and realized that he had all but jogged down the stairs. He took a moment to breathe and practice his easy airs before walking into the bright sunlit room. The wonderful aroma of bacon and pastries swept under his nose. Seated at the round table he found his mother, two of his sisters, and Robert. Mary was absent. Was she not feeling well? That thought gave him a sick feeling.

"Good morning to you all," he said walking fully into the bright breakfast room. There, that sounded unaffected. Carver crossed over to his mama and kissed her cheek in his usual way. "Mother you look lovely, as always."

She smiled and looked at him with a squint. "And you lie as always, but I'll allow it because it makes me feel good." She patted his cheek before he straightened back up. "Did you sleep well?"

"Wonderfully," he lied and turned his attention to Robert. "Is Mary well?"

"She was feeling a bit ill this morning and wished to rest in a little later than usual, but nothing serious." His smile was reassuring. "Is... Miss Bellows well? I haven't seen her yet this morning," asked Robert, his tone clearly conveying a question in the subtext. But no one else seemed to notice. Mother sipped her tea. Elizabeth broke the seal of a letter. Kate was engrossed in *The Lady's Magazine*.

"She should be down any moment. We have plans to ride this morning," he said with a discrete nod toward Robert. Robert nodded back his understanding and Carver turned toward the sideboard and picked up a plate with the intention to fill it.

"Well, then, she must have gotten a head start because Daphney left about an hour ago," said Elizabeth. Carver paused, set down the plate and turned to face his sister who had spoken without looking away from the letter she was holding.

"A head start?" he asked, hoping he didn't sound as worried as he felt.

"Mmhmm. I saw her walking toward the stables from my window. She was wearing a warm wool cloak, so I assumed she was going for an early morning ride." A surprising amount of panic gripped him. What if she had decided to leave after all? Surely Elizabeth would have mentioned if Daphney had been carrying a bag? He wanted to ask but knew it would raise too much suspicion if he did, so he swallowed his questions.

"If you are going for a ride, may I come along?" asked Kate, glancing up from her magazine for the first time.

Carver held his breath a moment. He loved his sister, he really did, but he also *really* did not want to spend the morning riding with her. He had too many questions for Daphney. Too much to figure out without having to worry about Kate's inconvenient presence.

His mother thankfully answered first, "No child, you may not. Never mind the fact that your brother looks like you just stuck a tack in his shoe," she tossed him a knowing grin, "but you cannot go because we have far too many things to tend to for the ball, and I need you and your sister's help." For once, he thanked God for an upcoming ball.

Kate pouted as usual, "But that's such dull work, Mama. Can you not manage without me for a few hours?"

Carver walked over to his baby sister and kissed her on the top of her dark blonde curls. At least this one still seemed like a child. "Sorry, love. Another time."

"You could at least try to look disappointed," said Kate with a put-on frown.

He let his mouth tug into a boyish grin, "I could, but I fear the effort would be too great." Kate's eyes narrowed, and she flashed him a taunting smile with a crinkled nose. He flicked her chin playfully and strode toward the door, intent on finding Daphney.

If he continued to look light and playful, hopefully they wouldn't see the worry he was feeling. And behind the worry, the ache that never seemed to leave. He didn't want them to know how broken he was. How frustrated. How tired. He had been gone too long, and they all needed him, not a shattered man.

His mother's voice stopped him before he reached the threshold. "Carver, when do you expect Oliver? I assume he is coming. He never misses a family event." There was such a fondness in his mother's eyes whenever she spoke of Oliver. His friend had been like a second son to the family. And it struck him how pathetic it was that he too already missed Olly, though he'd sooner jump in the path of an oncoming carriage than admit it to the man.

He turned around. Elizabeth put down her letter and seemed to wait for his answer. "He left on a hunting trip yesterday but expects to be here in time for the ball."

"But he is coming?" asked Elizabeth. It might be odd to others how close Elizabeth and Oliver were, but it never gave Carver any pause. Oliver acted as much like a brother to Elizabeth as Carver did himself. Except, Oliver had probably been a better brother to Elizabeth over the past three years than he had. Oliver had certainly spent more time with her.

"Yes, he will be here. And if I know Olly, he'll pop in at the most inconvenient time." Most likely at eight o'clock in the morning.

Elizabeth smiled. "That does sound like him." But then she picked back up her letter and continued her reading.

A glance out the window at the bright morning outside reminded him that he had a woman to find. "If you all will excuse me, I believe I'll go find Miss Bellows."

Carver walked out the front door and his boots thudded hard against the cobblestone drive. No matter how hard he tried, he couldn't shake the feeling that around every corner, he would find Claire, waiting to jump out and surprise him as she had done hundreds of times during their long and close friendship. Which was ridiculous seeing as how the woman died three years ago. And yet, his mind held on to her as if she were no further away than an arm's reach.

Was Robert right? Had he not accepted yet that she was dead? A week ago, Carver would have scoffed at the man for suggesting it. After all, he had a successful and busy life in London. But the more he thought about it, the more he saw the merit in it. Which is precisely why he needed to take a good beating from a long ride. He didn't want to think about what Robert had said or what Claire had smelled like or how the thought of returning to London made him feel empty.

Was there nowhere he could find peace? Certainly not in his family home, and as much as he didn't want to admit it, not in his house in London either. Yes—he needed a good ride. Carver considered asking Daphney if they could take their ride another day. He didn't feel like reining in his horse to keep pace with hers.

He walked into the stables at a quick pace. At first glance, he didn't see Daphney. He tried not to think the worst. She had given him her word that she would not run away in the night. But then, how much is one supposed to rely on the word of a criminal known for conning gentlemen?

Carver shook his head and continued into the stables, walking the familiar path to his horse's stall. He patted the snouts of two mares who hung their necks over the wooden stall doors and noted that Lucy —his sister's white and cream spotted horse—would be the perfect docile ride for Daphney. Where was she anyway? Most likely exploring the grounds before their ride. If that were true, he might actually have enough time to take Thunder for a quick ride before she ever knew he was gone. Except for one crucial problem.

Carver stopped just in front of Thunder's stall. Thunder's *empty* stall. Where the devil was his horse?

Just as he turned around, the head groom, John, came running to his side. "My lord!" He was slightly out of breath from running back into the stable. "I'd hoped that you were out riding Thunder."

Well, blast.

"Do you mean you don't know who took out my horse?"

The man's mouth pulled into a thin white line. He was clearly fearing for his position. "N-no, my lord. When I came out this morning to tend to the horses, Thunder was gone. I assumed your lordship had gone for an early ride since his saddle was missing as well."

That only left one person. Daphney. The blasted minx had nipped off with his horse! He wished she had taken the two thousand pounds rather than his favorite horse. And besides, there was no way the woman could hold the massive hunter. The beast was spunky and rest-less and never let anyone near him besides Carver and the groom. A heavy, familiar dread settled over him. He felt sick.

"Saddle up The Gentleman, John."

John bowed quickly and ran off to saddle the duke's horse. The Gentleman wasn't nearly as fast as Thunder, but he was the next best thing. And Daphney had at least an hour head start which meant that Carver needed every bit of speed he could get if he were going to find her. He only hoped he would find her in one piece.

But then the sound of pounding hooves drew closer outside of the stables and then came to a halt. Carver jogged out of the stables and relief flooded him when he found Daphney sitting proudly atop his large black hunter. She wore a simple olive dress under her wool cloak. The hood was down and the cloak billowed in the wind. Her hair was tied back in a nearly undone knot at the back of her head. She smiled at him, mockingly. "Good morning, dearest."

Relief was replaced with wrath.

"What do you think you're doing?" He stepped forward and took hold of Thunder's bridle. The horse tossed his head against Carver's hand, breathing heavily.

She smiled bigger, clearly not deterred by the ice in his tone. "I should think it was obvious." She leaned over patted Thunder's glistening black mane. A single lock of hair tumbled in front of her face. "Proving that I can saddle and mount a horse all on my own." She smiled and sat back up. "And the fact that I've been out riding this big prancer for the past hour should convince you that I know how to keep my seat." He refused to be drawn in by her twinkling eyes. She could have been hurt.

"You were supposed to wait for me. It was incredibly thoughtless of you to go gallivanting off on a horse that is much too strong for you without so much as a word as to where you were going."

Her head kicked back. Surprise clouded her eyes and then was quickly replaced by a dangerous look. "I suggest, *my lord*," her tone holding its own reprimand, "that you swallow your spleen before you attempt to rattle me off any further. As you can well see, I am quite capable of handling a strong horse." *That's what Claire had thought, too.* "Now, if you are quite finished acting the part of overbearing gudgeon, we can get on with our ride."

Any other time, he would find her blazing fury attractive. At this moment, he wanted to throttle her. Why would she not listen? He needed her to listen.

"Fine. We can go just as soon as you get down from Thunder. I've asked the groom to have another horse saddled. You may ride that mount instead." Just then John exited the stables holding the reins of The Gentleman—his father's light brown gelding. Carver blinked and tried to hold back his surprise at the now fat horse. When had that happened?

"He's ready, my lord," said John. "Shall I take him to the mounting block?"

"Yes, thank you, John. And replace that saddle with a side-saddle if you will."

But when he looked back at Daphney, he saw a sharp spark in her eyes. She smiled, only adding to the blaze threatening to engulf her. "No, John." She said, never looking away from Carver. "I thank you for your concern, but I plan to continue on this horse." Her brow twitched in a challenge.

"No, she will not, John." The words slipped through his teeth, slow and precise. "She will ride The Gentleman." Carver had been considering having John saddle up Lucy for Daphney to ride since he knew that his father's fat horse would likely be more than dull. But now—well, now he would make her ride the chubby horse as penance.

In his periphery, Carver could see John and The Gentleman doing a back-and-forth dance of indecision.

Daphney sputtered an incredulous laugh as the cold wind twirled tendrils of hair around her face. Thunder's ears twitched. "His name is The Gentleman? No—absolutely not. I have no desire to ride a slug, thank you."

Carver tightened his fist at his side. "He is accustomed to carrying my mother from time to time and would be much safer for a lady to ride." He could not, in good conscience, allow Daphney to ride his spirited and dangerous horse one more minute. His mind raced through different possible scenarios, all ending in a horrifying conclusion.

He hadn't been able to save Claire three years ago, but he could save Daphney now.

"Get down, woman."

She tapped her finger to her lip in feigned contemplation. "No." Was she enjoying his agony?

"Then I guess I will have to pull you off myself."

Those eyes—that looked more golden in the light than amber—glinted. "You will have to catch me first." With a graceful expertise that indeed proved her to be one of the finest horsewomen he had ever seen, Daphney tugged on the reins and kicked Thunder into a gallop.

Carver let out a low growl before hurrying to The Gentleman and tossing a leg over the saddle. He pressed his foot into the side of the horse and set him in motion. He was going to catch Daphney and ensure her safety. And then he was going to kill her.

Chapter Fifteen

R ose could not resist the urge to leave Carver in her dust. The
man was practically begging for it by demanding that she get
down immediately—as if she were a child. And if that wasn't enough,
implying that she wasn't a good enough rider to keep her seat! It was
unpardonable.

Carver had looked so tightly wound that she thought he would
snap. It was the same tension she felt from him in the hallway when
they had first arrived at Dalton Park, as though he was struggling,
unable to stifle something inside. There was some strong emotion that
held him prisoner. Really, she had no right to push him to a breaking
point—she herself had things she wanted to keep hidden—but she
couldn't seem to help it. She wanted to see the real Carver.

Rose had to hold back her laughter at the sight of the poor man
trying to entice that lazy, fat horse to match Thunder's pace. The spirited, solid black hunter must have shared the blood of a racehorse—for
when given his head, Thunder took the earth with a fierce drive that
could only be matched on the racetrack. Her breath pulsed through her
lungs as she held tight and leaned into the horse. Leaned into the
energy. Leaned into freedom.

It had taken every ounce of Rose's will not to go back on her word and flee during the night. But something in her was pulling her—demanding that she stay. And it wasn't the money. It was the look in Carver's eyes when he told Rose that he needed her to stay for his sister. It was the way his smile hung in her dreams. It was the suppressed heaviness she could see in him when he thought no one was looking. It was *something* tugging her to him. Anchoring her in that place.

Beating hooves sounded louder behind Rose and she realized that Carver had begun to catch up. She took a quick right and veered Thunder away from the expansive green rolling hills toward a copse of trees. Growing closer, Rose was able to see that just beyond the first little cluster of bright evergreens, lay the most lovely meadow. Patches of white wildflowers dotted the ground giving testament to the mildness of their winter. A narrow stream wound its way along the edge of the tree line. The sun danced through dotted clouds, almost giving the illusion of spring instead of winter. Wind twirled through the trees and flew over the stream, playing its own sort of symphony.

It was beautiful. Peaceful. Comforting.

Rose pulled Thunder to a stop—both woman and horse breathing heavily to refill their lungs. This place—it was the exact opposite of London's cold envelope, where the only nature to be found was in Hyde Park. Here, the air felt crisp and clean, inviting and promising. She felt the strongest urge to just lie down and breathe. To fill her lungs and let the promises of that place whisper to her. When was the last time she hadn't been running? Or hiding?

Her reverie was interrupted by the mad gallop of Carver and The Gentleman finally catching up. A new devilish grin replaced his previous scowl as he shouted over the distance separating them, "You're in trouble now!"

A flutter rushed into Rose's stomach. Without hesitation, she leapt down from Thunder, tossed his reins over a tree limb, and ran into the meadow like a Bow Street runner was on her heels. Her skirts plastered to the front of her body as she ran against the wind. She tossed an excited glance over her shoulder, and her hair rushed against her face.

Carver pulled his horse to a halt beside Thunder and dismounted. With strides twice as long as hers, he was behind her in less than a blink.

"Give it up, you rogue!" he said loudly but she could hear the smile in his voice.

Rose could hardly contain the laughter growing inside her. How many times had she run through the streets of London trying to escape a man in much the same manner? And yet, this was completely different. It was only for fun—no real looming threat to her safety. Something that Rose wasn't sure she had experienced once since Papa died.

Rose ran fast, tripping on her skirts and laughing like a child. Carver overtook her with a swift arm around her waist and Rose lost herself laughing. It didn't matter that she sounded ridiculous. She simply couldn't help it. Her stomach felt as if bubbles were turning round and round and were threatening to spill over.

Carver picked her up and threw her over his broad shoulder as if she were no more than a sack of flour. "You're going to pay now!" he said with his own laughter undermining the ominous threat.

"Where are you taking me! Put me down!" she kicked and squirmed trying to free herself.

With determined strides, Carver carried her in the direction of the stream. "You, my dear, are going for a swim."

"A swim! It's January, Carver! I'll catch my death!"

His hold only tightened around her legs. "I doubt it. You're much too stubborn to die from a little cold water." He was right, of course. She would never let herself kick the bucket from something so silly as that.

But the stream drew closer, and she found herself holding onto the back of his jacket a little tighter, trying to grip enough fabric to hold her there. "You wouldn't!" she said in a challenge.

He laughed a little menacingly. "Oh—I would." She found it very hard to be upset. It had been so long since Rose had done anything just for the enjoyment of it. It felt far too good to not allow herself a moment of fun. Even if that moment did end with hypothermia.

Rose continued to kick and pound her fists into his back as they reached the stream—her laughter still spilling over.

"You seem awfully happy for a woman about to find herself dumped in the stream," he said.

"Because I know you won't do it."

"Is that so?" He pulled her down from his shoulder only to hold her in his arms. She had never felt lighter. Rose looked him in his sparkling steely grey eyes. *That* was most definitely the look of a man about to throw a woman in the water and enjoy every second of it.

Rose began to feel a little more panicked at the thought but couldn't seem to stop laughing. Returning to the house dripping wet did not sound appealing.

He then began to count. With every number, he swayed her over the water—taunting her. "1…" *Sway.* "2…" *Sway.* "3…"

"Wait!" She yelled and clung to the lapels of his jacket, burying her head against his chest. "I'm sorry I took Thunder without your permission!" she shouted and spilled the words out quickly. It wasn't in her nature to apologize, but she also didn't wish to spend a miserable ride back soaked to the bone and shivering.

When he didn't speak, she lifted her head and eyed him cautiously. His face was no longer playful. His eyes burned into hers. His intense gaze looked fierce and protective in a way that she'd never experienced before. The temperature was frigid but she couldn't feel the cold. There were so many emotions racing behind his eyes.

"Promise me you won't ride Thunder again." She couldn't understand why he was so possessive of his horse. Had she not proved herself able to manage it?

But still, she sighed and said, "I promise."

His brows twitched down. "Really? That simple?" No, it wasn't simple for her. She hadn't relented to a single person since she was a child. Why did she feel compelled to now? His hold tightened around her, sending an unexpected feeling of safety down her spine. She refused to acknowledge it. Feelings were not always reality. *She* kept herself safe. No one else.

"Why?" he asked.

She avoided his eyes and instead focused on the lock of hair that curled up a little at the nape of his neck. "Because I recognize fear when I see it." Her fingers itched to touch that lock of hair. They were too close. She squirmed and pushed away from him. This time he gently set her down and released her. She faced him and tilted her face up to look him full in the eyes. "But what it is you're afraid of, I still haven't figured out."

"Are you never afraid, Daphney?" Would he stop looking at her like that? She couldn't breathe with his gaze holding her in that way. She turned her eyes away hoping he would do the same. He didn't.

It took a great deal of false security, but she looked up in his eyes again. "I gave up being fearful a long time ago." Or at least, she thought she had. But when he looked at her that way—like he could see through to her very soul and spot every weakness she possessed, she felt very much afraid.

In only two days this man had begun to undermine every wall and protection she had so carefully built around herself. Her heart ached to give in, but her mind refused.

"How?"

She looked down and adjusted her skirts. "If you have nothing to lose, you have nothing to fear." She had lost Papa—the last person she had ever loved—when she was only a little girl. The pain, the vulnerability, the fear of living without a home, guardian, or food, had crippled her. That's when she had learned to pick up her own sword. To never let anyone in. To never need anyone the way she had needed Papa.

Rose wasn't that frightened little girl anymore. And she never would be again.

Carver stared at the frightened woman in front of him. Her hair danced wildly around her downcast face. Did she think she was fooling him? Maybe her glinting armor convinced others, but not him. She was every bit as broken and bruised as he was. What kind of life had she been forced to live that could have left her so terribly jaded?

But to ask her would mean balancing a very fine line of confidence.

If he asked her about her pain, she would have every right to ask him about his. She turned away and walked toward the trees. He let her go.

The cool sharp breeze felt good against his skin. It worked to soothe the deep ache he felt as well as the stifling warmth he had begun to feel around Daphney. What was he doing? He couldn't actually be falling for the woman, could he? How ridiculous.

He shoved his hand through his hair and eyed the lush evergreens as he adjusted and readjusted his footing. But his mind would not let go of Daphney. She was literally being paid to spend time with him. She was a criminal. It wouldn't do to go losing himself in an infatuation with a woman who was going to leave in a week with an enormous amount of his money in her pockets. Never mind the fact that she was breathtakingly beautiful, felt like a balm to his heart, and made him want to smile more than anyone else had in years.

None of that can matter.

What he needed was to strike a friendly balance with the woman. One where they got along well enough to convince his family of their relationship, but keep enough distance so that she didn't end up in his arms with him pouring out his heart at every playful exchange.

After a few minutes of much needed space, Carver made his way to where Daphney hid behind a large tree. Her faded green skirts peeked out from behind the trunk of bare oak and he could see her hands breaking a stem of grass into tiny pieces. He walked around the tree and rested his shoulder on the trunk beside her.

A friendly balance...maybe even a harmless flirtation?

"You don't have to hide. I won't dump you in the water today," he said with a smile.

Her eyes met his, and a smirk pulled at the corner of her mouth. "That's a relief to a woman who cannot swim." It was clearly a joke. The water wasn't more than a foot deep. But he saw a rare opportunity to learn more about her and couldn't resist.

"Can you really not swim?"

She shrugged, taking on a look of playfulness once again. "Maybe. Maybe not." Apparently, their tense moment from beside the stream was behind them now. Good.

"Oh, come on," he nudged her shoulder. "You can't even tell me that much about yourself?"

"I'd rather not."

"Why? Afraid I'm accumulating ways to rid myself of you that don't include giving you my fortune?"

Daphney looked toward her boot. "As I told you last night—I think it would be better if you did not confuse Daphney's story with mine." A single lock of hair slipped from behind her ear. Having to practice more restraint than he would have thought, he resisted the urge to brush it back from her soft face.

"As remarkable as it sounds, I am both ruggedly handsome *and* intelligent enough to compartmentalize information."

She almost smiled. "Well…you are one of those things at least." Her eyes peeked up from below thick lashes. "But I'm not going to tell you which one."

"Why, Miss Bellows," he said with a grin, "are you flirting with me?"

She shrugged again, something he was beginning to recognize as a nervous gesture. "I'm just getting into character. Your family will expect to see a certain amount of attraction between us, after all."

His brows lifted as well as the tempo of his heart. "Will they now?"

Friendly balance.

She laughed. A glorious, beautiful sound. "You look the very picture of a rake when you do that."

"So what you're saying is, I was convincing in my role as Lord Newburry."

She angled her face toward him, leaned her head back against the tree and tucked her hands behind her back. His eyes instinctively traced the lines of her pale pink lips. They were so close to him. "No," she said. "That's what confused me. Even when trying to play the part I could tell there was something about you that was inherently… good." Would she still think that if she could read his thoughts right now?

He cleared his throat and turned so that his back rested against the tree and he was no longer facing her taunting lips. "If only my old governess could hear you now. She might regret having resigned from her post due to my having been a *horrible child*."

Daphney sputtered a laugh. "Really? What was it you did that was so horrible?" This time it was her shoulder that moved to rest against the tree. Her lovely scent carried on the breeze and he breathed it in. Did she realize her hair had begun to slip from its pins? He could tell by the bits that were already flying in the wind that she had beautiful, wavy hair. What would it look like loose?

"Hmm?" He blinked, forgetting what they had even been talking about. *Your ugly old governess!* "Oh." He cleared his throat. "Nothing so extravagant that warranted the title of 'horrible child.' Just the usual larks a schoolboy is inclined to play."

"Which are?" she asked with lifted brows. "I spent most of life on the streets. I'm afraid that has left me completely ignorant to the 'larks a schoolboy is inclined to play,'" she stated, as though his history were the more shocking between the two of them.

He wanted to linger. He wanted to know more. How had she ended up on the streets? Had she ever known her parents? But her expression was unguarded at the moment and he knew that the minute he started asking questions her walls would fly back up. Tucking his questions into his pocket for another time, he revisited memories of his crusty old governess.

"Let's see," he looked up and squinted at the sky. "Of course, there was the frequent bit of pepper in her tea, the occasional frog in her bed, worms in her boots, gluing the pages of her textbooks shut," he made a thinking noise, "oh, and the time I recruited one of my female friends to sew the bottom hem of Miss Blaine's Sunday dress shut." Claire hated that craggy old Miss Blaine just as much as Carver did, so she had been happy to help. In the end, it worked out just as they had hoped. Miss Blaine could no longer abide the larks and packed her bags.

"Oh, is that all?" said Daphney, her eyes dancing. "A horrible little brat indeed! I knew street urchins more well-mannered than you."

He laughed, relishing the lightness he felt when Daphney was near.

"Were you punished for any of it?" she asked.

"Not nearly as much as I should have been. Of course, my mother gave me a famous scolding, but I honestly think she despised the governess as much as we did. She would never have admitted it but I think she was thankful to see the woman go without her having to be the one to send her off. Mother despises confrontation."

"I can see that. She seems to be a very warm and tender lady." Daphney's voice sounded almost sad.

"She is."

"And what about your father? Was he angry?"

"Very little." Carver couldn't remember his father ever growing very angry. Reiterating what Mother had said, yes. Enforcing Mother's edicts that he write his governess an apology letter, yes. But never really becoming upset or raising his voice. "He has always been a very gentle and understanding father."

Guilt pinched him. His father had never been anything but kind and attentive. Even when his father had dozens of important things to get done in a day, he never failed to set it all aside and give his children his full attention when they needed it. And in return, for the past three years, Carver had pushed him away. He had pushed everyone away, but especially his father. When he looked into the man's eyes, he was transported back to that day. Back to hearing his father utter the words that had ruined Carver's life. *Claire had an accident. She's gone.*

So he avoided the duke. Avoided the tenderness he knew he would see in his father's eyes. Avoided the pain.

Daphney smiled softly. He wanted to run his hand along her soft cheek. "That's nice." But her smile turned sad again, and she tore her beautiful golden gaze away looking somewhere behind him. She looked as if she were caught up in a distant memory.

"What about you? Did you know your father?"

Her breath stilled. She held it in a moment, then released it. "We ought to be getting back. Your family will begin to wonder what's become of us." She pushed off the tree and started walking back toward the horses, leaving him no chance to reply or press her further. Hardly fair that she should be able to ask him as many questions as she wished but he couldn't ask her a single one.

How could he get her to open up? To see him as a safe confidante? And more importantly, why did he so badly want her to? Carver was unmistakably attracted to the woman. But he wasn't at all sure that he should be. He had never given his heart the chance to love again after...he couldn't finish the thought. He was tired of thinking of that day. Tired of it being an all-consuming part of his life. Maybe if he just stopped thinking about it, the pain would disappear.

But still, the question was whether he wanted Daphney—an untrustworthy thief—to be the one to teach his heart to love again. She was definitely not the most suitable choice. And yet, his heart was beginning to long for her anyway. Well, he certainly wouldn't figure it out by continuing to lean against that tree. Several steps and he was back at the horses.

Thunder tossed his head in ready anticipation of the ride back to the stables. The Gentleman grazed, leisurely, on a patch of grass. Carver smiled. After watching Daphney ride Thunder to an inch, she would be cursing him for forcing her to ride such a lazy roan. His eyes wandered to Daphney. She had not mounted yet. She was staring at him.

His heart quickened at the directness of her gaze. What was she doing? The look in her golden eyes tugged him toward her. One step, and then another brought him directly in front of her. She did not speak, did not smile, just looked. Did her lips just part? Yes. His gaze lowered to rest on that lovely mouth. Instinctively, his hand went to her jaw and his thumb brushed her lower lip.

Even over the howling wind, he could hear her breaths quicken. Kissing her was going to complicate things, but blast it all, he didn't care. All he could think about was how warm her skin felt against his hand. How sweet she smelled. And how right it felt to be near her. He leaned down slowly, cradling her face in his hands trying to hold the moment still, never letting it slip from him. He kept his eyes fixed on her lips and just before he closed the gap, he saw her smile. A wicked smile.

"I was only waiting for you to help me into the saddle," she whispered, and then very clearly bit her lips together to keep from laughing.

She had been playing him that entire time! No doubt getting him back for doing the same thing to her the day before outside her bedchamber.

His eyes narrowed even as he smiled. He dropped his hand. "Of course. I know," he repeated the same words she had used. But then he leaned in and whispered in her ear, "But I *was* going to kiss you." Her smile dropped, and he heard her take in a sharp breath. He wrapped his hands around her small waist and hoisted her up into the saddle before returning to Thunder without another word.

Chapter Sixteen

W*ell, that was a confusing morning.*

Rose marched down the corridor in search of her bedchamber with unstoppable determination. She needed a respite. One that offered more privacy than that of a tree—which obviously had not been enough of a barricade from the handsome gentleman she was trying to evade.

"Why couldn't he have been a cad?" She mumbled to herself. A cad would have been much easier to not develop feelings for. But no, Lord Kensworth—*Carver*—was nothing like a cad. He was honorable, thoughtful, funny and…attractive. She had intended to retaliate for his little stunt outside her room yesterday, and after learning about how much he enjoyed a good lark as a boy she had thought that he would appreciate some good-natured revenge. What she had *not* intended was to find it ridiculously difficult to not let him kiss her. And then to have him openly admit that a kiss was exactly what he had been intending! Every time she thought about it, her heart raced.

Oh, Rose, you blasted fool!

She was falling for the earl. And she was falling quickly. She should have never allowed herself to ask him those questions. It was the first step toward blurring the lines between target and friend. That was why she was so firm in her resolution to never tell him anything about her own life in the first place. There was too much danger in opening up to someone. Feelings would bloom. Her heart would warm. Then she would lose her heart altogether—and that couldn't happen. Not now, not ever. There was too much at stake. Too much vulnerability.

If you have nothing to lose, you have nothing to fear. She would never fear losing someone she loved again because she would never love again. Never again would she be left homeless and poor and heartbroken and afraid. She created her own safety, and this resolve strengthened with each pounding step she placed against the red rug beneath her feet.

That's when she suddenly realized that at some point during her inner rant she had made a wrong turn. Rose paused in the middle of the corridor and turned a quick circle trying to reorient herself. There was nothing for it. All of the hallways bore a remarkable resemblance to each other. Massive stone walls, floor to ceiling windows, and red carpets lining the floor. All Rose knew was that her room could not be found in this corridor. But it had to be on that floor, didn't it? The first floor holds all of the public rooms. The second was bedchambers. And the third housed the nursery. That meant she had just turned down the wrong hallway.

She turned around with the intent of going back the way she had come when the sound of ladies' voices drifted from an open bedchamber a bit further down the hall.

"What do you think of it?" came a nervous voice that sounded like Elizabeth. "No...it's all wrong! Oh, why did I ever let you talk me into green, Kate?" Yes, that was Elizabeth.

Rose probably should have turned around and continued walking. The ladies were clearly having a private conversation. But then another voice joined theirs, pulling Rose further into the exchange. The duchess spoke in a smooth tone, with a warmth that made Rose feel as if she were being wrapped in a hug. For some reason, she couldn't walk away from that. "Ah, my darling girl! How beautiful you look. Kate was exactly right convincing you to choose green."

Rose's feet involuntarily drifted toward the voices and the open door.

Elizabeth replied, "It's too bold and has far too much embroidery. I'll look ridiculous." There was the sound of a skirt swishing like she was turning in a circle. Were they talking of a dress? "I'm hoping to look like an eligible lady, not a ridiculous greenhorn screaming for attention."

At least three ladies laughed. "It is London, dearest. Everyone will be screaming for attention." That was Mary—Or Lady Hatley as Rose should remember to think of her.

Against her better judgement, Rose tiptoed beside the bedchamber and peeked inside. She had the strangest desire to get a look at that green dress. Sure enough, Elizabeth was standing a few paces away from a gilded looking glass, hands on her trim waist, assessing the pale sea-foam green gown she was wearing. Rose didn't think it looked too bold. In fact, she thought it complimented Elizabeth's golden blonde hair perfectly.

Elizabeth's overblown look of uncertainty, however, would not fly one bit in a London ballroom. Rose had graced enough of the suffocating crushes to know that a lady who looked on the verge of nervous vomiting would be eaten alive by the debutantes and matrons of high society.

To cut a dash in London, a lady needed to hold herself with a self-assured air—mixed with a touch of false modesty. Add in a polite blush here and there and she was sure to have her hand claimed for every dance. Also, it never hurt to have the size of her dowry bandied about the town. That is, assuming, she had a sizable dowry to offer. And Rose was sure that Elizabeth did. What did the girl have to worry about? She was stunning, kind, had a beautiful figure, and a purse full of money. What thoughts could possibly be running through her mind to warrant such a look of uncertainty and trepidation?

Although, on second thought, knowing what she knew about the London ballroom, Rose could easily see how a woman who was actually there in search of making an advantageous match would feel a bit daunted. Never mind the fact that most of those 'advantageous matches' were in actuality dishonorable coxcombs who took advantage of women in the lower classes while the *ton* turned a blind eye. And then there were the fortune hunters and the old crazies who hoped for a young bride that they could mold into their desired wife. Now that she thought about it, there really were very few good prospects for Elizabeth—or any young woman—in London to choose from.

But what did she really know about making a match? She had only ever attended the crushes to swipe a few jewels off the necks and wrists of unsuspecting debutantes. And maybe a few fobs and pocket watches from the dandified gentlemen. The task was ridiculously easy, considering the cramped rooms were stuffed wall to wall with swooning ladies and prowling gentlemen and Rose's touch was soft as air.

"But you are not even wearing your jewelry!" The youngest sister, Kate, moved to Elizabeth's back and began to drape a glittering diamond around Elizabeth's neck.

That's when Rose realized Elizabeth was one of those debutantes that she would have all too readily stolen from and never thought twice about. To Rose, they were all the same: overly privileged ladies who had never known a day of strife in their entire lives. And although that was most likely also true for Elizabeth, seeing her there, nervously preparing for her first season among her mother and sisters, caused a heavy remorse to settle in her chest.

"Daphney!" A surprised voice pierced through Rose. "What are you doing just standing out there? Come in!" Kate said in that exuberant way that Rose was beginning to realize was a constant for the young lady.

But Rose *did not* want to go in that room. She would likely feel as comfortable in that room full of gabbing women as a cat in an alley full of hungry dogs.

Daphney, however, would have been all too eager to enjoy a chat with her future mother and sisters-in-law. Summoning her courage as well as her most polite smile, Rose inched into the room. "Oh, I'm sorry. I didn't mean to intrude." She knit her brows together with false humiliation. "I got a little turned around and stumbled past your door trying to locate my room."

"Nonsense," said Kate walking to Rose's side to pull her into the gaggle of women. "You are not intruding in the least. We were only trying to convince my prudish sister that the color of her dress is not nearly as brazen as she believes."

"Yes, dear, please join us and share your opinion!" The duchess's voice felt like a siren call. Something wonderful that Rose couldn't—and didn't want to—refuse. How many times during her twenty-three years of life had Rose wondered about the sound of her own mother's voice? Was Mama's tone high or low? Was it soft like silk brushing against the ears or did it have a hint of rasp?

Rose forced a small smile, hoping that her pain was not evident. She quickly scanned the room and all who were there. The duchess sat in a chair near the fireplace. She was situated with her weight on her right hip, ankles crossed, elbow resting on the arm of the chair with her chin resting lightly on the tops of her knuckles. She somehow managed to look regal and relaxed at the same time.

Kate perched on the bed. Excited energy beamed from her smile. Elizabeth faced Rose, clearly happy to have her share in such an intimate moment. Lady Hatley stood beside the window, gazing out with a worn and tired expression. With a delicate hand, she tenderly caressed the small bump of her belly. The loss Carver had spoken about hung around her like a heavy blanket. Her eyes flicked to Rose's but her expression did not lighten. In fact, it only grew more concerned.

It would appear that Rose and Carver's pretend betrothal was causing the opposite of the desired result for Lady Hatley. Rose would just have to try harder to make the lady feel at ease. It was important to Carver that his sister not come under any stress due to their relationship. And Rose was being paid to keep in mind what was important to Carver and that was the only reason she would throw herself wholeheartedly into relieving his sister's anxiety. The *only* reason.

Rose turned her attention to Elizabeth. "What do you feel is wrong with the gown?"

Elizabeth's shoulders slumped the slightest bit. "It is too…green."

She turned back to the mirror, placed her hand on her middle, and stood up taller. "I feel like it makes me look like a..." Everyone leaned a little closer in anticipation of what term Elizabeth would use to finish that statement. "Child. I hope to be viewed as mature and refined, not like a loud trifling bit of shrubbery."

"Wait," said Kate, eyes twinkling. "Are you a child or a shrub?"

"Both. I'm a young shrub."

Everyone chuckled but Rose stifled her laugh and instead allowed a soft smile. She didn't want to embarrass the girl. "Well, for what it is worth, I think the color is lovely and unobtrusive. It brings out your eyes brilliantly, which, if I am not mistaken, is what a lady secretly hopes a gentleman will take note of."

Rose would have never known that to be true until Carver had assessed her own eyes. She had never thought hers to be anything special. But the way he had looked into them...described them thoughtfully as if it were important to get the likeness exactly right—sent a thrill up her spine.

Kate giggled like a girl and even Mary's cheeks were touched with a light blush.

"Has Carver taken note of your eyes, Miss Bellows?" asked Kate in a dreamy tone as if seeing into Rose's very thoughts. There was no way she would admit them. It was too stupid.

"Oh hush, Kate!" the duchess reprimanded in her soft way. "Daphney, you needn't tell us." But then, a mischievous smile pulled at the sides of the woman's mouth before she utterly betrayed Rose. "Although...we very much wish you would."

"Oh yes, do tell!" Kate clapped excitedly as Elizabeth joined in the persuasion.

Rose was the very center of attention, and it appeared that there was simply nothing to be done but give the expectant women what they wanted. Perhaps telling them would serve to alleviate some of Lady Hatley's stress. Rose took a fortifying breath. She could do it. She could confide in the ladies this much for the sake of the ruse. "Well, at the risk of being in your brother's black books, I will tell you all that Carver has taken a rather fond notice of my particular eye color." She swallowed. "He says they resemble a glass of…fine brandy." Rose had to bite her cheeks to keep from smiling from how silly she felt admitting Carver's flirtatious comment. But oddly enough, admitting something personal felt better than she had expected. Her heart lifted a little.

She tried but couldn't keep from smiling as each of the ladies erupted in various noises of delight and squeals. Kate flung herself dramatically onto the bed with her hand pressed to her heart. Even Mary pressed her lips together to keep from smiling too big. The duchess simply chuckled with contented delight. The same bubbles of laughter Rose had felt in the meadow returned, and she was taken over by them. They all sounded ridiculous. And it was wonderful.

For the first time in her life, Rose stood amongst a group of women laughing—earnestly. She was not trying to steal anything or squeeze any money from them. She was not bringing them into her confidence so she could find out which gentlemen in the ballroom possessed the largest wealth. She was simply giving in to a natural joy from telling the truth. It was freeing.

In the midst of their giggles, a male voice broke over the room. Strong and low. "And just what bit of gossip has you, ladies, splitting your seams this time?"

Carver walked fully into the room, a skeptical smile on his mouth before his eyes took note of Rose for the first time and his face molded into an unreadable expression. Was he upset to find her there among his sisters and mother? Did he want her to keep her distance during the week? They really should have discussed these things.

Rose attempted to smooth the lines of his forehead with her words. "I stupidly got lost on my way back to my bedchamber after our ride. I found Elizabeth's room in the process."

"And we are so happy that she did!" Kate sprung off the bed. "Or else Elizabeth would never have known that she wished to have gentlemen take fond notice of her eyes!" said Kate, skipping circles around Elizabeth and dancing a ribbon across her blushing face.

Carver's eyes narrowed as a teasing smile pulled over his mouth.

"What's this, Lizzie? Tell me now who this foolish young buck is so that I can strike the fear of God in him."

The duchess stood from her seat to cross to Carver. She tapped him under the chin. "Oh my boy, *you* are the foolish young buck." She smiled mischievously again and passed through the room to the door. "Excuse me, children. I must go find your father and demand that he remarks on the beauty of my eye color." Her Grace looked over her shoulder and winked at Rose.

Carver turned his eyes from his mother back to Rose. "Why do I get the feeling this bit of gossip has something to do with me?" She felt the urge to squirm under his gaze until she remembered one important fact. The family was present, which meant he was not looking at Rose, he was looking at Daphney. Knowing she could hide behind the persona made her breathe a little easier. But did the feelings she was experiencing belong to Rose or Daphney?

"Because it was about you, brother," said Elizabeth with her own attempt at teasing. "Daphney has been filling us with jealousy because our eyes will never resemble anything so wonderful as your favorite drink."

Rose's cheeks burned.

Carver crossed his arms over his chest and feigned a glare at Rose. "I see, she's taken you all into her confidence has she?" Suddenly, something in his expression shifted. The teasing vanished and was replaced with an intense and somehow also sad look. "That is something even I have yet to manage."

The air closed in. The girls continued to talk and tease but Carver didn't look away and in some way, Rose knew that what he said was a message just for her. Did he want to be in her confidence? Yes. She knew he did. But why? No good would come of that.

Had she not made it perfectly clear last night and again this morning that if she were to stay, her private life simply without question had to remain private? If Rose wished to keep any sort of emotional distance between herself and the man with the handsome grey eyes, she had to keep herself hidden.

Besides, if he truly knew who she was, he would wish that he didn't.

"Yes, and now you are decidedly in the way, my dear brother," said Mary moving away from the window for the first time. She walked to Carver's side and threaded her arm through his. "Walk me back to my room so your little sisters can prod Miss Bellows with all of the romantic questions their blooming hearts desire."

Carver's face softened as he looked at his sister. His regard for Mary was beyond evident, as was hers for him. "Very well, I'm not too thick-headed to know when I'm not wanted. We will leave you women to your chat." He turned once more to face Rose. "Daphney, my darling," Rose noticed in that moment that Carver had not used such flamboyant endearments one time while they were alone. Apparently, that flirtatiousness was part of *his* facade. Why was she beginning to wish it wasn't? "Do not tell anything horribly embarrassing or I'll be forced to throw you into the stream." He winked, and Rose refused to acknowledge the jump in her heart.

Chapter Seventeen

"Do you like her?" The words broke out of Carver's mouth before he had time to stop them. Why should it matter if Mary liked Daphney? Daphney would be gone in a week and neither he nor his family would ever see her again. Although he was keeping the woman around in order to secure Mary's peace, so maybe it would be good to know her opinion.

But when Mary did not respond immediately, he found himself wishing he hadn't asked. "She's a surprising match for you." Surprising good or bad? He decided not to reply right away in hopes she would continue. She did. "Miss Bellows seems a touch..." Oh, great. Here it comes. He should have known better than to try to hide something from Mary. "Meek for your taste."

If there had been a drink in Carver's mouth, he would have absolutely spat it out. Memories of Daphney, holding a pistol to his head, dashing off on his horse while riding astride, laughing merrily as he threw her over his shoulder and paraded her to the stream, all flew through his mind. If there was only one real thing that he knew about Daphney it was that the woman was anything but meek.

"I think the more you get to know her, the more she will surprise you."

As he and Mary continued walking, an uncomfortable realization prickled him. If they kept walking the way they were going, they would pass by the alcove that held too many memories for him to bear seeing it. But he wouldn't be able to get Mary to go the long way around without raising her suspicions or having to tell her why he was avoiding it. And that would cause her anxiety. There was nothing for it. He would just have to try to pass it quickly and not let his thoughts wander.

Mary pulled in closer to Carver hugging his arm, the way she had their entire life. Particularly when something was bothering her. "I'm sure you're right. It's just…" she hesitated.

"What is it, Mary? You can always tell me anything."

She bit her lips together clearly trying to debate her next words. Finally releasing a breath she hurried through her thoughts. "I just always imagined that you would end up finding someone with a little more spirit like—,"

He groaned cutting off her words and regretting his encouragement for the conversation. He didn't realize it was going to lead to that particular conversation. "Why does everyone suddenly feel the need to talk about Claire?"

Mary's eyes flashed to Carver's wide and unbelieving. "You said her name." And it hurt like the devil. But he wanted to ease Mary's burdens. And if he had to pretend he was okay with Claire's death to help her relax, he would.

"You can thank your obnoxious husband for that."

"Robert? What did Robert say?" What did Robert *not* say?

Carver stopped walking to look at Mary. "He said a few things I needed to hear. And a few things I wished I'd learned sooner." He allowed his look to grow more pointed.

Mary's eyes darted away and to the ground. She fidgeted with the fabric of her dress. "We are not talking about you anymore, are we?"

Carver lifted Mary's chin, still seeing the strong vibrant girl that he'd grown up with rather than the tired and mournful mother she had become. "Why didn't you tell me about what happened, Mary?"

Unshed tears hovered over her lashes. She blinked them away

forcefully. "I—," she slumped and her defenses all lowered. "It was simply too hard. And you were too far away. I didn't want to tell you in person, let alone write the words on paper." Each part of that statement settled heavier and heavier on his chest.

You were too far away. That had been intentional on his part. He had wanted to be as far away from Kensworth Park as possible. And if he were being honest, he had wanted to be as far away from Mary as possible, as well. She had a way of cutting right through his facade and exposing the raw bits of him that he simply couldn't stand to examine after Claire's death.

"And to be honest, I didn't want to add anymore pain to your heart. I was afraid you couldn't handle it." Wait. Wasn't that what he was trying to do for her? Trying to keep her from worrying on his behalf?

He let go of her arm to turn and cradle her face. "Mary, love. I always want you to share your burdens with me. I am strong enough to handle them. And as for everything else...Well, I'm sorry I've stayed away so long. But I'm here now—and I'm not as broken as everyone seems to think."

"Really?"

"Really." Could she tell he was lying? His eyes shifted away despite his effort to keep them fixed on her.

Just behind Mary sat that blasted alcove with the little blue window seat where Claire had liked to come and read on rainy days when they couldn't go for a ride. It was also where he had first confessed his love to her, fourteen and sixteen years old.

But he couldn't tell Mary just how wrecked he really was. Or that his stomach tied in knots just looking at that alcove out of the corner of his eye. Or that picturing Claire's sweet face shedding tears of joy while returning the sentiment made Carver's knees buckle. They had only been children at the time, but as they aged, time proved that their love was every bit as real at fourteen as it would be at six years later when she died.

"You have finally let her go, then?"

No. Never.

"Yes." He flashed her his most dashing 'man of the world' smile. "Would I be a happily engaged man if I hadn't?"

Mary's eyes narrowed. Apparently, she wasn't quite convinced either. "Have you told Daphney about Claire?"

Carver knew his smile fell, but he simply couldn't keep it up anymore. Hearing Claire's name so many times in one conversation was beginning to wear on him. But he knew that he needed to get through it to fully convince Mary that he was indeed healed and over the love of his life, or else this conversation would undoubtedly keep happening. And he didn't think he could stand that.

"I haven't. Why should I bring up the past with my future?" He attempted a light tone but still the words felt too heavy.

Mary only seemed more concerned, but she didn't say anything for a time. She picked back up his arm and they were walking again. "Robert was incredible during the whole thing you know?" He nearly sighed a breath of relief at the much needed change of topic. And that they could finally hurry past that alcove and he could forget about it.

Carver let go of her arm and put an arm around her shoulders instead. She was tall enough that the position wasn't awkward. "That doesn't surprise me in the least. The man is a deuced saint."

Mary laughed and the sound did Carver's heart good. "That he is. I was a wreck after everything happened. Still am in some ways. But he didn't expect me to pull myself together right away," she said. "He gave me the time and space I needed to hurt and grieve, all the while making sure I knew that he was nearby when I was ready to talk."

He swallowed and felt his Adam's apple strain against his cravat—which again, felt too tight. He wasn't oblivious to what she was doing. But still, he wanted to know, "Did that help you?"

"More than I will ever be able to express." She turned her face up to look at his as they came to a stop outside of her bedchamber, her grey eyes conveying the empathy he felt from her. "Tell Daphney. Give her the chance to help you heal, Carver. It's okay to let someone else pull you to safety when you're drowning."

He loved his sister and respected her experience, but there was no way on God's green earth he was going to tell Daphney about Claire.

She was his hired fiancé. One did not tell an employee their greatest sorrows.

"I have healed, Mary."

She smiled softly and patted his cheek the same way his mother often did. "Saying it doesn't make it true, Carver."

He felt a sinking feeling in the pit of his stomach. It was heavy and uncomfortable and it told him that she was right. They were all right. He hadn't healed yet. But they were also wrong about everything else. Talking about it didn't make it any better. It had the exact opposite effect.

"May I see your little miss today?" Changing the subject was good.

"No, but you can tomorrow. Robert has taken her to visit with the neighbor's other children this afternoon. I suspect she will be in desperate need of a nap when she returns."

It was odd for Carver to think of Mary as a married woman and a mother. In his mind, they were both still children hiding in the trees to escape their awful governess. Part of him wished they were still children. If that were true, he would be able to look down through the limbs of the tree and find Claire, climbing up behind them, all too eager to jump head first into whatever scrape he and Mary were tangling themselves in.

But they weren't children. And Claire was dead. That realization sank in more and more during his time at home. He rubbed the back of his neck as he walked back toward his room. This time, taking the long way around to avoid that deuced alcove.

He considered for a moment going to seek out Daphney. Was she feeling uncomfortable among his sisters? Finding her in the middle of the giggling ladies gathered in Elizabeth's room had been unexpected, to say the least. He was even more taken aback to see her smiling in a way he hadn't seen before, unguarded and joyful. Even more distressing was the fleeting feeling that seeing her there with his sisters and mother looked...right. *She* felt right to him.

He wanted to kick himself for being such a dunderhead. The woman was pretending to enjoy his family. That was what they had agreed on. Daphney had made it perfectly clear that she would not form any attachments to himself or his family during the visit and that if at any point it seemed like she had, he was to remind himself that she was acting. If that was true, the woman was a bloody good actress. And her fake smile was absolutely lovely.

Even if it was only for show, Carver found himself wishing he could see it again. He nearly went to find her, but in the end, his emotional fatigue won over and he decided to take a walk instead. What he really needed to do was to go to his bedchamber and sleep. Last night had not afforded him any rest, but he couldn't go there. He couldn't go anywhere. He left the house in hopes that he would leave the memories behind as well.

Chapter Eighteen

Rose was not given further opportunity to see Carver again privately after spending the afternoon with his sisters. They had been at dinner together, but that was hardly the right place to update him on all of the facts of their relationship that bloomed in her conversations with Elizabeth and Kate. The girls were relentless in their questions, wanting to soak up every detail of Carver and Daphney's love story. And Rose had given them more than one ridiculous tale to swoon over.

As if a lady really wished to sprain her ankle in the middle of Hyde Park, only to be rescued by a handsome gentleman, lifted onto his horse and escorted back to her home. It was completely ridiculous, but it was apparently the first moment Daphney had realized she loved Carver. Why that was the first thing she thought of when the ladies asked for the exact moment she knew she loved their brother, Rose would never know.

It was unfortunate that she would now have to repeat the story to Carver, along with a slew of other embarrassingly romantic tales about their sham of a love story. There was not a chance that Carver wouldn't tease her for the stories she made up, but there was nothing to be done about it now. The ladies had hoped to hear sweet tales of the two love birds and Rose hadn't disappointed them. And although she would deny it all the way to her grave, part of her—a very minuscule part—enjoyed the thought of Carver actually caring for her in the way her stories suggested.

She had attempted to find him after leaving Elizabeth's room. She didn't think that his sisters would question him about the stories, but he needed to be ready if they did. But she had only spotted him through the window. He was walking across the grounds, without his coat and with such a look of unveiled pain slashed across his face that she almost felt ashamed to have witnessed it. He wouldn't have wanted her to see it. His mask of strength had been, at all other times, perfectly in place. But then, she saw him broken, full of hopelessness and pain. What had happened to him? Would she ever know?

She had watched him from that window, behind her own mask and hiding place for far too long. But she had hoped that watching him would lead her to some hint of what had happened to him. It hadn't. And by dinner that evening, he had his mask firmly back in place.

Today, Rose was determined to find Carver and tell him all the embarrassing things that she hadn't been able to yesterday. Bright afternoon sunlight beamed in through the towering windows as Rose descended the stairs in search of Carver.

As Rose wandered through the house, she found it amazing that although the temperatures outside where anything but warm, the golden tint of the sun against the oak banister and deep red rugs made the house feel as if it were in the peak of summer—that, and around every corner she found vases filled with flowers that could only be found in a garden during the warmer months. How was that possible? There had to be a greenhouse nearby. And if that were true, she very much wanted to find it.

Rose lingered as she walked. A house of that enormity ought to feel cold and uninviting. Instead, it felt magical. Warm. Mature in only the way that a castle built two hundred years ago could be. If she were to listen closely enough, she figured she would be able to hear the stories that lived within those walls.

At the bottom of the stairs, Rose found Mr. Henley quietly

addressing a footman. Once he finished, Rose approached him. "Good day, Henley." To be honest, she wasn't entirely sure how to interact with a butler. In real life, she would rank far under the man. But in this pretend, upside-down world, she was a lady. So she tried to her best to appear as such.

He bowed politely. "Good day, miss. Is there something I might help you with?" The older butler had a kindness in his features that set Rose at ease.

"I was hoping you could tell me where I might find Lord Kensworth."

"Of course, miss." He leaned in a little and lowered his voice. "I believe he might be found in the nursery." Henley spoke as if he were telling an important secret. One just for her.

"In the nursery?" Visiting Jane, most likely.

The butler nodded and smiled. "I was instructed not to tell Her Grace or any of his sisters. However, seeing as he did not include yourself in those instructions, I believe it is safe to tell you where he may be found."

Rose smiled. "Thank you. I'll be sure to keep the secret." She winked and the older butler flushed a little.

After receiving detailed directions to the nursery, Rose made her way to the third floor of the home. It didn't take her long to locate it, mostly because of the bursts of girlish laugher resounding off of the walls.

Rose stood just outside of the door peeking in on the nursery. It could only be described as a child's dream come true. Tall windows lined the walls, allowing an abundance of light to fill the space. The walls were painted to resemble a lush garden, and a canopy of light yellow fabric draped from the center of the room all the way out to the corners and down to the floor.

Carver suddenly came into view. He was squatted down and... hopping across the floor? His jacket, waist coat, and cravat were tossed over a chair and Carver—Lord Kensworth, the fierce pugilist and future Duke of Dalton—was hopping across the floor of a nursery making croaking sounds. He looked ridiculous. And apparently that was the point because little Lady Jane sat in a child-sized chair having a fit of laughter.

"You're not supposed to be laughing, my dear. You're supposed to be guessing," said Carver in mock exasperation while continuing to hop around the room.

"A bird!" Jane giggled.

"No." He said before making another frog noise.

"A dog!"

"Ribbit."

"An elephant!"

Carver paused and flashed the girl a narrowed glare. "Lady Jane, you wouldn't be making the wrong guess on purpose to watch your uncle make a fool out of himself, would you?"

The little girl nodded proudly and released another giggle.

His jaw dropped in feigned astonishment as he stood to his full massive height again. He looked down to his sleeves and began to roll them up with a menacing grin on his lips. Rose looked from Carver to Jane who eyed her uncle with an expression that indicated she knew what was coming next.

He smiled. "You better run, little one."

Jane squealed and shot from her seat. She turned quickly around her chair and began to run across the room as Carver started chasing her. Jane could barely run, she was laughing so hard. Rose felt her own heart beat faster from the memory of Carver chasing her through the meadow yesterday morning.

Pretending to run at a slower pace than Jane, Carver would reach out just as he was about to catch the girl and then let her slip through his fingers. On and on this game went until Rose accidentally let a slight laugh escape and Carver's gaze flew to her.

He froze for a moment before a slow smile grew over his mouth in a way that made Rose's breath quicken involuntarily. "Well, well, well," he stalked toward Rose with a tipped eyebrow. "Jane, darling, it would appear we have a spy skulking about."

Carver continued to walk slowly toward Rose with his shirtsleeves rolled up, exposing his muscular forearms and looking far more handsome than was good or fair for anyone. He looked both ruggedly masculine and easily approachable. Those things, coupled with the devilish smile on his lips and mischievous sparkle in his grey eyes, ignited something in Rose that hadn't been there before. Something overwhelming that she couldn't ignore. She had to clear her throat to find her voice.

"I wasn't skulking. I just didn't want to interrupt." She tried to smile as naturally as possible. Could he tell that she was blushing? And why the devil was she blushing?

"A likely story." He raised a brow. "Should we believe her, Janie?" He moved closer.

Jane was bashful now and simply shook her head with a smothered giggle.

"I didn't think so. This beautiful woman means trouble." He stopped just an arms length away. Close enough she could smell his scent and notice that the cut above his eye had almost healed. "Suppose she means to do something dreadful to us, Janie." He spoke to the little girl but his piercing gaze never left Rose.

"Like what, Uncle Carver?"

"Like force us to eat vegetables."

"Ew!" Jane shouted, still standing behind Carver's legs.

"My thoughts exactly." He moved even closer and Rose's skin felt like fire. What was he doing? Why was he looking at her that way? More teasing?

With hands clasped behind her back, she forced a steadying breath but it came out trembly. "My presence here is purely innocent, I assure you." She didn't look away. Carver was clearly playing a game and Rose would not cower under his gaze. Never mind that it felt like ocean tides breaking over her one by one until she felt her balance slipping.

"Hmm. I'm afraid I cannot trust you. Suppose you have an instrument of torture hidden behind your back. I don't think I can risk it."

"Would you prefer I leave, then?" She swallowed.

He looked at her for a long moment, tilted his head the smallest bit and then whispered. "No."

Something in the way he said that single word, sent shivers running over her skin. Were they still talking about the game? Was there an encrypted message she was supposed to decode?

She didn't have time to think about it because he cleared his throat and then regained his theatrical expression. "It's to the dungeon with you, woman." He reached behind her and pulled her into the room and whispered in her ear, "play along." But what she wanted to do was melt on the ground.

She looked down at little wide-eyed Jane and remembered there was no time for melting. She had to play along. But how? Rose was forced to stop being a child so long ago she wasn't sure she even knew how to be one anymore. And the only time Rose had ever spent around children had been during her short visits back to Hopewood Orphanage. She would go back now and again to make sure the children were getting what they needed and bring any extra funds she had...acquired. But she intentionally limited her time at the orphanage. She wanted to help the children as they deserved to be helped, to allow them to be children and see to their well being, but she would not let herself grow attached to them. No, that's what she had hired teachers and nursemaids for.

"Over here, Uncle Carver!" cried Jane, gesturing toward a small table and chairs in the corner of the room.

Rose looked back to Carver. "You heard the girl. Off with you!" He pointed to the little child's sized table.

She wanted to play along, she really did. But she simply couldn't think of any playful words. "Very well, I'm going." She sat down in the tiny chair. "Now what?"

Jane leaned forward, her eyes dancing. "You try to get away," she whispered, helpfully.

Of course! Why hadn't she thought of that? It's precisely what she would do if she were ever imprisoned in real life. "Look over there! I think I see a dragon," said Rose pointing behind Carver.

He didn't miss his cue. He took on a look of horror and spun around to face the beast. "Where?"

Rose darted from the chair before he turned back and made for the other side of the room.

"She got away!" yelled Jane gleefully.

"Well, don't just stand there, Janie. We have to catch her!"

Both Carver and Jane turned to Rose and began their pursuit just as a high voice interrupted their game. "Alright, little miss! It's time for your nap." A portly middle-aged lady with rosy cheeks walked into the room carrying a bundle of freshly laundered nightgowns. Lady Jane puffed out a bottom lip and attempted to protest.

Carver knelt down on one knee and took her tiny hands in his. "Never fear, my darling. I'll be back to play tomorrow." He leaned in and kissed her forehead. Rose couldn't look away. How had she ever thought the man capable of any dishonorable behavior?

Jane, reluctant yet compliant, walked with her nursemaid toward a room just off the nursery. She looked back and blew Carver a kiss before disappearing into her bedchamber. Carver caught it with a smile and then glanced to Rose.

"I t was good of you to play along," said Carver from across the room but coming closer to where she stood beside the window. Thick clouds were rolling in, beginning to hide the sun. For once, it actually looked like winter.

"I'll be honest. I hadn't the slightest idea of what to do."

He feigned shock. "Never say so!"

"Do not laugh at me or I'll box your ears," she said trying to hold back a smile.

He smirked, leaned his shoulder against the wall beside the window, and crossed his arms. "I'm sure you would try, but I doubt you could reach them."

"I could stand on a chair."

"And just how would you get me to stay still for my punishment?" Carver had a unique way of smiling with his eyes before his mouth.

"I'll aim my pistol at you," she smiled with one side of her mouth giving him a look that she knew was flirtatious. Why was she doing that?

"Ah…" he smiled fully. "That's a much better threat. The fact that you didn't think of it first leads me to believe you might not be such a good criminal after all."

Rose leaned her shoulder against the wall on the opposite side of the window. She wondered why it was so easy to banter with Carver. Easy to smile with Carver. In some odd way, it felt as if they had known each other for much longer than three days. "So you think I should have threatened a bullet from the beginning?"

He shrugged. "I would have. But you do as you wish, my dear."

She couldn't help but chuckle. "Do you even own a pistol, *my lord?*" She exaggerated his title because they felt too close now for real formality.

He gave a disbelieving smile. "Do I even…of course I do, you insulting woman! I don't, however, carry it strapped to my leg like you do."

"Of course not," she said. "I don't either, when I'm wearing breeches."

He looked just as shocked and bewildered as she hoped he would. "When you're—? Do you mean to tell me that you really do wear breeches?"

"Only when I'm pretending to be a stable boy."

His brows flew up. "Goodness, woman. Do I even want to know why you pretend to be a stable boy?"

She blinked innocently at him. "To steal horses. Why else?"

"Oh, yes of course. How stupid of me." He paused and looked at her from the corner of his sparkling grey eyes. A silence fell over the room but something inside Rose feared that the awkwardness of it would end their conversation. And for a strange reason, she didn't want that. She wanted to keep talking to Carver, and, against her better judgement, learn all she could about him.

"Are you a good shot?" she asked.

He smiled, more with his mouth than his eyes this time. "I could go get my dueling pistols and we could find out."

"Are you calling me out?"

"Unfortunately, my gentlemanly honor forbids me from challenging a woman," he said. "But I'd be willing to have a competition. Perhaps even a friendly wager?" His eyes glinted.

A wager? The idea made her both excited and nervous. Or maybe it was the way his eyes were shining with a secret. "How much?"

He shook his head. "No money."

"What, then?" her heart sped up just asking the question.

He held a soft smile for a long moment. "If I win, you tell me your name."

My name! Why did he seem to want to learn her name so badly? She couldn't imagine why it would matter to him. Unless…No, she banished that thought.

To agree would be a steep wager indeed. But she knew something that Carver did not. She was a devilishly good shot and rarely missed her mark.

A boost of confidence made her feel daring. "And if I win, I get to ride Thunder for the remainder of the stay, and you will ride the slug."

He smiled playfully. "Oh no, you pretty rogue. If you win, I will most certainly send you packing. My pride will be far too bruised to let you stay any longer."

She extended her hand to him across the window, "Do we have a deal then?"

Carver's eyes looked down at her hand, the hint of a smirk still marking his mouth. His gaze held her hand for a moment longer before his eyes narrowed on it and his brows pulled together. He reached out and she expected him to shake it in agreement of their wager, but her heart sunk when he instead cupped his hand around the backside of hers and tipped it over so that he could look closely at her palm.

She stiffened, knowing exactly what had caught his eye.

Rose tried to yank her hand away but Carver's grip tightened and he tugged her more fully toward him. It was not a painful or violent motion, but it certainly conveyed that he didn't mean to let her get away easily. She quit resisting and resigned her gaze to the floor as Carver lifted her hand up to look closer at it.

"What happened here?" he asked in a low husky voice.

Rose didn't need to look to know what he was referring to. It was the thick, rippling, purple and white scar winding its way from her middle finger down to her wrist. How had she been so careless to extend that hand to him? She usually tried to keep it hidden. The memories associated with that time of her life were not ones that she enjoyed reliving. They reflected her years of vulnerability and uncertainty. Times of grieving and heartbreak before she leaned to pick up her own pieces and become who she was now.

"An accident," she said still looking at the floor.

"Try again," his voice was tender but authoritative. He had a way of making her feel both completely safe and also horribly off-balance at the same time.

Rose pressed her lips together. He was evidently not going to let her go until she told him the truth. But she didn't want to tell him anything about herself. Easier to walk away when everything was done. And no matter how much she liked being around Carver or his family, she would walk away when this was all done. She had to.

Still, something inside her ached to be known by him, even if only in the slightest.

She kept her eyes focused on the floor, bouncing her gaze back and forth between Carver's black top boots and the swirling designs on the light blue rug. "I…was orphaned at ten years old when my papa died. I needed to find work. I did not enjoy living in the streets as a young vulnerable girl so I opted instead to cut my hair and wear a pair of breeches. I pretended to be a boy for the next two years…"

She tried to push away the horrifying memories of those first two weeks after Papa's unexpected death. She had quickly gone from a girl who was loved and cared for to a girl who was completely alone in cold dark alleys. She could still remember how badly her stomach ached from hunger. And the intense discomfort that crawled over her skin when she received ogling looks from the men when they passed her in the streets. She was exposed. Scared. Hungry. Alone.

Carver was still and quiet, holding her hand gently as he waited for her to talk again. "During those years I worked as a climbing boy." She took a deep breath. She was almost done with the story. The last part of the story all came out fast. "I was high up on a third story roof when I slipped. I slid down the roof and would have fallen to my death had I not caught a shingle that was protruding off the edge." She gestured toward the hand he was holding. "And I came away with a trophy for the whole adventure."

Carver remained perfectly still, not saying anything. She couldn't bring herself to look at him. They were standing too close, and she feared that if she let him look at her eyes, he would see the pain and fear that she tried to keep hidden. Rose had kept her heart guarded for nearly all of her life. She knew that if she let this man in, it would come at a high cost, just like the scar twisting down her palm.

But when Rose felt Carver's callused finger gently trace the line of her scar, she couldn't help but look up at him. His touch was so tender and sweet, that she was almost shaken to see the fierce look in his eyes and the firm set of his jaws. Was he angry? She swallowed and tried to not think about how much his touch affected her. How much she liked it.

"I'm sorry. I wish..." he let the words hang a moment as if hoping to find better ones. "I wish your life hadn't been that way." It was simple, but his voice, low and soft, drew her in. She wanted to lay her head against his strong chest and let him comfort her. The last time Rose had been comforted was the day before her papa's heart had abruptly stopped working. He had held her in his arms and sang her a lullaby after she had woken from a bad dream.

She tried to tug her hand away. She needed space to remember her rules. But he still refused to let her go. "I don't need your pity, Carver," she said, trying to push him away the only way she knew how.

He gently lifted her hand to his lips where he kissed not the back of her hand as was customary, but the inside of her palm where her scar twisted and buckled. "Good," his breath washed across the skin of her hand. "Because I will never give you pity. I promise you that." What, then, would he give her? Rose couldn't let herself think about it.

Chapter Nineteen

C arver watched in the mirror as Brandon, his valet, finished tying the knot around his neck for the fifth time. The man stood back with a weary expression while Carver looked at the linen again in the mirror. He was in a mood, and unfortunately for Brandon, the only thing that soothed his annoyance was ripping off his cravat over and over.

He needed to rip it off again. He lifted his hand but Brandon spoke up with wide nervous eyes. "My lord! If we have to start over again, I'm afraid that you will be late for dinner."

Carver eyed his valet, and Robert, sunk lazily into a chair by the fireplace, interjected with a chuckle. "Poor Brandon. You're setting him in a quake with that thunderous look, Kensworth."

Carver turned. His brother-in-law was smirking. "Do you not have a wife somewhere to annoy?" asked Carver.

But Robert just smiled at the valet. "Best leave us, Brandon, before you're made to tie a sixth knot. Or worse—find a new post."

A nervous-looking Brandon bowed and hurried to the door.

Coward.

Once the door was shut behind the servant, Robert re-situated onto his hip and leaned his elbow on the armrest. "Now, what's put you in such a devilish mood, Kensworth?"

Carver kept his eyes on his reflection in the looking glass as he messed with his hair. He let something of a growl escape, but no words. He didn't feel like talking. The afternoon with Daphney had upended him in a way that he hadn't seen coming. It had ruined everything.

"Come on," Robert said, in a tone that was probably meant to be rallying. "Get it off your chest. I don't know how much longer I can take seeing you this moody."

Carver turned his head to look at his brother-in-law. "Moody? Careful, Robert. It's been too long since I've visited Jackson's. My body is aching for a good fight."

Robert chuckled and sat back. "Well, you won't find one in me. You'd level me down before I had time to blink, and I'm not too proud to admit it. Now talk. And preferably while you're seated. You're making me dizzy pacing circles around the room like that." When had he started pacing?

He stopped, one hand on his waist and the other in his hair. So much for the polished style Brandon had arranged earlier. "If I tell you what's bothering me will you go away?" He said, annoyance burning through his tone.

"Very likely. Let's try."

Carver wanted to scowl, but instead he smiled. Is this what Daphney meant in the carriage when she said that he had forced her to smile? He sobered again at the thought of Daphney, the source of his dark mood. He moved to the chair by Robert and flopped down. "It's Daphney," he said tilting his head back to rest against the leather.

"That much went without saying. What has the elusive Miss Bellows done now?" She had begun to slip into his heart, that's what.

He was such a fool for bringing Daphney to his house. What was supposed to be a diversionary prank had turned out to be far more involved and taken more of him than he had been prepared to give. He had dreaded coming home because he had not wanted to confront the painful memories of Claire that lurked within its walls, memories that would torment his thoughts and dreams.

And with Daphney there, everything was worse. Now, he was not only faced with the thought of what could have been with Claire, but his mind obsessed over thoughts of a certain brown haired thief with ridiculously beautiful eyes and the ferocity of a lion. And she made him laugh…fully laugh, something he hadn't done in years.

Honestly, he thought he *had* healed and put Claire behind him, or at least had learned to become content without her in his life. But after spending time with Daphney, he was all too aware that he hadn't been content at all—but lonely. With Daphney, that loneliness was disappearing.

You are an idiot.

He was pining away for two women, neither of whom could he ever have. One was gone. And the other had made it astoundingly clear that he was not to fall for her. Unfortunately, she was making it blasted difficult not to.

"She broke her own rules and told me more about herself," said Carver. But it was unfair of him to say, and he knew it. It hadn't been her idea to tell him about the scar. He had pushed her, wouldn't let her go until she had told him. It wasn't her fault that hearing those stories had made his chest tighten and had filled him with a desire to draw her into his arms and keep her there.

She had been right to not tell him anything about her life. That made it fairly easy to keep their business-like arrangement in check. But the moment she had let him in to her confidence, the last bit of his will had died and buried itself and he could no longer keep his feelings at bay. Could no longer avoid the realization that he had fallen for her. Wanted to keep her safe, to make her smile, to hold her, to make her laugh.

And all of that made him feel like a traitor to Claire's memory and the love they'd had.

He groaned, exhausted of his own thoughts, and rubbed both of his hands over his face.

"I can't pretend to understand what you mean by that since I do not know the particulars of your arrangement with Miss Bellows. But I'm assuming whatever you learned is changing your feelings toward her in some way?"

He looked at Robert from over his finger tips. "Something like that." But then he shook his head. "Or...no. Because honestly, I've been attracted to her from the moment I met her. She's fiery and hot tempered. Nothing like the insufferable ladies in London. Daphney is strong and isn't the least bit afraid to come to points with me." He smiled. "Literally. Do you know that she held a gun to my head the first night she was here?"

Robert grimaced as if he was not happy to learn about that but didn't end the conversation. "Not something a gentleman would usually admit with a smile. So, what's the problem? Is she too far beneath your touch?"

"There's that. Not that I give a dash about social standing or what I owe to my family name..."

A smirk swept over Robert's mouth. "A given, I think, considering the trouble you raise in London."

Carver grinned. "My reputation's not so bad. It's not as if I have any lady birds warming my bed or angry brothers calling me out."

"And you have our undying gratitude for that. But I would be easier if I knew you weren't racing your curricle at break neck speeds after drinking all night. Or getting into fights outside of White's over a wager. Do you know that I've seen your name four times this month in the betting books? And the wagers are grim. Men are starting to bet higher and higher that you will die from overturning your curricle sometime in the next six months."

Carver laughed a mirthless laugh. "Keeping tabs on me, Hatley?"

"Unashamedly. What kind of brother would I be if I didn't?"

He didn't actually mind that Robert was watching him. In truth, it gave him an odd sort of comfort knowing someone was looking out for him. When he had first gone to London, his father had tried to check up on him, too. But Carver couldn't bring himself to look his father in the eyes after Claire's death. So eventually—after several excuses as to why he couldn't see his father day after day—the duke stepped back and let Carver have his peace.

Robert continued, "You've always been rowdy, of course. But I worry that your adventurousness has turned into recklessness after—"

Carver held up his hand. "I'll listen to your sermonizing, Robert but I don't intend to walk down memory lane with you tonight." He didn't need to hear that he'd become reckless after Claire's death. He didn't need to hear Robert say that boxing, racing, and drinking were only his attempts to hide from the truth. He didn't need to hear any of it because he already knew it was true. He could feel the toll it was taking on him.

Robert nodded and said, "Fair enough. I'll say no more about it. But what about Daphney? Do you like her? It seems to me that it would be easier if you did."

"How do you figure?"

"It would be easier to go through with the marriage than end the betrothal. You wouldn't have to make up excuses or lies. Just marry the woman and go on with your life."

Carver stood up and walked to the window. Darkness was beginning to take over the sky and in a few minutes they would need to go down to dinner. There wasn't a chance that Daphney would be walking outside, and yet, his eyes searched for her as they seemed to do every second since meeting the woman. "It doesn't matter if I like her or not. She and I cannot be."

"Because of your different stations in society?" It was difficult to convey all of his worries without revealing the true nature of his and Daphney's relationship, so Carver shrugged.

The problem was not Daphney's station in life. The problem was Daphney herself and the insurmountable walls she had constructed around herself. Then again, she had opened up to him that afternoon. Hang it, he had to tell Robert at least a little bit of the truth. He couldn't navigate it all on his own anymore. "When I first asked her to stay here, she made me promise not to fall in love with her." He chuckled sardonically at the memory. "Said she had no desire to be romantically involved with me."

"And you believed her?" Robert surprised him with the question.

"Any doubts I had were banished when I had to grease her palm handsomely to get her to stay. Two thousand pounds, in fact."

Robert just chuckled and pulled a golden snuff box out of his pocket. He held it in one hand and opened it with a lazy flick of his thumb. He took a pinch of snuff and smirked, enjoying a secret that only he was privy to. "Perhaps. But I've seen the way she looks at you when you're not watching." He shut his snuff box and slipped it back into his pocket as he stood. "And if you think she's only hanging around here for the money, you're more daft that I expected. You are the only one holding yourself back from that woman, Kensworth."

Carver looked away, out the window again. He could feel Robert's examining gaze and resisted turning around. After a silent minute Robert finally said, "Oh, I see it now."

"See what?"

"You already know, don't you? You already suspect that Daphney is growing just as attached to you as you are to her...and that upsets you because you think you're not ready for it."

His cravat felt too tight again. He tugged at it with his finger but it didn't help. "That's ridiculous." He paced away from Robert. For some reason, he couldn't stand still. He needed to keep moving like he always did.

But Robert stayed where he was. "Did I tell you what I did when Mary informed me she was with child again?"

The sudden and odd change in topic grabbed Carver's attention. He sighed and narrowed his eyes skeptically. Apparently, Mary and Robert shared the same conversational tactic. "No, you didn't."

"I just said, *No.* And then I turned around and left the house for the entire day." Carver almost couldn't believe that his saintly brother-in-law had ever done something so unthoughtful.

Reading the disbelieving expression on his face, Robert said, "Really. I swear I did." Robert walked to the dying fire and leaned his elbow on the mantel.

"I can't picture you doing anything so insensitive."

"No, because you didn't see me in my darkest days of grief." That familiar sting of guilt pinched at him. Once again, he had not been there when someone he loved had needed him. He wasn't there the day Claire had come to see him...the day she died. And he hadn't been there for Mary and Robert when they lost their child. "The truth is, when Mary told me that we were going to have another child...I was angry. And so I said *no* and left because in my head, if I acknowledged that we were having another child, it meant the one we lost was truly gone. And I wasn't ready yet to do that."

Carver pushed out a breath. "And your point is that I'm angry—because if I let myself love Daphney, I'll be finally admitting that Claire is not coming back."

Robert smiled and started walking to the door. "Do you think everything revolves around you?" He turned back around in the threshold of the door, twisting his smile into something more conspicuous. "Can a man not simply share a heartfelt story with his brother?"

"A man, perhaps—but not you, Robert."

"Whatever conclusion you take is up to you."

Carver smiled. "Parables are your favorite parts of the holy book, aren't they?"

Robert chuckled. "They are the most interesting to read, don't you think?"

But Carver's mind wouldn't release what they had been talking about before. "I know she's gone, Robert."

"Do you?"

Again he had to look away from Robert's narrowed eyes, away from the truth, and away from the answer glaring at him. He took in a deep breath. "Are you happy now, Robert? With the new pregnancy, I mean?" He couldn't bring himself to look at him while he asked the question.

"Yes. But I would be lying if I said that Mary and I don't still have moments of sadness, or fear that this child will face the same fate," said Robert. "We don't try to hide it from each other anymore. Talking about it together has gone a long way to helping us both feel better." Was there another option? Talking about it wasn't something he particularly wanted to do. Especially if that meant talking about it with Daphney.

After Robert left, all Carver could do was move back to his chair by the dwindling fire and stare at the embers as they faded. If Claire could see him now, she would have undoubtedly laughed at him and said that he was being unbearably tragic. She had a way of always finding the humor in things, and he needed that outlook right now. He leaned back and pictured her sitting across from him, her eyes sparkling with amusement, her cheeks dimpling in a glowing smile.

He ached with loss and darkness and an overwhelming need to hold her again, and then something else. Something new. A different, smaller emotion that sat quietly just below all of the others and, somehow, cast a new light on his pain. It was changing him. And he knew it was because of Daphney.

Being with her those past few days had eased some of his hurt. Her wit and unique view of the world made him feel like laughing again. Like he wasn't so lonely—and never had to be again, if he didn't want to be. And when he was with Daphney, he almost felt...like himself again.

He sighed when he realized that he was beginning to love Daphney. He let the weight of it all sink over him. Was she falling for him too? Or were her feelings an act? Hope glimmered as he thought that maybe the answer to truly moving on was as simple as pushing into Daphney and seeing where his feelings for her led.

Chapter Twenty

How was it possible that one man's smile could make her heart race so quickly? He was too dashing in his black double-tailed dinner jacket and handsomely tousled hair. And the way his grey eyes sparkled in the warm glow of the evening candlelight made Rose feel the sudden urge to fidget with her gloves. How absurd everyone must think their match. Carver looked like he had just been pulled out of a painting of an ancient Titan who no one man could ever possibly resemble. And Rose...well, she was short and plain. And as she had discovered earlier that evening when spending far too long in the looking glass, she had developed a few new age lines in the corner of her eyes, and one on her forehead. No matter how many times she pulled the skin tight, it had sunk right back into the skin of a twenty-six-year-old woman. Which was especially bad, considering she was only twenty-three years old.

She had even considered letting the maid arrange her hair, but in the end it just felt too wrong allowing such a thing. This wasn't her life —and it wouldn't even be her fake life after the duke's ball. She knew it would only be foolish to let herself enjoy the luxuries of such a privileged world. Easier to say goodbye if she never let herself have it in the first place.

Which is exactly why she should not let herself give a dash whether Carver found her beautiful or not.

He means nothing to me.

Or maybe if she reminded herself of it enough, it would start becoming true.

Carver walked to Rose as the rest of the family continued to trickle into the drawing room. He smiled with his eyes, in that way that was uniquely his, and Rose silently reminded herself to remain detached. She said it in her head over and over before she realized it wasn't working. She had been unbelievably stupid in the nursery that afternoon when she let her guard down. Telling Carver about her childhood had been a serious misstep. How had she almost let herself fall into his arms and feel the warmth of his comfort? *That* could never happen. Everything and everyone around her was only there temporarily and losing sight of that would only create heartbreak in the end.

Which was why her situation was starting to become very complicated. Rose needed to remain distant and detached. Daphney however, was sweet, charming, and fervently in love with Carver. And it was becoming impossible to separate the two.

Carver's voice pulled her from her thoughts. "You look lovely tonight, Daphney."

I don't care.

"I do?" Blast. When had she become so delicate and missish? It wasn't at all like her to need reassurance or to feel nervous or to blush like she was doing currently.

When she locked with his eyes, she couldn't help but see his sincerity and feel glad she had asked.

"You do," he said, his kind smile molding into something else. He had flirted with her before and she had seen a warm look of attraction from him before, but this was something entirely different. It was intense and meaningful and…oh—she couldn't decide what, and that frustrated her.

His gaze flicked down to her lips, and she felt a heat rush over her entire body. She couldn't breathe. Thankfully, it was only a quick glance before he smiled and looked back at her eyes. "And when you blush like that, it puts your beauty over the top."

Rose bit her lips and looked away from this new look of his. That's when she realized everyone else had begun entering the drawing room. Her heart sunk as she realized that he had just been acting the part of her fiancé.

"What's wrong?" he asked, studying the expression she must have let slip past her guard.

Rose quickly pulled herself together and turned back to him with a smile. "Just a little headache is all." This was beginning to be too much.

His brows pulled together. Was it true concern, or something put on? "Are you well? Do you need to go lie down?"

She laughed. "Do you really think I have such a delicate constitution?"

He smiled and stepped in front of her so that he was facing her and his back was to his family. He reached out and gently adjusted her shawl so that it rested higher on her shoulders. She tried to reject the feel of his fingers against her arms, or how incredible he always smelled.

"Not at all. But I wouldn't blame you in the least if you wanted to forego dinner tonight," he said. "I'm afraid that we have a little bit of a challenge ahead of us tonight." He dropped his hands back to his side. "My mother just informed me that we are to have *guests* for dinner." His tone was not lost on her.

She tossed him an amused smile. "You say the word as if you were talking about some sort of poison rather than having people over for dinner."

"Believe me, poison would be preferable to the Gardeners."

Rose chuckled, feeling both intrigued and thankful for these people who were taking her mind off of whatever it was that was happening between her and Carver. "And just who are these poisonous Gardeners?"

"Our insufferable neighbors, unfortunately, in Town as well as here at Dalton Park. I have no idea why Mother sees the need to be kind to them. Not only is Mrs. Gardener the most obnoxious woman to ever walk the earth, but she insists on foisting her eldest daughter on me every chance she gets." An unwelcome pang of jealousy struck her. How stupid. It wasn't as if she didn't know that Carver was probably the most eligible gentleman in Society.

"Would you like for me to pepper her tea when we move into the drawing room?" Rose smiled, feeling oddly triumphant that she knew something about Carver that Miss Gardener did not.

Carver tipped a flirtatious smile. "I would be forever in your debt."

Chapter Twenty-One

"Betrothed!" Mrs. Gardener exclaimed after Carver finished introducing Rose. "Good heavens! But, my lord, we saw you not three weeks ago in town and you did not mention any sort of attachment."

Mrs. Gardener put Rose in mind of an overripe hog dressed in ruffles, snorting her disappointment at having been denied a juicy apple. There was no doubt that Carver was the apple and the matchmaking mama had hoped to snatch him up for one of her two daughters, both of whom were looking daggers at Rose.

The eldest daughter, Miss Gardener, was certainly beautiful with her tall and trim yet curvy form, and blonde locks piled softly upon her heart-shaped head. Rose wondered if Carver thought Miss Gardner beautiful, even though he claimed to find her annoying. She didn't look to be in her first blush, but had such a unique beauty that Rose was sure *the ton* would have seen fit to give her a nickname such as the Incomparable or the Unattainable.

"Did I not?" said Carver in the tone that Rose had come to know as the precursor to a sarcastic comment. "Forgive me. How thoughtless of me to not have discussed my marriage intentions with you in the middle of Bond Street." Carver shook his head made a *tsk* noise that forced Rose to bite her cheeks to keep from laughing. "Very shabby of me indeed."

The rotund Mrs. Gardener did not look amused. She shot her beady brown eyes at Rose. How fitting that the pig woman's eyes really did look like mud. "And pray tell, Miss Bellows, where are you from?" She all but spat the words.

"Bath, ma'am, where I reside with my uncle," Rose said with a soft smile that she hoped would only make the woman angrier. Maybe if Rose was cunning enough, she could get the woman to really snort.

"And just who is your uncle?" If Mrs. Gardener's eyes narrowed any further, they would completely close. "I have a few friends in Bath. Perhaps he and I are acquainted." *Unlikely.*

Rose smiled, not feeling the least bit ruffled by the question. There were few things as enjoyable to her as getting to spin a new tale on the spot. It made her heart race and blood pump in her neck. She was good at lying. Definitely not a noble ability, but an enjoyable one none-theless. "My uncle is Mr. John Bellows. Do you know him, ma'am? Although, I highly doubt it since he often suffers with the gout and has unfortunately become something of a recluse."

"John Bellows, you say?" said Mr. Gardener, sparking up with his bushy eyebrows and booming voice. "Ah! You know, I do believe I am acquainted with the fellow!"

Rose held back a smile. "Are you really, sir? How wonderful!"

"A very tall gentleman, isn't he?" A picture of Uncle Felix's short round figure flashed into Rose's mind, leaving her hard-pressed not to release a laugh. "I dare say I met the man when I was taking the waters myself! A nice fellow, indeed! Was kind enough to give me a very thorough recommendation of the best sights to visit during our stay."

Poor Mrs. Gardener looked as if she had just been offered a leveler. Evidently, the woman had been hoping to find some major fault with Rose's family connections that would justify a snub. But thanks to her husband's high praise of Rose's fictitious uncle, the lady was forced to keep her pouty mouth shut.

She decided that was the very moment to further prove her eligi-bility to the Gardeners. And although the duke and duchess had never asked outright, she knew they had been harboring the same thoughts. "Oh yes, that must have been him. Uncle John is everything kind and hospitable. Even while plagued with such a dreadful affliction, he never fails to smile." She sighed. "I must say it breaks my heart to see him set down from what he really loves."

"Oh, and what is that?" asked Mrs. Gardner, her expression skeptical. Rose could feel Carver's eyes on her, too.

"His work," she said. "He wouldn't like me saying it, but Uncle is a marvelous businessman. One does not acquire a fortune such as his without having an impressive mind." Rose tossed a rueful smile to Carver, "I am almost fearful that Lord Kensworth has offered for me only out of the rumors of what a *benevolent* guardian my Uncle has been." Her words came out playful and bouncy and not at all like her own personality.

But Carver played along. "You wound me, my love! I would have been grateful to marry you even if you were a thief."

Rose's eyes snapped to Carver's and held his gaze for entirely too long, but she was unable to look away. Was she mistaken, or?—but no he couldn't have been serious. And yet, something in his tone sounded remarkably honest. Rose decided that Carver was a better actor than she had first given him credit for and pushed his words from her mind —at least until later when she was free to dissect them in private. Which she definitely would.

The eldest Miss Gardener's slithery voice brought Rose's thoughts back to the present. "And is that where you and Lord Kensworth first became acquainted? In Bath, that is?" The look on her face somehow conveyed to Rose that she was not asking out of interest, but rather fishing for an opportunity to put her down in some way.

Rose raced back in her mind to all of the stories she had already told Carver's sisters. "No. We first met last season in London, but were fortunate to further our acquaintance in Bath during Lord Kensworth's visit." Rose kept her smile impassive and only hoped fear wasn't showing on her face. She knew Carver had not been home to Dalton Park for several years, but didn't know if his family had spent the summer months in London. If they had, they would know straight away that she was lying. She glanced around the room and noted that only Mary was sitting close enough to overhear, and she looked to be attending a different conversation. Rose relaxed.

"How odd that I don't recall seeing you last season. I usually have a very reliable memory," the young lady smiled prettily, but Rose did not miss the challenging glint in her eyes. Why was she pushing those questions? It was more than looking for a set down. Apparently she sensed a scandal, as well as an opportunity to free up Carver for herself.

"Odd indeed." Rose matched her smile and gave a slight shrug, hoping that would be the end of the interrogation. It wasn't.

"And Bath? I must say, I'm most surprised to hear that Lord Kensworth would ever venture to visit such a place!" It was amazing the lady could see anything with her nose stuck so far into the air like that. "I confess that I've always found it excessively dull for my tastes. Did you not find Bath society a dead bore, my lord?" Rose did not like Miss Gardener. Not one bit. And it wasn't because she was jealous of the woman's milky complexion and pale pink, voluminous lips. Or the nagging thought that maybe Carver found the woman equally stunning. It was that she represented every member of Society who had ever cast Rose aside as a disgusting street urchin unworthy of help.

Carver smoothed over some of her bitterness when he smiled and said, "I could never be bored in Daphney's company."

Dinner did not prove to lighten any tensions. Mrs. Gardener only continued to pepper Rose and Carver with questions as Miss Gardener —the little minx—continued to look at Carver through her excessively long dark lashes. Mr. Gardener seemed to be thoroughly bored with the whole party and did not attempt to control his wife's impertinent questioning at all.

Rose found it interesting how proper and refined the noble family was when company was present. Gone was the excited energy and joyful hum of conversation from the previous night. Instead, the ladies were somber and polite and the gentlemen all held an authoritative air. Not unkind. Just different. Rose liked the idea that she had been able to see the family as they really were.

It wasn't until the second dinner course was complete that Rose felt she could truly relax. After what felt like an agonizing amount of time, the Gardener females abandoned their interrogation of Rose and begrudgingly allowed the conversation to be steered toward different topics. The eldest Miss Gardener however, rarely took her eyes off of Carver. Why that filled Rose with the desire to take hold of Carver's hand and rest it right on the table for everyone to see, she would never know. Maybe she was simply invested in the role she was playing. Still, it was an odd urge and one she'd never felt before.

"Mr. Gardener—," the duke spoke from across the table, drawing everyone's attention. "What ever happened with your valet? I heard about the scandal from my man and I must admit I'm curious to know how it all ended."

The plump Mr. Gardener groaned. "Devilish business, Duke. Had to send him off and haven't been able to find a single reliable replacement. I'll be dashed if I employ another crook."

Rose's eyes shot up and her spoon full of turtle soup fell back into the bowl. "What happened?" she asked before her brain could tell her mouth to keep shut. Rules of proper society were very strict. A lady speaking up across the table to enquire about a conversation between two gentleman was forbidden. But it was too late to retract her breech of propriety.

Mr. Gardener's displeased eyes settled on Rose before turning back to the Duke. "Nothing I haven't had to deal with a dozen times from the likes of those vulgar commoners. I say it's too bad that we even have to deal with any of them."

Rose could feel the tension growing in her back, as well as Carver's eyes burning into the side of her face. But she resisted the urge to look at him and instead kept her eyes fixed across the table.

"It's just horrible!" Mrs. Gardeners shrill voice pierced the room. "We give these servants a roof over their heads and they repay us by stealing a watch out of Mr. Gardeners own jewelry box! Can you even believe it?" She spoke more to the room than to anyone in particular. Although, her gaze did rest on the footmen standing at the sides of the room more than a few uncomfortable times.

Stay quiet. Don't comment. It's not your place.

But her intrigue got the best of her. "Why did he steal the watch?"

Mrs. Gardener looked physically disgusted as she puffed up further, her enormous bosom swelling with indignation. "How should I know why the man took it? An employer should never have to even ask such a thing of their servants." She looked around the quiet room for support.

"True..." said Rose. "On the other end, a servant should also be provided with adequate wages which they very rarely ever are."

Every eye in the room flashed to her. Even the two footmen across the room who, until that point, had been doing a remarkable job of pretending not to listen to the conversations happening in front of them.

"I beg your pardon!" said Mrs. Gardener. The woman's eyes narrowed. "Are you implying that I do not pay my servants adequate wages?"

This was not at all the polite sort of conversation that normally took place at a dinner party. It was rude and almost unthinkable in London Society. But this wasn't London, was it? Maybe the rules were more relaxed in country parties and the guests were free to insult each other as much as they wanted.

Rose took in the table as she weighed her options. Miss Gardener looked far too pleased at the scene Rose was making. The duchess watched Rose with a wary expression. Mary, Robert and Elizabeth had all taken a very sudden interest in their soup bowls, but she didn't miss the slight smiles hovering over their pursed lips. And as for Carver, she couldn't see him without pointedly turning her head in his direction.

Should she say what she really felt? Daphney would have never understood anything about servants wages or the horrid living conditions of the lower class. But Rose did, and she ached to speak of it. But what she wanted to say was from her heart, not Daphney's. It would mean pulling her facade down for a moment and exposing herself to those people. Could she risk it?

A last look down the table took her eyes to the duke. He locked her gaze for a moment and then gave her an almost undetectable nod. It was so discreet she wondered if she had imagined it. But the confidence granted by that single gesture was enough to make her square her shoulders at Mrs. Gardner. "Forgive me," she began, "it's only that in my experience, servants are very rarely paid what is actually needed to provide for themselves and their families."

"Now we are expected to provide for their families?" The woman let out an incredulous laugh and looked anxiously around the table again. "Upon my word, Miss Bellows! Who gives you the authority to speak on such matters? I think you forget your place and would do well to not pursue such unladylike subjects."

"On the contrary." The duke's voice carried down the table. "I should very much like for Miss Bellows to speak her mind on the matter." He smiled at her and she felt a fatherly approval. She tried not to linger on that thought and how much it tugged at her heart.

For once in her life she had been given permission to speak freely among those above her station, and she would not waste it. She only hoped that Carver was also as approving of her opinion as his father. "Respectfully, Your Grace, I have always felt that those who are fortunate enough to enjoy wealth and standing in society often do not do as much as they ought for those who are less fortunate than themselves." After a brief thought, Rose amended, "As *ourselves*, that is." But it was difficult for her to lump herself in with those she had been angry with and felt dismissed by for most of her life.

Rose had her faults, but turning her back on the hungry and needy was not one of them. Uncle Felix had always said it was her biggest fault, giving away almost every guinea that she had ever earned on their jobs. She knew that underneath his tough exterior he shared her views. It was impossible to ignore the hungry stomachs of orphans when she herself had been one. When she had felt the sting of loneliness. The fear of death.

"And you do not think it just to release a servant for stealing?" His tone was not accusatory, but inquisitive.

The duke carried an intimidating air, when he chose it. Had she not seen the same kindness in his eyes that she often saw in Carver's, she might not have continued. But it was there. "I believe that the world is often more gray than black and white, Your Grace. And as such, every person ought to be treated with compassion before justice." She took a breath. "I can't help but wonder how the world might be better if a servant—or even a thief for that matter—were given the chance to explain what situation might have brought on such a desperate act before being released without recommendation or turned in to the magistrate."

Mrs. Gardener gave a huff from across the table. Her husband looked unwilling to comment until the duke had first stated his opinions on the matter. And Carver...well she didn't know what Carver thought of her words because she still couldn't bring herself to look at him. Why was she so afraid of what she might see? It wasn't as if his opinion of her mattered. Or did it?

"And a better way is increasing wages?" asked the Duke after a thoughtful moment.

"It's a start, yes," she said. "When we have more to give, I think that we have a responsibility to give it. Especially if what is needed is compassion and sympathy."

The duke took in a deep breath and leaned back in his seat, intertwining his hands over his stomach, holding the attention of everyone at the table. No one uttered a word. Not even the sound of a spoon clinking against the side of a bowl penetrated the silence. Blood whooshed through Rose's ears. Never had she said something so bold to a Peer before. And yet, she didn't regret it.

Chapter Twenty-Two

Rose hadn't realized that she had been holding her breath until the duke spoke. "I agree with you, my dear. I think you said it very well. And I'm thankful to see that more young ladies exist, besides my own daughters, who care more about the welfare of other's than the embroidery of their neckline."

Her mouth felt dry. "Thank you, Your Grace." She swallowed and caught a glance of the glowering Miss Gardener before taking her eyes back to her bowl of soup. She raised a trembling spoon to her lips but hesitated before taking a bite. She had seldom been so nervous, or cared so much what a member of the gentry thought of her. But she was beginning to realize that she did care very much about how Carver's family viewed her.

And Carver. She could feel his gaze, but nothing in her dared meet it. Did he think her impertinent? Brass faced? Or did he think that she had simply defended criminals because she was one?

He knew too much about her now for her comfort. And when he looked at her with those stormy grey eyes, like he had in the nursery, she felt he could see right to her soul. It wasn't a good feeling. It was uncomfortable and overwhelming and left her feeling as if the world was turning over on itself and she was losing her hold.

Dinner dragged on endlessly. Eventually the duchess stood from the table and suggested that all the ladies move into the drawing room and leave the men to their port. The gentlemen stood along with the ladies and Rose could feel Carver trying to catch her eye. But she resisted and hurried out of the room like a coward. When had she become this way? Avoiding the gaze of a man because she feared that he might be disappointed in her? It was stupid. And she wouldn't allow herself to act that way when the gentlemen rejoined them.

The ladies trickled into the drawing room. Each of the Dalton women looked desperate to hide their misery as they settled onto the various sofas and chairs scattered about the drawing room and took on the task of entertaining their guests. Rose, however, took the opportunity to retreat to the window. Night had saturated the grounds, making it impossible to see anything other than her own reflection in the glass, and, unfortunately, the additional reflection of Miss Gardener as she approached.

With a determined posture, Rose turned around to face the woman. Miss Gardener held the smile of a lady who thought herself highly superior to the one she was addressing. Rose resisted the urge to roll her eyes and inform the woman that Carver enjoyed the thought of poison more than her company.

Miss Gardener spoke with a false sweetness. "Do you know, Miss Bellows, I find it increasingly odd that I cannot recall ever having seen you in London last season. I make it my business to know each and every one of the debutantes, you see." Her voice dripped with barely veiled accusation.

But Rose had graced enough society functions to know how to play the game. "Don't worry, Miss Gardener. I don't fault you for not remembering me. It must be very difficult to memorize the faces of each London lady with your eyes fixed so determinedly on my fiancé." She let her gaze grow pointed as a grin touched her mouth.

Miss Gardener's face flushed hotly as she narrowed her blue eyes. "I'm sure that I do not know what you mean."

Rose wanted to chuckle but didn't, thinking it would make her sound too menacing. "Don't you though, Miss Gardener?" she said settling for a smile. "I cut my wisdoms a long time ago, and it's plain for me to see that you, as well as your meddlesome mother, have been trying to belittle me in front of Lord Kensworth and his family this entire evening. And although I find it very entertaining, I am getting tired of it and must now insist that you give up the hunt and move on to some other unfortunate gentleman." It was likely more than she should have said but Rose wouldn't allow herself to regret the words until tomorrow. Tonight, she was enjoying the chance to give the pompous lady a much-needed set down.

The blush already touching Miss Gardeners cheeks turned into a dark crimson before dropping away all together. The woman's pretty lips curved into a vicious smile. She stepped closer. "There is something very odd about you, Miss Bellows. And believe me when I say that I fully intend to uncover just what it is."

Her moment of enjoyment left her. She *had* said too much. Shown too much fire. Drawn too much unwanted attention. Was Miss Gardener threatening to dig until she found out the truth? Rose knew she wouldn't have to dig very far. Although the woman didn't know Rose's real name, there were already several warrants out for her arrest with her detailed description. One inquiry into Bow Street and the woman could easily figure out the truth.

But Rose was a professional criminal and knew how to never let her worry show to an adversary. Instead, she smiled softly and blinked. "I'll confess. I have always thought of myself as odd. Please don't hesitate to let me know if you can figure out the cause."

Her jest was not appreciated. Miss Gardener sneered and then turned to join her mother on the yellow settee. Rose relaxed and turned her eyes back out the window, noticing that her body was trembling slightly. If she were in the middle of any other job, she would have aborted the con right then, knowing that she had been compromised. But Carver was counting on her.

Rose still had three days left until the duke's ball. Three days for Miss Gardener to dig into Daphney Bellows's life and find out that the real Daphney was none other than a maid recently released from her post due to an indiscretion and living on a farm in another part of

England. A thick lump formed in her throat. Was three days enough time for Miss Gardener to uncover enough incriminating facts? Probably not, but there was no way to know for sure.

She needed to leave. Her feet ached to run. To protect herself. To get as far away from potential danger as possible. She ought to claim a headache that very night and go pack her things. If she rode all night, she could be at the orphanage by dawn. She would need to spend a few weeks in hiding until Miss Gardener and her mother tired of asking questions. Or perhaps she and Uncle Felix could flee to Scotland and work a few jobs there. She would figure out the logistics later. All that mattered now was that she leave Dalton Park as soon as possible.

But then, the door to the drawing room opened and Carver stepped through, filling the doorway with his strength and authority. His direct grey gaze settled immediately on Rose and it felt as if the world stopped moving. He smiled, warm and slow. She couldn't look away. Nothing else mattered. A tense breath released from her chest and her hands relaxed. And there, caught in the current of his eyes, Rose realized something for the first time. She loved him. And she wasn't going to leave.

Chapter Twenty-Three

The next morning, the sun felt just as reluctant to start its day as Rose. A chambermaid had come in about an hour before to open the curtains, and had left a fresh can of water on her vanity, but Rose hadn't gotten up. She nestled under her warm coverlet and peered out at the grey, gloomy sky, wondering what in the devil she was doing with her life.

She wasn't supposed to like living at Dalton Park. She wasn't supposed to like Carver's family. And she definitely wasn't supposed to let herself imagine what it would be like to really be engaged to Carver, or have him love her in return. Yet there she was, lying in bed, dreaming about the way his eyes crinkled in the corners when he really smiled. And how his lips had felt against her palm when he kissed it in the nursery. What would it be like to *really be* kissed by Carver?

Rose groaned and threw the covers off her body. She sat up and swung her legs over the side of the bed, letting them fall to the floor with a satisfying thud. What she needed was to splash her face with water and get a grip on her heart. So she loved the man. No matter. She was a self-sufficient woman who worked better alone. In a few days, the whole ruse would be over and she would be free to rip her heart back from his hands and move on with her life. It would definitely be painful, but she would force herself to forget Carver Timothy Ashburn. She would force herself to forget his handsome smile, and the way his laugh sounded when it boomed through the meadow, and his eyes, and his strength, and his funny stories.

This time she cursed. A splash of water wasn't going to be enough to remedy those feelings.

Rose took her time dressing that morning, hoping the extra alone time might be enough to sort out her twisted and conflicting emotions. It wasn't. After donning her slate blue walking dress, worn half boots, and tying her hair up in a simple silver ribbon, she left her room intent on exploring the house.

That early in the morning, Rose knew the family would be in the breakfast room, so she decided to explore the opposite side of the house. It wasn't that she was cow-hearted and afraid of running into Carver. She had simply already seen that side of the house and thought it would be nice to see what else the expansive home had to offer. And she only tiptoed down the stairs because…well…she was cow-hearted.

Rose made it to the bottom floor and quickly swept down the hallway leading away from the breakfast room. As she walked, she noticed the massive family portraits lining the walls and the occasional porcelain busts that rested on the wall's inset ledges. There were so many doors in every hallway. She couldn't imagine owning a house with so many rooms.

She paused in front of a painting she recognized was Carver as a young boy. He was maybe thirteen or fourteen and had clearly not yet formed the broad muscular stature he possessed now. She immediately recognized the same mischievous twinkle in his grey eyes. She had never before seen grey eyes on anyone—it seemed that even the painter had a hard time capturing the particular soft light of his iris.

Beside Carver's painting was one of the duke, around thirty years old. Rose realized—stupidly, for the first time—that Carver would one day take possession of his father's title and become the duke himself. He would own Dalton Park and his wife would become duchess.

How could she have been so ridiculous to even entertain the idea of giving into her feelings for him, for even a moment? It was absurd. She was a wanted criminal—not a lady. And he was the son of a Peer of the Realm. He was part of the nobility and probably the most desired suitor in all of London. Every eligible woman in that blasted town had to have her cap set on Carver. She could never compete with them. Would not compete with them.

It was time to give up any idiotic illusions and see the situation for what it was. A job. She and Carver were playing parts and it would all be over soon. It was time to get her deuced heart to obey her again.

"Rose, you stupid fool," she whispered after looking once more at Carver's painting.

"Pardon?" A male voice sounded behind her.

Rose jumped and spun around to find the duke standing in the threshold of an open door behind her. He had spectacles on the bridge of his nose and a smile on his mouth. Gone was the intimidating duke from dinner with the Gardeners.

She curtsied. "I'm sorry. I didn't mean to disturb you, Your Grace."

"You're not disturbing me in the least. Did you need something from me?"

"Oh—no, sir," she said feeling nervous that he had overheard her name slip. "I was just exploring the house and paused to look at this painting." She gestured toward Carver's likeness on the wall. "Again, I'm sorry to have disturbed you."

The duke stepped out of the doorway and narrowed his gaze to the painting of young Carver. He pushed his spectacles closer to his eyes and smiled. It was astounding how much he and Carver favored one another. Both men shared an imposing figure and strong jaw, and the same disarming smile.

"Ah. He was a young one, here. I miss the days when he was a mischievous little bantling running wild across the park, playing pranks on his governess." The duke smiled fondly as if he were looking back in time rather than at a portrait.

She smiled, too, thinking of Carver chasing her across the meadow and threatening to toss her into the stream. And playing in the nursery with Jane. It struck her that he had made her smile more in these few days than she had smiled in years. "Is he so very different, now?" she asked.

The duke's smile fell a little and a sadness entered his eyes. "Yes." His brows creased and then he looked at Rose. "Or, at least, he was. Before you came along. But you've managed to bring back a piece of Carver that I—" he smiled tentatively, "—*we* haven't seen in a long time." He smiled again but this time it was more than sad, it was regretful and weary.

She remembered the pain she often saw hidden in Carver's eyes. The heaviness that lurked just behind his playful mask. She ached to know what had happened to him—to all of them.

"My study is just through there," said the duke. "Will you come in and talk with me a moment?" A sudden nervousness built inside Rose. Why would the duke wish to speak with her alone? Did he suspect something? Did he not approve of her? Had Miss Gardener said something to him?

She smiled and tried to keep the worry from reaching her eyes. "It would be my honor."

Trying to swallow her nerves, she stepped inside the duke's study. A wave of masculine smells filled her senses: tobacco, firewood, leather, and smoke. It was an oddly soothing blend. The sun had finally begun to peek from behind the clouds and was streaming through the windows, revealing a few stray particles of dust floating in the air. The warmth of the room hugged her as she stepped further inside.

The duke gestured toward a navy leather wingback chair situated beside the crackling fire. Rose sat down and he took a seat in the matching chair adjacent to hers. When the duke did not immediately speak, Rose searched the room for anything that could spark a conversation. Guilty people usually kept their mouths shut and avoided eye contact. She held a confident posture, smiled and looked the Duke in the eyes. "There is an impressive amount of game mounted on these walls. I gather you enjoy hunting?" More like a frightening amount. Rose wasn't usually easily intimidated, but she was finding herself hard-pressed not to squirm under the sight of the wolf baring its teeth above her head.

The duke smiled and crossed one of his long legs over the other. "Do you truly wish to discuss a topic that I imagine you would find intolerably dull, or should we put the civil whiskers away and get right to it?"

Rose swallowed and forced herself to hold his gaze. "With pleasure, Your Grace." She admired his ability to cut through the pleasantries just as much as she was worried by it.

"Let me start by insisting that you call me Charles. Or Duke if you'd prefer it. But I think we can both agree that Your Grace is a touch too formal for our relationship, hmm?" It wasn't too formal, given the fact that she wasn't actually going to have any sort of relationship with him or his family in a handful of days. But it would look too suspicious to refuse him.

"Perhaps *Duke* until after the wedding day?" Rose asked.

"That will do." He smiled again and Rose began to relax. Perhaps he hadn't suspected anything after all and only wanted to get to know her better. Get to know *Daphney* better, that is.

He rested his chin between his thumb and forefinger, looking completely at ease. "I wanted to tell you how much I admired what you had to say over dinner last night."

"Really? I was afraid it wasn't the right time or place to share those opinions."

He waved her off with a good-natured smile. "It's my opinion that truth doesn't require a specific time or setting to be spoken."

She wrinkled her nose in an awkward honest smile. "I'm not so sure that the Gardeners would agree with your opinion on that. I'm certain I thoroughly offended them."

He chuckled. "Oh, hang the Gardeners! I've wanted to be rid of their unwanted friendship for years but my wife is far too sweet to cut them out. I hope your statement finally accomplished the thing." Oh, yes. Rose liked the duke. There wasn't a hint of starch or pomp in his manners. He was authoritative and commanding, but not in a way that belittled anyone. In fact, he treated her with the same care and respect that he gave his daughters.

But she couldn't let herself hang onto that thought. She wasn't his daughter. And she never would be.

"But I'll tell you, Daphney, there was something that kept me up last night." His look turned searching and all of Rose's apprehension returned in a rush. "The circumstances you spoke of last night are not usually known to gently bred young ladies like yourself." The fire crackled and popped, but those were the only noises in the room. Rose didn't dare speak, not until she knew where he was going with that topic. "But *you* spoke with authority on the subject, almost as one who had been on the other side of the argument." His gaze grew even more speculative. "One might be led to suppose that you were not actually a genteel lady after all, but rather a female who had lived such a life of poverty and theft herself."

He knew. But how was that possible?

Rose held his gaze and carefully chose her words. Maybe she was changing, or growing, or just going soft, but for some reason, she really did not want to lie to the Duke. Neither could she tell him the whole truth. Not only would Carver be upset, but by admitting who she was, Rose would open herself to possible arrest. She couldn't trust the duke with that, no matter how much she liked him.

Rose pursed her lips and then said in a calm voice, "One might be led to assume that, yes. But I dare say Carver would not appreciate it if they did."

Rose and the duke stared at each other for an agonizing moment as she felt her palms grow damp with sweat. The duke's face was unreadable. He did not look upset, but he also did not look happy. Rose was certain of one thing: the duke knew she was not who she claimed to be.

Finally he smiled and gave the most subtle of nods—similar to the one from the night before. In this voiceless exchange, the duke communicated his alliance. How could this be? Why?

He leaned forward in his seat and spoke quietly. "Daphney. My son has carried a deep pain that has kept him from returning home for several years. Nothing I could ever say or do would bring him back to us." He leaned back in his seat and steepled his fingers together in front of him. "But with you by his side, he came home. And even more than that, he's seemed like our old Carver again, which is something we never thought possible. So my dear, because of those things, your past doesn't matter to me. You have a friend in me and I hope you never forget that."

Rose gritted her teeth, pushing down the tears she felt welling up in her eyes. Had she really made that much of a difference in Carver's life? And if the duke knew the extent of the crimes she had committed, would he still say those things? She doubted it.

Dash it all, she was failing in her attempts to detach herself from this family. On the contrary, she felt more attached to them than ever. How was she going to make it through the remaining days with all of those feelings warring within her?

Rose looked down at her hands in her lap. "Thank you, Duke," she said in a shaky whisper.

He leaned forward and clasped his hand over hers. "Are you alright, dear?"

A rogue tear slipped down her cheek and she shook her head. "But I will be." She hoped. But the truth was, she wasn't so sure. She felt exposed and vulnerable—and those were not feelings she'd experienced in a long time.

She tried to imagine going back to her normal life once Carver had no need of her anymore, but the prospect was starting to look bleak. Going back to a lonely existence of stealing, living on the run and hiding behind different facades sounded lonely and exhausting.

But what other choice did she have? She had no family. Carver's was only on loan. She needed to start distancing herself from him.

"Do you want to talk about it?" the duke asked with a tenderness that reminded her too much of Papa.

Her eyes met his, and she wished she could unload all of her worries on his capable shoulders. "I can't," she said. "But I wish I could."

"Well, if you change your mind, you know where to find me."

She smiled and stood. "Thank you. I'll remember that."

Before she had fully left the room, she turned back around. "Carver loves you all very much. There is nothing he wouldn't do for any of you." She said it in hopes that the duke would remember it if word ever came out about their ruse.

The duke frowned a little. "I just wish he knew that the same was true for us."

Chapter Twenty-Four

Carver tapped his index finger on the table, matching his rhythm to that of the clock ticking away on the mantle. Where was she? The breakfast hour was nearly over and most of the house had already come and gone. But not Daphney. She hadn't come down to breakfast. Why?

"Oh, for goodness' sake, will you just go look for her already?" A shockingly perturbed Elizabeth shook him from his thoughts. Robert and Mary, the only other two people besides Elizabeth remaining in the breakfast room, stifled laughs.

Carver stopped his tapping and turned his eyes to Elizabeth. "And just what have I done to earn your ire this morning, Elizabeth?"

She patted her tight lips with a serviette. The girl looked tired. "Nothing. It's just that you've been tapping your finger on the table for ten minutes. I've never been able to hear the seconds of my life pass by with such clarity before." Now he had to stifle a laugh. Usually so easy-going and good-natured, something had certainly happened to put Elizabeth in a foul mood.

"Robert, dear, I have a strange feeling that something is bothering our darling siblings," said Mary.

"So do I, love. And if we are quick about it, I think we can extricate ourselves before they drag us into their fits of the dismals."

Mary chuckled and Elizabeth glared at her. "Normally, I would disagree with you, Robert. But I don't quite have the energy for it today."

Carver watched as Robert's teasing gleam fled his eyes. "Are you unwell, Mary? Should I call for the physician?" The concern that colored his words brought a smile to Mary's face. She placed her hand on Robert's cheek with a look of such adoration that Carver almost felt he should look away. He felt a deep longing for a woman to look at him like that again. And not just any woman.

"Nothing concerning, darling. Just the expected fatigue." But then his sister's smile turned a touch too flirtatious for his comfort. "I think I need to go lie down for a bit. Would you mind very much to see me to our room?"

Robert's brows creased as he assessed his wife's not-so-subtle twinkle. And then one of his brows lifted and his smile matched hers. "I believe I can make the sacrifice."

Carver resisted the urge to both gag and punch his brother-in-law in the face. "Oh, dear goodness, will you two just go before Elizabeth and I both start retching?"

Mary flashed him a saucy glare. "No need to unleash your sour moods on us!" She—and Robert as a result—stood from the table. "We're all too happy to go."

"Yes—that's the problem," murmured Elizabeth from behind her tea cup. Her lips twitched and Carver commiserated with his own suppressed grin.

Mary and Robert left the room and Carver turned in his seat to look fully at Elizabeth. "Now, my dear, what is it that's put you in a high dudgeon?"

She rolled her eyes and waved him off. "Clearly you have enough on your plate as it is without adding my bad mood to it." What a very Elizabeth thing to say. She was always practical and levelheaded, which was why her temper was so puzzling. She eyed his own quizzical look. "Really, I'm fine. Now…why do you suppose it is that Daphney is avoiding you?"

He felt his brows shoot up. "Avoiding me? I hadn't formed that conclusion yet. I only thought she was ill or something. Do you think she's avoiding me?" The thought made him nervous. He searched his mind for anything that he could have possibly done to offend her. Not a single thing came to mind other than the fact that he'd kissed her hand in the nursery the day before. Now that he thought of it, she had seemed to avoid looking at him through most of dinner last night. Had he made her uncomfortable? Had he been reading all of her signals wrong?

"Goodness," Elizabeth said with a chuckle. "I don't think there's any need to pull that face! If I were you, I would train it into a less desperate expression before you make Daphney run for the hills."

He released a sigh, knowing that she was right. "When did you become such a knowledgeable young woman?"

Elizabeth's smile fell. "I'm not a child anymore, Carver. There's really no need for you to continue to treat me as one." With a scrape of chair legs across the floor, she stood and left the room.

Carver sat gaping at the door after Elizabeth. What had he done wrong? He had the feeling that he was in two women's black books and was at a complete loss to understand why. His last few years of avoiding the opposite sex had certainly not done him any favors when it came to navigating his relationships with his sisters and Daphney. With a sigh, he headed out to look for Daphney.

His search was unfruitful until he reached the garden, where a flash of navy caught Carver's eye around a corner. He had spent two hours after breakfast scouring the house for Daphney, only to reach each room shortly after Miss Bellows had recently left it. Daphney had apparently won the maids over to her side. He worried that if she could remain hidden so easily within a house, how much easier for her to hide in the busy metropolis of London?

The thought of losing Daphney was beginning to tear at him. Before he knew what had happened, his heart was bending toward the woman in a way he never thought it would again. He longed for her.

But he needed to know if she returned his regard before he was willing to broach the topic with her.

And now, in the garden, he had found her.

Carver maneuvered quietly around the hedges of the garden and entered through the opposite side. As he had learned from that first night, it was not very wise to sneak up on Daphney. But still he couldn't help it. There was something freeing about playing and teasing with her.

Walking lightly across the gravel path, Carver slipped down the row behind her. She continued to walk slowly, occasionally holding out her hand to run it across the leaves of a bush. He kept advancing toward her from behind but still kept his distance, not making a sound. Her face was far away in thought. Perfect.

She turned the corner and began to walk down the next row of hedges and trees. None of the flowers were in bloom, but the green shrubs had been well-maintained and created a frustratingly opaque wall. He hurried and took the corner to catch up to her. This time he was planning to pin her arms down when he caught her so that she couldn't draw her pistol on him.

But when he turned the corner she was gone. He hurried down the path, remaining half bent over as he walked, and made to turn the next corner when he heard the click of a pistol being cocked. He froze and looked sideways at the gun being pressed to his temple.

Blast, she's good.

"Why are you following me?" asked Daphney. But she didn't sound playful. Her voice was all authority and distance.

He looked at her from the corner of his eye. There was a tear stain on her cheek but he didn't dare acknowledge it. Instead he asked, "Why are you avoiding me?"

A pause met his question and then she lowered her pistol. "It's not very smart to sneak up on a criminal, you know."

He turned to face her and resisted the desire to reach out and touch the line on her cheek where a tear had dried. "Not very smart, but exceedingly fun," he said and was glad to see a small smile touch her lips.

Carver noticed something else was not quite right about Daphney. She looked cold, the usual blush to her cheeks absent, her eyes were guarded. This strong desire to wrap his arms around her took him by force. He felt every bit as protective as Robert had looked when showing concern over Mary's health.

The wind howled around them and Daphney pulled her wool cloak more tightly around her. For once, the weather seemed to match the month, leaving the day bitterly cold and dreary. That gave him a thought. "Come with me," he said, reaching out and taking her hand. Her *gloveless* hand. The chill of her fingers prickled through his own gloves to his skin. Did she not own any gloves other than the one pair of dinner gloves he had seen her wear? He paused and dropped her hand. "But first," he used his teeth to tug off his own gloves. "Take these."

Her beautiful dark brows drew together, and she looked from his offering back up to his face. "You're giving me your gloves?" Her voice was thick with emotion.

It wasn't that big of a gesture, really. He had at least five more pairs in his wardrobe. "Of course. Your hands are cold." But he could see she was about to cry and wondered if he had done something wrong. "What is it?" he asked placing a hand on her arm.

She shook her head and accepted his gloves like they were a sacred offering. "I've been on the streets most of my life, Carver. And you are the first gentleman who has ever offered me his gloves." She smiled. "Thank you."

❦

"Ah, so this is where all of the lovely flowers come from," said Rose as Carver lead her into a hothouse situated to the back of the manor.

The warmth and humidity of the room pressed around her. It was a welcome relief from the bitter cold day, but she was sure that her hair would suffer the consequences. Her waves had an unfortunate tendency to frizz in excessive humidity. What would Carver think of it? She shook that thought away. She was supposed to be putting this man out of her mind.

They stepped further into the glass house and Rose let go of Carver's hand. She refused to read anything into the fact that he had held it all the way to the greenhouse. It was probably just for show. They needed to appear to be in love. Too bad she really was.

"Do you like it?" Carver asked. A new sense of pride sparkled in his eyes that Rose had never seen before. For the first time since arriving at Dalton Park, Carver looked proud of his family estate.

She ran her fingers over the stem of an orchid and breathed in its heady scent. "How could I not? It's beautiful. There are so many different species of flowers in here." Her eyes bounced joyfully over each of the different hues. She relished the deep fragrances that filled the room. But most of all, her heart raced from the realization that Carver was barely taking his eyes off of her. She could feel his gaze like needles prickling over her skin. "It's so different from London where there is very little color amidst all the stone and smog."

He stepped closer. "I can't believe we've both lived in town all this time and never crossed paths until you knocked on my door."

She laughed and took a step away from him with the excuse of further examining a pretty pink flower. But really, she just didn't trust herself to be so near him anymore. "How do you know we haven't crossed paths?"

"I would have recognized you."

She turned around and eyed him. "Oh really? I doubt it. I'm very good at assuming disguises. Usually, I wear a wig and add several layers or pillows to my wardrobe to alter my figure. I've even been known to wear a patch or two." She had always thought that the out of mode fake beauty marks were ridiculous, but they were successful in helping change her appearance. If no one among high society had ever been able to recognize her thus far, she doubted Carver would have either. She was very good at hiding and disguising herself.

His mouth tipped into a smile that made Rose's stomach flip upside down. "You can change your hair all you like, but I would still know those eyes anywhere."

Detach yourself. You're leaving in a few days.

Rose blinked and turned away feeling fearful that she had already given too much of her heart away to this man and would never get it back.

She tried to put some space between them by walking a few steps away until she paused in front of a dark red rose bush. She felt Carver's approach and forced herself to slow her breathing. Her eyes skipped over each bloom, none of it really registering. Rather, she was wishing that Carver had granted her the space she had needed to stick with her resolve. A little more time was all she needed to get ahold of her heart before she saw him again, but he had sought her out and found her. He always found her.

Rose's senses were all attuned to Carver's looming presence behind her. The air felt stiflingly warm. Why was she still wearing her cloak inside the hothouse? Sweat began to gather on her hairline. She reached up and tried to undo the ribbons at her neck but the gloves Carver had given her were too big and she couldn't feel the strings. He touched her shoulder and turned her toward him. He lifted her chin and undid the ribbons to remove her cloak, the back of his fingers brushing against her neck.

Well, that certainly didn't help anything.

The cloak lifted from her shoulders and then he draped it over his arm. At least now she didn't feel as if she were being smothered by the wool fabric—but by his direct gaze instead. Rose turned her eyes back to the bright red blooms.

"They are beautiful, aren't they?" he said. "I believe my mother planted these herself." He finally looked away from her to inspect the roses.

She couldn't help but smile at the irony. Rose slipped her fingers below the flower that she had always thought felt like velvet. Beneath the bloom of her namesake. "They are lovely. It might be a little narcissistic of me but I've always loved this flower the best."

She glanced up and saw Carver's brows stitch together. "Why is that narcissistic?"

She froze. *Oh no.* Her stomach leapt into her throat when she realized what she'd done.

No, no, no, no.

She frantically searched her mind for a way out. She hadn't at all intended to tell him her name. In fact, she was trying to pull her heart away from the man, not hand it to him on a silver platter.

Rose reluctantly met his gaze. Carver's heavy brow softened as realization overtook him. "Is...your name...Rose?" That was it. She had moved off the edge of some high unreachable cliff and was falling. Hearing her name slip off his lips undid her. Every last ounce of fight she had disintegrated. She felt scared. Vulnerable. And like she had everything to lose.

Tears burned her eyes and her legs felt weak. She did the only thing she knew how to do. Rose turned around and ran.

Chapter Twenty-Five

R ose. Her beautiful name had tumbled over and over in Carver's mind ever since he had learned it that morning in the hothouse. It suited her perfectly. And the moment he had heard it, the last bit of hesitancy and uncertainty fell away and he knew what he wanted—no, needed.

But the look on her face, the unshed tears that hovered in her golden-amber-brown eyes told him that she hadn't been ready to reveal it. He should have pretended he hadn't heard her slip. It didn't feel right knowing that he had breeched her privacy…even if it was by accident.

And *Rose* had looked more fragile in that moment before she had darted from the greenhouse than he'd seen her yet. She'd looked frightened and unsure of the very world around her. Seeing her that way, knowing her heart was fragile and cracked, had made him want to hold it and be strong for her, no matter that he didn't feel it. He could be anything for her.

Surely, he could hold together his own pieces enough to keep hers together, too?

"I'm concerned about Daphney," said Mother, breaking through his thoughts. She sat beside him on the settee, eyes focused on the needle work in her hands. "I heard she didn't come down for breakfast this morning, and then she requested a dinner tray be sent to her bedchamber. I hope she is not feeling unwell. Perhaps I should go check on her." He smiled at his caring mother.

But what could he say? *No. She's just avoiding me because she unwillingly revealed to me her real name.* "I believe she has a touch of a headache, that's all." Most likely she did.

His mother sighed beside him. "Poor dear. Headaches can be the very devil at times. I think I'll have a maid send up some lavender water and see if that helps."

He reached out and squeezed her hand. "I am sure she would appreciate it, Mother." But he had a plan to find out himself just how Rose was feeling.

He waited until he knew everyone had already retired to bed and were likely asleep before he quietly walked down the dark hallways and wound his way to Rose's room. The floors creaked beneath his boots but otherwise, not a single sound touched the halls. He stopped outside her room. How to get her attention without alerting the house? He had no desire for any of his family members to find him visiting Rose's door in the middle of the night—even if they thought them to be engaged.

Carver reached up and gently scratched Rose's door. He held his breath and pressed his ear to the door listening for any signs of movement within. Silence. He scratched again, this time a little louder. A small rustling noise came from within. He laid the barest of taps on the wooden door so that she would know he was the one trying to gain her attention and not just a mouse lurking in the walls.

He heard footsteps and as the door knob turned, his breath quickened. The door peeked open, "Carver?" Rose's hushed voice came through the narrow opening, breathy and raspy and still heavy with sleep. All he could see was one of her eyes through the crack. What must she be thinking of him? "What are you doing here? It's one o'clock in the morning."

"I should think the answer is obvious." He let the statement hang in the air a moment, contemplating exactly what it felt like to be Lord

Newburry before he smiled and added, "Stealing you away for an adventure."

She let out a breath of relief that made him laugh.

"What sort of adventure has to take place in the dead of night?" she asked, still skeptical.

"The secret kind."

She opened the door more fully. His breath caught. Her wild waves were let down and tumbling over her shoulder where they fell to the waist of her night gown. The warm glow of the candle danced in her eyes and fluttered against her soft skin. He'd never seen her that way before. Now that he knew her name, she felt more real to him, softer and more beautiful. She was everything beautiful and nighttime and hope and...

"Carver Timothy Ashburn, tell me right now if you have any ill intentions toward me during the course of this *adventure*." She was waking up enough for her voice to carry its usual authoritative edge.

He grinned and crossed a hand over his heart. "I swear to be the pattern card of a gentleman." Though, he didn't swear that it would be easy. He had the strongest desire to run his hands through her hair. He clasped his hands behind him.

"*Gentlemen* in my experience usually have the worst of intentions," she said.

"Fair enough. A saint then."

She eyed him for a minute, weighing the odds in her mind. And then, without preamble, she shut the door. He blinked at the solid wood door, now nearly touching his nose. Was that it? She didn't trust him? He was about to turn and walk away, dragging his bruised ego in tow, when the door reopened and she appeared wrapped in a thick blanket, a mischievous grin on her face. "I'm watching you, Kensworth," she said, eyes narrowed as she walked passed him, sweeping her warm sweet smell under his nose and straight through his good intentions. But he mentally shook himself and re-focused.

He took up her hand and allowed himself to relish how good and right it felt in his. He guided her up the stairs to the third floor of the house.

"Where are you taking me?"

"Shh. You'll see," he said.

They made it to the top floor, and he steered her toward the last window in a long row. Aside from the lantern he'd brought along, everything was shrouded in darkness. They stopped just beside the window. Carver reluctantly dropped her hand to undo its latch.

"What the devil are you doing?" she asked, a small panic rising in her voice. If she wasn't thrilled about him opening the window, she definitely wouldn't be happy when he asked her to climb out of it.

He turned to face her. The night air was cold as it pushed through the open window. She pulled her blanket tighter around her. "Do you trust me?" He thought of her past and he knew about the scar that marred her hand from having nearly fallen off of a high roof top. He was asking a lot of her, to trust him in this way, and he knew it.

Carver extended his hand. Rose's brow's pulled together as she eyed his hand and then the roof line just outside the window. Her gaze met his, patent fear in their depths. "The last time I was on a roof, it didn't go so well."

"I know. But I won't let you fall. I promise."

She took a deep breath and grabbed his hand. It was a little sweaty and shaking but he didn't care. She was trusting him, and his hopes soared at the thought. He smiled and leaned down to pick up the blankets he had placed in the corner earlier that night, then climbed out the window. Rose followed closely behind and he was careful to never let go of her hand. "We don't have far to go," he said looking back at her, the darkness urging him to keep his voice lowered.

The cold winter air made him feel alive and energized. It somehow felt more pure and tangible than it did in the summer time. When you breathed in the chill, it had a presence in your lungs. Did Rose feel the same way? Judging by the way her teeth were chattering, probably not.

They walked a little further on the steep roof taking careful and determined steps. Carver squeezed her hand now and then to let her know he was paying attention to her and would not let her go. Rose did not say a word. Finally, they arrived at a small portion of roof that was nearly flat with only the slightest incline, tucked almost like an alcove into the steep roof. Carver had no idea why this part of the roof existed. Nor did he care. It had been his own personal hiding place since he was a boy and that was all that mattered to him.

He took one of the quilts draped over his arm and spread it out over the roof. When he was a child, he had never been so prepared as to bring a quilt with him. But he had a woman with him this time, and he thought she would appreciate a few small comforts while being forced to endure the cold January night on top of a roof. Really, it had seemed much more romantic in his head.

After arranging the blanket, he turned back toward Rose. He was shocked to find a smile on her face. Her hair flew all around, and her whole body trembled, but she was smiling. "What are we doing out here, Carver? Other than catching our death."

He took her hand and brought her into the little hideout. "You'll be warmer in here. The wind is blocked by the roof peaks."

She stepped inside and sat down beside him, wrapping her blanket so snuggly around her that he wondered if it would become a permanent fixture on her. "Do you know where else the wind doesn't reach?" Her tone and grin were cheeky. "My bed."

He tipped a brow. "Yes, but I could hardly join you there, now, could I?"

She sat up a little straighter. "No. You most definitely could not." He was sad that it was too dark to see her blush, as he was certain she was. Rose adjusted and faced out for the first time. "And I also don't have a view like this from my bed either."

"It's beautiful, isn't it?" This was what he had wanted her to see. Sitting up here felt like sitting on the clouds. The twinkling stars reflected off of the lake in front of the house, making it look as though hundreds of stars had fallen across the grounds. One could see for miles and miles from that spot.

In the distance, smoke billowed from tenants' chimneys, tree lines swayed with the wind, and the world looked peaceful. He had missed being here. It was his own secret. A place to hide away that not even Claire had known about. He doubted that Rose knew how significant it was that he had brought her here.

He kept his eyes on the horizon. "I'm sorry that I found out your name. I know that you were not ready for that revelation and I'm sorry for putting you in the position to confirm it." He felt her stiffen beside him. "I cannot unlearn your name. But I can level the playing field a little bit."

She looked at him. "How?"

"Well, for starters I've brought you here." He gestured to the view ahead of them. "I know it's not quite the same as learning your name but it is somewhere that's special to me that no other soul—besides you—in the world knows about." Her lips tugged into a soft smile as she looked from him back toward the horizon. She took a deep breath and looked out over the world as if she were seeing its meaning for the first time, savoring the significance of it all. The surrounding view was incredible, but he couldn't tear his eyes away from the face of the woman beside him.

His stomach knotted with anticipation and dread at his next words. "And now, I give you permission to ask me anything you've ever wanted to know about me." He knew what she would ask. There was not one part of him that wanted to utter the words, but it was time she knew. Without a doubt, he had fallen in love with this woman. With *Rose*. She deserved to know the ghosts that haunted him.

Chapter Twenty-Six

S hould she ask him? Carver, the mysterious earl, sat beside her and basically gave her a key to any secret he kept locked away. But it didn't feel right to ask him. Especially since he was only letting her ask because of her name slip earlier. Yes, her name was deeply personal to her, but the more she thought on it through the day, the more she realized she was happy that Carver finally knew it.

She felt almost free for the first time in her adult life. This man had given her the ability to stop trying so hard. To smile. To laugh. To hope. And because life had ingrained certain truths in her mind, she was afraid it would all come at a great cost. All wonderful things did. But it was a price she was now willing to pay. Even knowing that she would be leaving in only a few days, it was still worth it to feel the wonder and freedom of loving someone. She would deal with picking up the pieces later. Right now, she wanted to savor every moment, every smile, every secret they shared.

It probably wasn't right to ask him. But she had to. She had to know. "Fine, then. I do have a question for you." He took in a deep breath through his nose and held it. She looked up at him, their eyes meeting. "What...is your favorite dessert."

The air all rushed from his lungs at once, along with a laugh. *"That is what you've always wanted to know about me?"*

She shrugged a shoulder. "It's important."

He smiled and looked down at her from the corner of his eye. "I love a simple chocolate cake."

She scoffed. "Everyone loves chocolate cake," and rolled her eyes at his unoriginality. A moment of silence lingered and her heart pounded harder and harder until she couldn't take it anymore and gave into asking what she really wanted to know. "What happened three years ago?"

Carver's eyes shut tight. It was the exact look someone wore when they had just been shot, or stabbed. His mask had dropped away and Rose could finally see the wound he tried so diligently to keep hidden. Three whole breaths came and went before he said in almost a whisper, "She died."

Two words. That was all he said, and all she needed to hear to understand. Those two words hung in the air around them feeling heavier, more meaningful, with every passing second. Rose didn't know to what *she* Carver referred, but instinctively Rose knew that whoever she had been, the woman had held Carver's heart.

Rose scooted closer to Carver. She knew he expected her to explode with questions. But she wouldn't. Rose knew what it was like to lose someone dear. It didn't matter to her who the woman was or what had happened to her. All that mattered to Rose was that she had died, and her death had left Carver shattered. She couldn't bring the woman back for him—although she would have if she could—but she could sit here with him and share his pain.

※

C arver froze as Rose scooted closer. She wrapped both of her arms round one of his arms allowing him to truly appreciate her petite size. Her personality had always made her seem so much taller and more commanding. Here on the rooftop, she seems so small and gentle as she hugged his arm and laid her head against his shoulder.

The warmth of her body pressed into him with a new, unfamiliar comfort. He and Claire had never gone through any difficult situations that would have required her comfort.

He waited for more questions to come, but they never did. Rose just sat there and held onto him. His body slowly relaxed into something like peace. Like hope.

"I'm sorry," she whispered into his arm. He leaned over and kissed the top of her head. Eventually he would tell her more, but tonight, that bit felt like enough.

The silence stretched on until he thought it might end the night. But then she spoke, quiet and with hesitation marking her words. "I...was named after my mother." Then, he was sure everything changed between them. It would never be the same again—nor did he want it to be. "Her name was Emily Rose Wakefield. She contracted a fever during birth and died the day after I was born."

Carver shifted his arm out of her grasp so that he could wrap it around her shoulders instead. He pulled her close, unwilling to let her go. She laid her head against his chest as he asked, "Is your middle name Emily?"

"No, it's Amelia. That was my aunt's name." Whatever wall that had stood between them was gone. "She was my papa's sister, and they were apparently very close." She paused. "But all of my relations had died by the time I reached five years of age. So I never really knew them."

"I'm sorry. That must have been terrible." He couldn't imagine not knowing his family. Especially his mother. He imagined it would be all that more difficult for a woman to grow up without the guidance and reassurance of a mother. "You said you lost your father when you were ten?" He shouldn't have asked that. It was unfair of him to ask such a question when he cringed at the thought of answering any more himself.

Rose didn't seem to mind his questions anymore. If anything, he could feel her lean further into him. "Yes—heart failure. It was so sudden. I had no idea it was coming," she paused and took a breath. "One moment he was happy and dancing me around our little rented apartment and the next..." her voice shook with emotion, and instead of making her finish the sentence he tugged her in closer and rubbed her arms. She buried her head into his chest and cried. His strong, stubborn, self-sufficient woman, was crying in his arms.

After a minute, she sniffed, righted herself and fiercely swatted away a stream of tears. "It was so long ago, but I still miss him just as much as the day he died." How frightening life must have been for her to lose the only living relation she knew. Suddenly, her strength and formidable personality made sense to him. "Everything changed for me that day. Papa was only a street merchant, so it wasn't as if I had lived a luxurious life before, but it had never felt like anything in our life was missing. I never truly knew what hunger was. But after he died, and I was all alone...food suddenly became a luxury. That is until I met Uncle Felix and he and I began running jobs together."

"Uncle Felix was the accomplice you spoke of?"

She nodded. "Though, he would likely huff and puff if he knew that I had described him as such. But—ever since Papa died, I've tried my hardest to not become attached to anyone again. To never truly allow myself to rely on another for support." He could hear the insecurity in her voice, begging to be understood. "There's a quiet comfort in knowing that I provide my own food, clothing, and shelter. I've worked very hard over the years to learn how to live in this world on my own, and it scares me to put that trust in anyone else." Those words were for him and he knew it. She paused a moment. "Especially after Papa's death and seeing how quickly everything can fall apart. It's just been easier to be on my own. But Uncle Felix,"—she let out a single quiet laugh—"Well...from the moment he met me, he's refused to let me go."

Carver had a strong desire to meet this man. To shake his hand and to thank him for caring for Rose, even though he had no right to do such a thing. And Rose would likely shoot him in the head if he did.

"How did you meet him?" he asked, running his fingers gently down the side of her arm.

That brought a beautiful tickling laugh from Rose's mouth, one he hadn't heard before. It was innocent and almost childish in a wonderful way. "I tried to steal from him on the street. It was shortly after I had fallen off of that deuced roof and couldn't climb anymore. So, I tried my hand at pick-pocketing, but I was horrible at it. And little did I know, I was trying to pickpocket from the most notorious thief in London.

To this day I don't know why he took me under his wing. At the time, he said that I was the most pathetic, clumsy urchin he'd ever seen. He said he would teach me a few things and then send me on my way. But one day turned into a week. And after a week a month. And then we were running jobs together, and he was teaching me every-thing he knew. Although I've sworn that I don't need him, the truth is that I would be dead without that man. I owe him everything."

He almost couldn't believe this woman beside him. All she'd been through. All she'd endured. And she was there with him, not hiding or running away. She was honest and transparent and he felt completely unworthy of her. His heart was whispering—no clawing—at him to open his mouth and let the words out that he'd kept shut away for so long. But his fear was thick and determined to stay. What would she think if he told her all he felt about Claire? It would push her away and he couldn't risk that.

So he kept the conversation on her. "I seem to remember you saying you didn't have anyone in your life that you cared about. But if I'm not mistaken, I hear at least a little fondness in your voice for your Uncle Felix."

She smiled up at him. "It's true. And now that you've learned my secret, I might have to shoot you."

"No need. I'm good at keeping secrets."

He saw her smile turn softer. Sadder. "I know you are." And then she tucked her chin back in and curled up next to him where she spent the rest of the night.

The night was bitter cold, and the roof was a hard and uncom-fortable seat, but neither of them minded. Rose seemed just as content to remain there with him as he was to be with her. They traded stories of childhood. He learned how to remove a man's pocket-watch during a dance—though he didn't think he would ever have the chance to try out his newfound skill—and he taught Rose how to ball up her fist to throw an effective punch without breaking her thumb.

Every new detail he learned, every smile he received, every time she leaned into him a little more, felt like a gift. He loved her in a way that he hadn't thought would be possible for him again. And now that he had it, he could never let it go. Could never let *her* go.

But did she want that too? Would she stay if he asked? Would she let him love her? He may never be whole again, but he could make sure that Rose was. He would spend the rest of his days carefully removing the splinters in her heart if she would let him.

The golden peaks of dawn tiptoed over the horizon. Had they really spent the entire night like this? He looked down at the woman who was almost asleep on his chest. He could hear her heavy breaths and feel her shoulders expanding and releasing and knew she was slipping into sleep. Nothing in him wanted to disturb her. But he had to. He needed to walk her back to her door before anyone else in the house woke up and discovered them.

Absolutely nothing inappropriate had taken place between them that night. Unfortunately, not even a stolen kiss. Blast his promise of saintliness. But still, he didn't want to set Rose's name—or Daphney's—on the servant's tongues. If she stayed and became his wife as he hoped, he wanted it to be by her own choice, not by his family's force or because of a scandal. He wanted to give her the freedom to make choices in her life based on her own desires and not a governing circumstance.

He stroked the loose waves that had fallen against her cheek and moved them back behind her ear. "Rose." It was the first time he had called her by her given name. She made an adorably sleepy *hmm* noise that made him smile. "What if I asked you to stay?" He released the words and felt the lightening of his heart. The rightness of what he had just asked.

Rose took in a deep breath and held it for a moment as if she was turning the question over in her mind and wondering if she had just heard him correctly. She finally adjusted to sit up and look at him. She was all golden and morning and light and happiness and everything that he wanted in his future.

"What do you mean?" she asked, squinting against the heaviness in her eyelids from a night spent awake.

He smiled as he traced the lines of her waves tumbling over her shoulder. "I mean that I love you." He reached up and ran the back of his fingers down her cheek. "And I don't want you to leave—ever. I want you to let me tell my family the truth and have you join our family as Rose and not Daphney."

Rose bit her lips together as tears pooled in her eyes. "Carver…are you proposing to me?"

He wiped a tear that fell down her cheek with his thumb. "Yes, I am."

Her breath increased as he held his own. "I told you not to fall in love with me," she said sounding almost desperate.

"I know."

She looked up at the gold and pink sky, trying to blink away her tears. "I'm a con woman, Carver. I've stolen from a lot of people."

"I know."

"And…I don't even know the first thing about being a countess." She laughed without amusement. "Or a duchess for that matter." She shook her head and her brows were pulled together. "I don't deserve to be your wife."

He cupped her face in his hands and looked in her eyes. "*That* is definitely not true. And you don't have to be a thief anymore, Rose. I can take care of you, if you'll let me." He knew what he was asking of her. "And my mother can teach you everything you need to know about holding the title of a duchess, and my father will love you like his own."

She swallowed and tears were still escaping from her uncertain eyes. "I'm not sure I know how to be cared for."

"I know," he said again and smiled. "I'll show you."

The silence tugged and twisted between them. Rose's gaze burned into his, making them somehow feel both connected forever and also moments away from potential fracture. He wanted to kiss her more than anything, to show her that he loved her in a tangible way. But he knew the decision was already difficult enough for her and wanted to give her emotions the respect they deserved without adding any further complications.

"Can I think about it?" she finally said into the quiet.

No. "Yes, of course. Take all the time you need."

But tell me now. Say yes.

He felt a desperation that he hoped to God he didn't show. He needed to be strong. He needed to prove to her that he was secure without her. That he would be a dependable strength for her to lean on, even if he wasn't so sure himself.

She leaned in and laid a soft kiss on his cheek. The sensation sent a wave of heat and hope through his entire body. "Thank you, Carver," she said. "For everything."

Chapter Twenty-Seven

W as this real? It had to be a dream. But a quick pinch told Rose she was very much awake, and she should not have pinched so hard. An offending red splotch now marked her arm but still all Rose could do was smile. She laid in her bed, staring at the golden canopy draped over her and mentally re-lived her entire night with Carver. Their night together had been wonderful and sweet and intimate. Carver had asked her to marry him. She still couldn't believe it. He knew her shortcomings; he knew her sins, and still he wanted her.

The very idea of him wanting her felt almost too good to be true. It felt like a lovely dream. A false reality. A continuation of their ruse.

A new feeling settled in Rose's stomach. Something about it all felt unreal. But the more she thought of it, the more it did not feel like a good kind of unreal. There was something off—some unknown warning that she couldn't name or understand. Perhaps she was sabotaging herself? Maybe this was her fear of a new life speaking. But no. She didn't think so. Rose very much wanted to marry Carver. But somewhere deep within her she could feel a hesitancy that needed consideration.

Rose took her pillow and pulled it over her face. She felt like screaming. Why did she have to think so much? Why couldn't she have just said yes right away and not given any of it another thought? She gave into her anxiety and released something like a growl mixed with a screech into her pillow. She kicked her legs and twisted around like a child throwing a tantrum, hoping she could simply will away her misgivings. It didn't work. Now she just felt stupid and tangled.

She sat up and smoothed down her mass of wavy hair. She stared at the closed window curtains. A line of orange light seeped around the edges. That's exactly how Rose felt. Like there was some truth trying to creep its way into her consciousness but it was obscured by her hope and longing to become Carver's wife.

He was perfect in every way. And she loved him, she was sure of it. So why the hesitancy?

Later in the day, the duchess invited Rose to clip flowers in the greenhouse for the ball, along with Mary and Elizabeth. Having only spent the morning staring at her closed curtains, Rose readily accepted. The change of scenery was much needed. Maybe it would even help her sort out her feelings.

"Still nursing your bad mood, I see, Elizabeth," said Mary, eyeing her sister who had been just as quiet as Rose during their time in the humid house of flowers. Rose watched from the corner of her eye as she clipped a pink bloom, not wanting to be observed eavesdropping, but very interested in the turn of conversation.

"I am entitled to a sour mood now and then, Mary," Elizabeth's words were clipped, confirming her sister's statement.

Mary's body seemed to soften as she moved to lean her hip against the short garden wall. "I'm sorry," said Mary. "I didn't mean to imply that you were not allowed to have bad days. You wouldn't be human if you didn't. But I do wish you would tell me what is bothering you. I love you, and you know you can tell me anything."

Suddenly, understanding dawned in Rose's mind. She knew what had kept her from saying yes to Carver right away. She loved him. And he loved her—she didn't doubt that—he just didn't seem to love her enough to trust her with whatever pain he kept hidden away. At first, it hadn't bothered her and she understood his need to stay quiet about it all. But now, she wondered at it. Could she live like that?

Rose would be turning her whole world upside down if she married Carver. There wasn't a question in her mind that he would be an attentive, caring, and tender husband. Carver was the sort of man who would see to her every need and not stop until he knew she was completely and utterly cared for. But that's not exactly what Rose wanted. But to be fair, she also hadn't even realized that she wanted to be married until Carver came along. But even so, she knew that she did not want to be married to a man who didn't need her care in return. She wanted her marriage to be a partnership. If Carver never opened up to her, never trusted her with his past, could she ever truly be happy with him?

Elizabeth clipped—a little violently—a long stem from a bed of flowers. "I know, but it's nothing. I'm going to go clip some greenery."

The greenery, Rose noticed, was conveniently on the other end of the greenhouse. Something was definitely bothering the girl, and if Rose was even considering accepting Carver and stepping into this tight-knit family, she needed to learn to act the role of a sister. No, she corrected herself. No more acting. No more roles. If she sought out Elizabeth, it would be from her heart, not because of a need to be someone she wasn't.

I'll think about Carver's proposal later.

Part of her didn't want to. She was afraid that she already knew the answer.

Rose shook off her thought and squared her shoulders toward Elizabeth's direction as if going into battle. She crossed the humid room to where a very menacing Elizabeth was ruthlessly murdering a green plant. It wouldn't survive her scalping. Rose moved her gaze from the pathetic plant to look at Elizabeth. The girl was looking a little pale and sallow. Rose opted for a lighter tone. "Heavens. That must have been some offensive plant."

She had the privilege of watching Elizabeth's lips twitch. "You should have heard the things it said about me." Rose smiled at the quip. She liked Elizabeth. Actually, she loved the entire family. But she felt a special connection to Elizabeth that she didn't feel with the rest of the Dalton ladies. Did Elizabeth like her as well? An even more terrifying thought…would she still when she found out the truth of Rose's true identity? Would the family even allow Carver to marry such a criminal? Maybe all of this contemplation she was doing was for nothing.

She couldn't focus on those things now. What did one say to a sister? If Rose was in a foul mood, she certainly didn't want anyone commenting on it. No one ever enjoyed having their bad mood declared.

She decided on a more honest approach and said, "Elizabeth…I'm not sure how to talk to you." But that was definitely too honest and didn't come out at all right.

Elizabeth's eyes widened but showed more amusement than shock. Rose added, "What I meant was, I've never had a sister, and this sort of relationship is completely new for me. So I cannot promise to be of any profound assistance, but I wanted you to know that if you wished to talk, my door is always open." There. She said it. She felt stupid and clumsy, but she said it.

Elizabeth's sincere smile warmed Rose, making her feel a little lighter, a little more capable of sisterly affection. "Thank you, Daphney." And then the sound of her false name brought her back down to earth.

R ose stood outside of the drawing room, taking one step toward it and then away again. She'd been about this for far too long; the footman standing outside of the room, pretending scrupulously not to notice her indecision, was probably convinced she should be admitted to Bedlam.

She had avoided Carver all day, and she knew that if she stepped inside that drawing room where he and all of his family were gathered, she would no longer be able to avoid him. She didn't feel any closer to a decision and he would be wanting one soon. Rose did know that she wanted to marry Carver. She wanted to be his countess. She wanted to start a new life with him in London. And she also wanted to shake that blasted feeling of hesitation—but couldn't. It was there and it was real and it was demanding to be heard.

"Practicing your dance steps, love?" She jumped and whirled around at the sound of Carver's voice behind her.

"Carver!" she said in too high of a voice. She cleared her throat lightly and tried for an easier tone. "I thought you were already in the drawing room."

He grinned and tipped his brow. "Clearly." Did he know she had been avoiding him? "Should we go in or would you like help practicing your dance steps? A waltz perhaps?" How did he always make her smile so easily?

"As much as I would love to dance with you, I think we had better go in."

A dimple creased his cheek as he grinned. "Dinner with my family will not be nearly as much fun as waltzing in the hallway." He took a step closer and picked up her hand. How was it that one simple touch from him could send a tingle all the way up her arm? She wanted to lean into him. To kiss that dimple on his cheek.

"No," she lowered her voice. "But I suspect I've already given the footman over there enough reason to toss my name around downstairs. I don't think Daphney's reputation can withstand any more marks this evening."

His smile didn't drop, but his eyes narrowed slightly, making the grin look more intimate and thoughtful. He lifted his hand and tucked a hair behind her ear. "Hopefully soon, *Daphney* will no longer be a consideration. Your name is too beautiful to keep hidden any longer." He leaned down and lightly kissed her cheek. She closed her eyes and breathed in his intoxicating scent. But the rush of flutters to her stomach and the overwhelming feeling that being kissed by Carver felt *right* confused her. If they were as perfect for each other as she suspected, why couldn't she bring herself to simply say *yes*?

"I forgot to tell you," Carver said after they had gone into the drawing room and greeted all of the family. "Oliver arrived this afternoon and will be joining us for dinner."

Rose whipped her head up to look at Carver's face. "Your best friend?" she asked. Carver had told her all about his and Olly's friend-ship last night on the roof. Nervousness twisted in her stomach at the thought of meeting the one person she was sure would have the strongest opinion about their match.

Carver chuckled. "You really have a way of making a man feel mature and masculine. But yes, he is my best friend."

Just then, the butler entered the drawing room and announced, "Mr. Oliver Turner." Rose's heart sunk through her stomach and all the way down through the floor where she wished she could melt and never return.

No. Surely not? It couldn't be...

But as the tall, blonde, blue eyed man stepped through the door, Rose felt for the first time in her life like she was going to faint.

His eyes immediately caught hers and he blinked as if questioning his own sense of reality. "Kitty?"

Chapter Twenty-Eight

C arver prided himself on his ability to think on his feet, but as he looked back and forth between a confused Oliver and ghostly white faced Rose, his pride failed him.

Rose was the first to speak, although her words sounded a touch nervous. "Mr. Turner, how lovely to see you again." Each member of his family took a turn looking bewildered. No doubt they had heard the personal—and wrong—name Oliver had used to address her. Why *had* he called her by that name? A sinking feeling told him that Oliver and Rose had already been acquainted. And knowing all that he now knew about Rose, that could not be a good thing.

A discreet jab to his ribs snapped Carver back to the moment.

"Olly!" he released Rose to advance toward his friend and clap him on the shoulder. "Glad you finally made it. How were the roads?" He hoped he could gain enough of Oliver's attention to send him a signal that conveyed he was not to acknowledge Rose again until after they had spoken alone. Had they been friends long enough that a single look could tell the man everything he needed to know?

Apparently not.

Oliver looked around Carver, dismissing his existence. "The roads were dirty and bumpy as always." He pushed by Carver and began addressing Rose. "Kitty, what are you doing here?"

Carver thought he could physically hear Rose swallow from across the room. His parents crossed to stand by Rose and Oliver with skeptical looks. Rose's eyes bounced around the room as if she were searching for an escape route. Oliver reached for Rose's hand with far too tender a touch. Not good. Carver needed to get Oliver alone before he opened his mouth again.

"Oliver," said his father with deeply creased brows. "How do you and Miss Bell—,"

"Olly!" Carver interrupted a bit too loudly. "Have you seen the newest addition to the east wing?" He grabbed his friend by the arm and began dragging him toward the door.

"Do you mean the addition that was added two years ago?" said Oliver, annoyance running through his voice. "Yes, I've seen—,"

"Wonderful! Let me show it to you." He was making a cake of himself again but he didn't care. He needed to protect Rose. His family would know the truth eventually, but not now. And definitely not in the drawing room before dinner with the servants present.

"But Carver," Mother called after them. "Dinner will be announced any minute. Can showing Oliver the expansion that he's already seen wait?"

He was vaguely aware that Robert was laughing somewhere along the edge of the room but of course he wasn't going to help. "Feel free to start without us," Carver called back before yanking a reluctant and agitated Oliver from the room.

Oliver shared Carver's height, but thankfully, not his broad build or else Carver might not have been able to maneuver him the way he did.

"Kenny, what the devil was that?" said Oliver, shoving Carver's hand off of his arm as they both tripped into the hallway.

～

R ose looked around the room at each set of shocked eyes, all aimed at her. She blurted out the first excuse she could think of that would get her out of there. "I...feel a little bit cold," she said. "Excuse me while I go retrieve my shawl." And then she pulled the shawl she was already wearing around her tighter and rushed from the room.

She really was getting worse at her job.

Rose plunged out into the hallway and paused. One quick sweep of the hallway revealed a smiling Henley. "In the library, miss." With a quick nod to her coconspirator, Rose was propelling herself toward the library, faster than was considered ladylike, but oh well.

Rose reached the library and burst through the door, sending it to slam against the wall. Her shoulders tensed at the noise, and both Carver and Oliver jumped as if an elephant had just knocked the door down. Her less than graceful entry reminded her too much of Uncle Felix and a chuckle escaped her before she realized that the two men in front of her did not share her amusement.

Carver sent his hand raking through his already disheveled hair. He looked frazzled. "Rose," he said and then looked to immediately regret the slip of her real name.

"Carver," she said with a reprimanding tone.

"Kitty?" Oliver asked.

"I meant, Daphney!" Carver unsuccessfully recovered.

"Daphney?" Asked Oliver. "What is he talking about, Kitty?"

This was madness. Never had so many names been flung around one room before. "Stop," she said a bit too loudly for the space and both men's eyebrows shot up. She took a breath and smoothed her skirt. "Now, can we all just take a deep breath and collect our senses?"

"No time, love. We need to be at the dinner table soon or they will grow even more suspicious."

"Love?" Oliver's bright blue eyes bounced wildly back and forth from Rose to Carver.

It was time that she confessed. She wasn't entirely sure why that thought made her shake. It wasn't as if Carver didn't already know she was a con woman. But now he would learn she was a con woman who had scammed his best friend out of five hundred pounds. Would he want to still marry her after that?

"What's going on, Kitty?" Oliver asked again.

Rose sighed, turned around, and shut the door. She might be about to confess everything to Oliver but she didn't wish to enlighten the whole family simultaneously. "I am not Kitty," she said while turning back around to face him. She looked briefly to Carver and could relax a little when she saw him smile. "As Carver accidentally pointed out, my name is Rose. Rose Wakefield."

Carver crossed his arms and his supportive smile turned amused. "I suppose this is a belated question, but do you two have a prior acquaintance?"

She narrowed her eyes. "Don't think I don't see your lips twitching, Carver. Yes, we are already acquainted, and this is not at all funny."

"It's a little funny," he said tipping his head to the side. Actually, it was a little funny. She had to fight her own smile.

Oliver stepped closer to both of them and waved his hand as if they had forgotten he was in the room. "Can someone please tell me the joke?" Humor didn't reach his voice. He reached out and grabbed one of Rose's hands. "Why did you pretend your name was Kitty?" Rose pulled her hand away as fast as she could.

"Mr. Turner—,"

"Wait," Carver said with wide eyes looking back and forth between her and Oliver. "Olly, is this?...Do you mean to tell me that this is *her?*"

"Yes, of course it's her!" said Oliver. "And will someone please tell me what *she* is doing *here?*"

Now Rose felt bewildered. "Who is *her?*"

"You," both men said looking a little pained.

Rose resisted the urge to growl. "Not this again." She turned on her heels and moved to sit on the sofa in the middle of the room. The fire was lit in the grate and she wished it wasn't. It felt difficult to breathe. She placed her hands under her legs and bit her lips trying to find the right words to explain their unfortunate situation. "Mr. Turner—"

"Oliver," he and Carver both corrected once again in unison.

"Very well." She looked back and forth slowly between the men, unsure whether to feel amused or frightened by their seemingly connected thoughts. "Oliver," she directed her attention to the blue eyed man. "I am..."

"A criminal," Carver answered her pause unhelpfully. She flashed him a tight lipped look, but he just grinned back at her reminding her of the unaffected rake she had originally thought he was.

"More specifically," she turned her gaze back to Oliver, "I am a con woman—a swindler if you will. I focus my attention specifically on hoaxing gentleman out of their money." Did he see where this was going yet? "And I am by no means pleased to tell you that..."

His face went pale. "Don't say it."

She winced and then looked at him. "I pretended to be Kitty in order to scam you out of your five hundred pounds." She paused and pointed a finger at Carver. "And if you keep snickering like that, I'm going to shoot you."

"My dear, you can only threaten something so many times before it loses its edge. Now, tell me, Olly, did you decide to marry her before or after she relieved you of your burdensome money?"

Oliver stepped toward Carver. "Did you decide to steal my woman before or after I told you I was going to marry her?"

His woman? Marry her?

A more somber expression fell over Carver's face. As if he were just now realizing that Oliver wasn't finding the situation as humorous as he was. "I didn't steal *your* woman, Oliver. She was never yours to begin with. She was only using you to get your money."

But that only made things worse. Oliver took another step toward Carver, his face looking hard and angry and a little dangerous. "Were you behind this, Kensworth? You've played a lot of pranks during your time but this was too far."

"It wasn't a prank—," but before Carver could fully get the words out Oliver had advanced to Carver and thrown his fist into Carver's eye. Rose stood up but then quickly sat back down when she realized that getting between two angry men was not something she particularly wanted to do.

Carver didn't hesitate even a second. He grabbed Oliver by the cravat with one hand and punched him in the jaw with the other. Oliver fell back a step and swatted the blood from his split lip before lunging at Carver again and ramming him into the wall, pinning him against it with his fists. The two huge men stood there staring at each other and breathing hard before Oliver said, "I hate that you let me win just now."

Carver shrugged as much as Oliver's grip on his jacket would allow. "Felt like the right thing to do. Are we alright now or do you want to hit me again?"

Oliver sighed and let go of Carver's jacket. "I want to know what the deuce is going on."

Rose swallowed and stood from the settee. She glanced between the two men—one with a swelling eye and the other with a split bloody lip. Their cravats were falling off, shirts were halfway untucked, their hair looked ridiculous, and it was all her fault. It was all because of what she had done. The weight of it sunk over her.

"I'm terribly sorry, Oliver," she advanced toward him feeling an odd current of emotion running through her. "It was nothing personal, I assure you. I tried to scam Carver, too," she said, hoping that would take some of the sting out of it. "It is, or rather, *was* my job. But I have decided to give up that way of life from now on."

Carver's gaze fell on her. It was intense and searching and hopeful. "You have? Does that mean what I think it does?" Blast. Why did she have to say that?

The only thing that Rose had officially decided over the course of that day was that no matter what happened between her and Carver, she did not want to continue lying and stealing. After meeting Oliver and Elizabeth and the duke, she just couldn't do it anymore.

Chapter Twenty-Nine

Carver walked past Oliver and grabbed Rose's hand. "Rose, are you accepting my proposal?"

Her hands felt soft and warm and tender. Carver had been able to sense all day that Rose wished for distance and time to think. He had happily given it to her and felt content to wait for her answer forever. But now all contentment fled, and he was desperate for her answer.

Her brows creased and then she looked down to their hands. What did that mean? Was she going to reject him? How could that be? He knew from some deep place within him that they were meant to be together. He released one of her hands so he could lift her chin up. He needed to look into her eyes, to help her feel the connection he knew was there.

"Are you going to marry me?" he asked again.

Those brandy colored eyes burned into his. She didn't say a word, just looked at him. Such depth—such meaning behind her gaze. She looked at him as if she were searching for an answer to something but couldn't find it. "Carver," she said, her words thick before she paused to swallow. She was killing him slowly. "If I become your wife, I'll need to be able to help carry your burdens."

His shoulders relaxed. She was only afraid that she couldn't shoulder the weight he carried? It was understandable. Rose had lived her entire life caring for herself. She was likely weary and tired, and if he married her, he would make sure that she never had to feel the weight of them again. And absolutely never make her responsible for his. He would be the husband. He would bear the world for her from then on.

He took her face in his hands. Her wide searching eyes looked into his. "Rose, my love. You needn't worry yourself about that. If you allow me to become your husband, you will never need to carry a single one of my burdens." What else could he say to ease her mind? "Any weight I carry is my own. I will make sure that you are happy and well taken care of. It won't be the other way around." Never had his thoughts come out so clearly before. So why did her eyes drop away like that? And why did it feel like she was pulling away from him?

His doubt rang in his ears as he waited for her answer. Rose opened her mouth to speak but then movement toward the door caught both of their eyes. *Oliver*. He was attempting to discreetly shuffle toward the door. He had completely forgotten Oliver was still in the room.

Oliver froze when he realized they were both looking at him. He grinned tensely and gestured his thumb over his shoulder. "I was just leaving." He looked like he was going to turn around and leave but then he paused a second and his eyebrows drew together looking thoughtful and serious. "Kenny, I...I concede." And then he smirked. "But I'm not sorry I punched you." Then he looked at Rose and smiled. "As for you, Daphney, or Kitty, or Rose or whoever you are...don't worry about what happened between us. I'll be over it soon."

She smiled looking both emotional and relieved. "Thank you, Oliver." Rose looked back at Carver, an unnerving sadness hiding behind her fake smile. "We can talk later. You two should clean up before we go into dinner."

$\sim$

The entire room gasped when the three of them walked back into the drawing room. Carver and Oliver had both changed their shirts and smoothed over their appearances but were not able to hide their various wounds and swelling faces.

"I hope you didn't hold dinner on our account," Carver said to his mother as if nothing in the world had just happened.

The duke crossed his arms and leveled a look at Carver and Oliver. "I think I speak for all of us when I say, what the devil just happened?"

Rose wanted to sink into the couch. She wasn't ready to tell them everything. Not yet. Maybe not ever. But definitely not yet.

But what other choice did she have? She opened her mouth to let the ugly and shameful truth fall out but Oliver spoke first. "It's an embarrassing tale that I'd rather not discuss but Kenny and Miss Bellows played a rather—" he peeked at Rose from the corner of his eye, "realistic prank on me. I found out and gave Kensworth his just deserts for it." Relief flooded her and her regard for Oliver only grew. He didn't have to say that. He had no reason to be kind to her.

"I see," said the duke only looking mildly pacified and still a little skeptical.

Lord Hatley laughed from the corner of the room. "I'm impressed you managed to land him a punch, Turner. I would have liked to see that."

"So would I," said Mary with a twinkle that Rose had never seen on the woman before.

Carver chuckled but didn't have time to defend himself before the duchess gave them both a maternal scowl. "Well, I think you two look like overgrown children in need of reprimanding. I'm tempted to tie your legs together for the rest of the evening like I did when you two quarreled as boys."

The duke laughed this time. "But Darling, don't you remember that it never seemed to punish them as much as it made them laugh over trying to coordinate their steps and falling over?"

She smiled and moved to stand beside the duke, wrapping her

hands around his arm. "Of course. That was the point. Did you think it was supposed to be a punishment?"

He smiled a fond warm smile down at the duchess and said, "You are a brilliant woman."

"Yes, I know," she said with a smirk.

The love between the duke and duchess made Rose ache. She ached because it was beginning to feel like she would never experience a love that was long and lasting and able to weather the harsh storms of life.

In the library, Carver had confirmed her fears. Even if she married him, he would not share his grief with her. He would continue through life masking his pain, pretending to be a perfect and happy man. Rose didn't want a perfect man. She didn't want a hero. It might be nice at first, but eventually it would grow old. Tiring. She would always feel like there was a wall between them. But she loved him. And her heart hurt to think of ever having to say goodbye to him. Maybe she could learn to be the only one in a relationship who needed help. The only one to be vulnerable. But another whisper somewhere within her said it would never work.

"We can go into dinner just as soon as Elizabeth comes down," said the duchess. "Her maid sent word that she had something of a wardrobe issue and needed a moment to recover it." It seemed that everyone was having an odd night.

An uncomfortable silence settled over the room and Rose resisted the urge to look at Carver. She was afraid he would see her disappointment. Her uncertainty.

Finally, Elizabeth entered the drawing room. Rose had to hide her surprise at the vision of vivacious beauty in front of her. She tossed a sideways glance to the duchess and found that her wide eyed reaction mimicked Rose's. The entire family looked fascinated by Elizabeth's transformation. Of course, she had been beautiful before, but in that pale pink dress hugging her figure, with a slightly lower neckline, she looked like *a woman*. Elizabeth's golden tresses were even arranged in a more intricate and fashionable style, and the glittering sapphire on her neck only enhanced the intensity of her bright blue eyes.

But the most striking change was that a smile had replaced the scowl that had accompanied her most of the week. What could have inspired such a change? But when Oliver stood up with a grin and crossed to Elizabeth, the answer was obvious.

He smiled and kissed her hand, not just the air above it. "Hello, Little Lizzie," said Oliver.

Rose saw Elizabeth's smile drop before she quickly recovered it and tossed Oliver a cutting remark about his swollen bottom lip making him look even uglier than before. But Oliver laughed and the whole room seemed to lose interest in the conversation. Apparently, it was nothing new to them.

"How long has Elizabeth been in love with Oliver?" Rose whispered to Carver as they sat down to dinner.

Carver looked sharply down at her with creased brows. The surprise in his eyes was real. "Elizabeth doesn't love Oliver. The two act more like brother and sister than she and I do. They've been that way since Oliver and I started spending our summers here during our Eton years."

Rose turned her attention down to the first course of cream soup, but couldn't keep her eyes from moving toward Oliver and Elizabeth.. And the more she saw, the more certain she was that Carver had no idea what he was talking about. Rose now knew what it was to be in love. And the look that Elizabeth gave Oliver when he wasn't paying attention—the look of longing, pain, and hope all mixed together—was the look of a woman very much in love with a man who didn't return her affection.

Rose suddenly realized that she had never actually told Carver that she loved him after he had declared himself. Why hadn't she said the words back? Even if she hadn't accepted his marriage at the time, she should have at least told him that she returned his regard. What had she said as a reply? *Thank you.* She cringed.

She peeked up at the strong handsome man beside her. He didn't know she was watching him, and he looked...sad. His shoulder hung a little heavier and his brows were pulled together. He looked weary and exhausted. Rose wished more than anything that he would let her in.

Let her take care of him just as much as he would take care of her. There was so much about each other that they both still didn't know. Of course, if she married him, they would have the rest of their lives to figure those things out. Rose didn't need to know them all before they married. She just needed to know that there was the potential for her to learn them.

Carver had fully accepted her as she was. She wanted to be able to do the same for him.

Chapter Thirty

C arver's eyes fluttered open to the sight of Oliver hovering over his bed. "Blast!" He jumped and wielded his coverlet as if it were a shield rather than a piece of fabric.

"Effective," Oliver said dryly and with a raised eyebrow. "If I had been attempting to murder you my plans would surely have been thwarted now."

Carver rolled his eyes and tossed his shield away. "I have not missed your early morning wake up calls." He scraped his hands over his face, trying to cast off the last bit of sleep.

"Are you going to get up, or should I get in there with you?"

"I'd rather you didn't." His feet met the cold floor. Oliver had Carver's robe at the ready and tossed it at him. "I'm beginning to think you've missed your calling, Olly. Would you consider taking Brandon's position? At least then your presence in the morning would be justified."

Oliver sunk into the chair across the room. "You couldn't afford me," said Oliver with a smirk. "Alright. From the top. How did you find Rose?"

Carver grinned and dropped into the other leather chair across from the one Oliver was in. "She found me." His fingers traced the cracks in the leather. "Her accomplice got his information mixed up and sent her to my home instead of Newburry's. She arrived on my doorstep with a pillow stuffed under her dress and the unfortunate news that unless I paid her off handsomely, word of my impending fatherhood would be made known to London."

Oliver laughed just as Carver suspected he would. "What I wouldn't give to have seen your face. No doubt Newburry would have pushed his money into her purse faster than she could snap. But you haven't so much as flirted with a woman since—," Oliver caught himself, "—well, in a long time. So did you call her out on it right away?"

Carver then poured out the tale of the carriage ride, the night in the stables, how he fell in love with her almost instantly, and everything else leading up to the moment of Oliver's untimely appearance.

"I cannot believe you're engaged," said Oliver. "When I left you in London only a week ago, you were set against the idea of ever courting again." But that was before he had met Rose — the woman who made his heart race and his arms ache to hold her.

A quiet fear overtook him and his smile dropped. "I'm not engaged yet. She hasn't given me an answer." And at this point, he wasn't so sure that he wanted to hear the answer she was going to give him.

"I know. I was there for that little chat, if you'll remember," Oliver smirked with too much amusement and then winced as he touched his fingers to his cut lip. "But I don't think you need to worry. She'll accept you. A woman doesn't look at a man the way she looks at you and not hope for a future with him." Was that true? Did Rose look at him with longing? He didn't even know if the woman loved him or not.

"I'm happy for you, Kenny. And I hope you know that Claire would be, too." At the mention of Claire, Carver's whole body stiffened. He wasn't thinking of Rose anymore.

Would there ever come a time when the sound of Claire's name would not affect him in that way? He was in love with another woman for, goodness' sake. That should be enough to ease the pain. He had thought, by confessing his feelings to Rose and proposing, his heart would heal. So why didn't he feel healed yet? He had no doubt that his love for Rose was real and lasting, but his heart still ached for Claire with a fierce, unstoppable determination. And that made him feel like the worst sort of man.

"I know that look," said Oliver, pulling Carver from his thoughts.

"What look?"

"The, *I'm wallowing in what could have been*, look."

Carver smirked. "Really, Oliver. Your sympathy is just too much. You'll put me to the blush if you keep it up." But Oliver didn't laugh like he had anticipated. Oliver just leaned back and eyed Carver beneath creased brows.

Carver couldn't take it anymore. "What?"

"I'm not sure yet."

"Well, stop it. You're looking at me like I'm a drowning puppy."

"How's it been being back home?" Carver had wondered how long it would take Oliver to dive into that topic. Sometimes it was deucedly inconvenient having a friend who had grown up with him and knew almost every aspect of his life.

"Obviously, it's been entertaining," he tried for a smile.

"Have you been sleeping?"

"Yes, darling. A solid eight hours every night."

"The circles under your eyes tell me you're lying." Oh, now he was a physician, too? Apparently, he was a good one because Carver actually was lying. He had barely slept more than two hours every night. But that wasn't exactly anything new.

"Are you trying to tell me my beauty is wilting?"

"Would you like to go ten more rounds or will you cut line and tell me how the deuce you're really doing?"

Carver looked to Oliver at first with a smirk, ready to shoot off another joke. But then his smile faded and his shoulders slumped. He didn't want to admit that he wasn't doing well. Especially since in someways, he really was doing better. He was laughing more. He was in love with a beautiful woman. He was throwing himself headfirst into a new life. Wasn't that what everyone meant by moving on and healing? But always in the back of his mind, was *Claire*. Her light blue eyes still plagued his dreams and the memories of all they had planned together clawed at his determination to put her out of his mind.

"I'm...fine." Some days he felt finer than others. When he was with Rose, he felt lighter, happier, like everything was right with the world and all of his pieces were in place. But when he was away from her...the pain would find him again and guilt's heavy hand pressed on him.

Oliver's eyebrow raised, but he looked unimpressed. "Really? You don't look fine right now. You look devilish, and that's putting it mildly."

"Is this the sort of flattery you give ladies? I can see why you're still a bachelor."

Oliver rolled his eyes and shifted further into his seat. "Well, since you're clearly not in a mood to answer me honestly, we might as well talk about something else." Yes. Anything.

"If you insist. By the way I never apologized for stealing your bride out from under your nose. Do you think you'll recover?"

A smile grew on Oliver's mouth. Carver knew that he was safe from returning to the previous undesired conversation. "I think we both know it won't take me long to bounce back from losing out on Kitty— er—Rose's perfection." That was the truth. Oliver was forever falling in love with some new lovely female. The only problem was that he usually fell out of love as quick as he fell into it. Enchanted one night, horrified the next. Carver was used to the pattern.

"Olly, how *do* you manage to find so many perfect women in such a short span of time?" Oliver wasn't exactly a rake. But the man teetered terribly close to the line.

"It is a blessing, indeed," said Oliver with mock sincerity. "If only they remained perfect, I might actually be able to shackle my leg to one of them."

Carver thought of several of Oliver's latest loves. "What was wrong with the woman you walked with in Hyde Park? If I remember correctly, you spent nearly every morning with her for a week."

"Unbearable laugh. Never heard such a nasally thing." It was always something ridiculous that eventually turned him off to a lady.

"And the one they called The Exquisite?"

"Exquisitely dull."

"Miss Oak?"

"Too mousy," Oliver said, as if Carver should know what the devil a term like mousy would even refer to.

Carver wondered if Oliver would ever find the right woman. There seemed to be something tragically wrong with every female he met. Oliver was not critical by nature. He was fairly easy to please, in fact. But when it came to women, it was almost as if he had a perfect imaginary ideal woman who he was measuring everyone else against. If such a woman really existed, Oliver had never mentioned the woman to him.

"Do you think Lizzie is awake yet? I was hoping she and I could get a ride in before she needs to get ready for the ball tonight." Carver narrowed his eyes on Oliver. Odd that he would think of Elizabeth after the conversation they had just had.

"What have I done to earn that look?" asked Oliver.

"Nothing. It's just..." Carver sat up straighter and leaned toward Oliver as if he were seeing something for the first time. He searched the man's eyes, hoping to find the answer he was looking for. But the blank look Oliver returned told him nothing. Absolutely nothing. He sat back. "Never mind." He was being stupid. Whatever Rose thought she saw between his sister and his friend was simply the comfort of familiarity between old friends. Nothing to be worried about.

Oliver chuckled and stood up. "Alright, then. I'll go see if I can find her."

"But don't go in her room," Carver blurted out, startling Oliver as well as himself.

Apparently, he felt a little worried.

Oliver blinked at him as if Carver had taken leave of his senses. "No..." he said. "Of course not. What's gotten into you, Kenny?"

Carver shook his head. "Nothing. I suppose Rose just has me a bit on edge." He paused and rubbed his face again. "I wish to God that she would give me an answer. I have this devilish feeling that she's going to slip out during the night without me knowing. I just want her to give me the chance to love her like she deserves."

That was partly why he hadn't been sleeping. Ignoring the thought that he might truly be losing his mind, Carver woke up almost every hour last night and went to listen at Rose's door until he heard a rustle or some sort of indication that she was still inside. Still hadn't given up on him.

Even once he had cracked the door and peeked in just long enough to be reassured that she was safely under her covers. Was that a normal thing to do? But the fact that he would rather die than have anyone find out about his snooping told him that it probably wasn't.

The more he grew to love Rose, the more he worried that he would lose her, just like he had Claire. And he refused to let that happen again. He refused to fail Rose the way he failed Claire.

He felt Oliver's hand grasp his shoulder and jostle him a little. "You're going to be okay. No matter what Rose's answer is." Not exactly the positive reinforcement he was looking for.

Chapter Thirty-One

R ose ran her fingers down the fine champagne silk gown, savoring its luxurious feel. Elizabeth's maid had dropped the gown off earlier that afternoon with the specifications that it be altered for Rose's shorter height so she could wear it to the ball tonight. It was the kindest of gestures, and yet Rose's pride still prickled at the realization that Elizabeth had noticed her wardrobe and found it lacking. And standing there in front of the looking glass in a ridiculously beautiful dress with her hair curled, braided and pinned in the most elaborate arrangement she had ever worn, she almost didn't recognize herself.

She smoothed the fabric's nonexistent wrinkles for the hundredth time. This didn't look like her. She no longer bore the dark circles under her eyes from the endless string of sleepless nights. Her cheeks were tinged with a slight blush of excitement and her cheekbones didn't seem to stick out so far. Rose hadn't been forced to skip a meal the entire week, and her body was certainly responding favorably to the effect.

She unrolled one of her long evening gloves—that Elizabeth had also provided—until she could once again see the purple twisted scar of her palm. The proof that she was still the same little urchin from the streets. The wounds in her heart were healing, but part of her was thankful that the wounds on her body never would. She would need them in the months to come.

Because of those wounds, Rose had learned how to be strong, how to take care of those in need and to keep going when she wanted to give up. It was a small sort of comfort to know that those physical reminders would never let her forget. Rose pulled her glove back up and smiled. It was fine that she was different now. Good, even.

A scratch sounded at the door followed by Elizabeth's head of blond curls peeking inside. "May I come in?"

"Of course," Rose said with a smile.

The dazzling Elizabeth stepped through the door revealing her cream gown with white satin overlay. She walked to Rose and touched the sleeve of Rose's gown. "Carver was right, gold brings out your eyes."

Rose ignored the blush she felt creeping up her neck at the thought of Carver describing her eyes. "Elizabeth, I can't thank you enough for this dress. It's lovely."

Elizabeth waved a hand and crossed to her side. "It looks much better on you than it would have looked on me."

Rose's brows tucked together and apprehension broke over her. "Do you mean this was a new dress of yours?" She had assumed it was a dress that Elizabeth had worn before and no longer needed. If Rose had known the dress had never been worn, she never would have accepted it.

Elizabeth reached up and began adjusting a few of the pins in Rose's hair. An odd sense of sisterly affection flooded Rose's heart. It was a feeling that she hadn't realized she had been missing out on. "I was supposed to wear it for my come out this season in town. But I like it much better on you," said Elizabeth. "And before you open your mouth to protest again, just know that the gold washed me out in the very worst way so really you're doing me a favor by taking it off of my hands." The girl smiled mischievously.

Rose ought to have given it back. But the truth was, she really did like the dress and there was no time left to change before the ball. Rose's stomach fluttered with nervous anticipation. Soon she would walk into the doors of the very first ball where she would truly be welcome. And it would be especially memorable because she had decided to accept Carver's proposal.

After tossing and turning in her bed the entire night before, Rose had decided she was being unfair to Carver, to expect him to completely open up to her over the course of one week. To be honest, she couldn't even believe she had opened up to him as much as she had. Even the very idea that the man would propose to her after only a single week of acquaintance was ridiculous. She couldn't expect too much ridiculousness at one time.

She felt lighter now that she had made her decision. So light she felt as if she could fly. Carver loved her, she loved him, and that was enough. They would figure out the rest as they went along.

The ball was a disaster. Nothing so far that evening had gone as she'd hoped. Dinner before the ball had not been the informal relaxed meal she had grown accustomed to enjoying with Carver's family. Rather, with all of the duke's elite friends and their esteemed wives packed around the table it had more closely resembled a session in the House of Lords. She and Oliver seemed to be the only people at the table who did not have a title before their name.

Rose would not have minded had she been at Carver's side. But as it was, the duchess had followed strict seating protocols and Rose found herself nearly at the bottom of the table and at least seven place settings away from the man she loved. The elderly yet exuberant vicar seated to her right had held her in such confined conversation for nearly the entire dinner that Rose had barely been able to even look in Carver's direction. And the baron seated at her left was so large that she could not have seen around the man had she even wished to sneak a glance at Carver.

After dinner, things had only gotten worse. The baron practically snatched her arm and begged to escort her into the ballroom, leaving her little room to actually refuse him. Carver was then left to escort the obnoxiously beautiful and doting Lady Sophia—who had fluttered her lashes at Carver all evening—into the ballroom. From there, Rose had been swept around the ballroom and introduced to nearly every person she would never care about in a million years instead of having any one-on-one time with the man she really wanted to see.

The ballroom was packed full of dapper gentleman and beautifully dressed ladies, but Carver was no where to be found. For the most part, Rose had been able to keep track of him above the heads of the rest of the guests. Where had he gone? Rose knew he had been trying to make his way to her the entire night. The one time they had made eye contact, he had smiled apologetically and gestured toward a spot in the room for them to meet, only for him to be intercepted and accosted by yet another matron with too many feathers waving obnoxiously in her hair.

But even when she wasn't looking at him she could feel the warmth of his gaze on her. It made her feel grounded and secure despite the fact that he was not beside her. Now, she had lost him and felt as if she were being tossed around in the ocean rather than standing against the wall of a crowded ballroom.

Rose felt stuck between two worlds, not truly belonging in either one. She had left the world of stealing and conning behind her, and seemingly along with that old life, her confidence. She knew without a doubt that she could slip the diamond bracelet off of the wrist of that slightly tipsy woman standing in front of her. She could do it in three seconds flat without anyone suspecting a thing. And the boisterous rake in the corner would be all to easy to convince out the emerald pin glittering from the center of his cravat. But no, she didn't want to do those things anymore.

But neither was she ready to be herself in such a place. She didn't even know how. The only man she had ever been truly herself in front of was absent. And the more time she spent away from him in that ball-room, the more she began to doubt again her decision to abandon her old life. She felt weary from all of the doubting. If only she could talk to Carver, hear his reassuring voice.

Rose's eyes darted around the room, hoping to find those striking grey eyes looking back at her. Instead, across the room, she found the piercing glare of Miss Gardener's haughty smirk. The odd, smug look in Miss Gardener's eyes was enough to make Rose look down at the glass of lemonade she was holding and contemplate the probability that the woman had spat in it. She set the lemonade down and decided to get some air.

She headed for the room the duchess had set aside as a ladies' retiring room, but decided to keep walking and slipped instead into an empty hallway. It was dark, but she didn't mind. She pressed her back to the wall and her hands to her cheeks in attempt to cool her body. The lights and sounds of the ball trickled into the hallway, not fully reaching her. Tears formed at the backs of her eyes as she thought about the disappointment she felt from the night.

She closed her eyes and let the salty tears drip down her cheeks and over her lips. She was stupid to have even considered a life with Carver. She couldn't even manage spending an hour in a ballroom without him.

"Crying at a ball is strictly forbidden." The husky rumble of Carver's voice washed over Rose like a sea of comfort. He was there. And all of her doubts vanished beneath his words.

"Carver," she whispered and opened her eyes.

He stepped close to her, his cool masculine scent wrapping around her as he wiped the tears from her cheeks. "My love," he leaned in and whispered over her lips. Rose placed her hands on his chest and relished the feel of his heart pounding against her hand. "I've been trying to get to you all night." His arm wrapped around her waist and pulled her closer, locking her in for what she hoped could be forever.

She smiled and breathed in his nearness. "You found me."

Rose fidgeted with the gold buttons of his dark blue evening jacket before looking up to meet his impassioned gaze. Her heart raced as he bent his head forward. And then finally, his lips met hers with such an aching tenderness that she feared her legs would give out beneath her. Everything felt right. Whole. Secure. She pushed her hands up over his strong shoulders and clasped them behind his neck, trying to memorize how his lips felt pressing into hers, never wanting the kiss to end. But the sound of a man clearing his throat ended it.

Carver broke away from her and squinted into the dark. "Robert," said Carver, clearly as perturbed by the interruption as she was. The music and light was spilling out the ballroom and illuminating over Robert's amused expression. "Well, Kensworth. It's a dashed good thing you're going to marry that girl or else I would be forced to call you out for a kiss like that."

"Go away, Robert."

"Not a chance, young blood." It was evident that the married earl was enjoying his power over Carver. Rose was glad she had the cover of darkness to hide her blush. "Her Grace is requesting your presence and I think now is the perfect time to hand you over to her," said Lord Hatley.

"I don't think I need to remind you, Robert, of all the times I found you stealing a kiss from my sister during your courtship and betrothal." Carver looked every bit the dashing gentleman in his tight fitting jacket, dove pantaloons, and imposing physique. But he sounded like a guilty boy.

Robert smirked. "You get one minute, Kensworth. After that, I come looking for you." He turned to walk back into the ballroom but called back, "And your clock started thirty seconds ago."

Rose pressed her lips together. That was hardly enough time to declare her love—but she would try.

But she couldn't because in the next moment, Carver was kissing her again. This time with enough fervency to wipe every single thought from her mind. With a groan he broke away and took a step back. "If I don't go he really will come looking for me. And likely bring my father for assistance," said Carver, his mouth curving into an impish grin.

"Go," she said, with her own grin. Rose didn't feel worried about not being able to find him in the ballroom again. Everything was going to be okay. She just knew it.

He reached out and ran his thumb across her cheek, looking reluctant to leave. "No more tears?"

She leaned her face into his hand and kissed his wrist. "No more tears."

He smiled that breathtaking smile, his eyes crinkling in the corners. "I'll come find you later." And then he was gone.

Rose leaned her head against the wall and attempted to catch her breath and still her racing heart. She smiled and smoothed a hand over the front of her dress before making her way back toward the ballroom. Life was going to be different, but she was feeling more optimistic that Carver would be patient with her as she adjusted. They would find a new normal. A balance between who she had been and who she was becoming.

Before she stepped back through the door of the ballroom, her eye snagged on someone familiar. She froze and took a sharp inhale of breath. There, standing with Miss Gardener, and engaged in a quiet conversation was a familiar man. A tall, boyish looking man. The man she had seen crossing the street in London. It was the Bow Street runner.

Mind spinning, Rose slunk back into the shadows. How had he found her? But the answer was obvious. Miss Gardener must have made good on her word and begun digging into who Rose really was. But how, in so few days? It would certainly explain that villainous smile the woman had given her earlier in the night. Miss Gardener had planned a trap.

But what was it? To lead the runner to her in the middle of the ball, having her ousted as a wanted criminal in front of everyone? Did Miss Gardener really think that Carver would then view her as some sort of hero and wish to marry her instead of Rose? No. Most likely the woman would never reveal that she was the one to have set the runner on her scent. She wouldn't need to since he had been hunting her these past three years.

Rose's blood whooshed through her ears as she debated her options. She forced herself to breathe.

She peeked back into the ballroom and spotted Carver on the opposite side of the ballroom. His back was to her as he spoke with his parents and another couple. Her heart sunk. She wouldn't be able to get his attention and she definitely wouldn't be able to make it across the ballroom without being seen.

Her eyes scanned the rest of the room, taking a moment to land on each one of Carver's family members. Elizabeth was smiling and dancing a cotillion with Oliver. Robert and Mary stood together, a little away from everyone else. He smiled fondly at his wife and then kissed her hand as she gently rubbed her hand across her growing midsection. Kate was also laughing and dancing with a young gentleman—no doubt enjoying the freedom of attending her first ball. Everyone was happy.

Rose's heart broke. She had to leave. There was no doubt in her mind that Carver would have told her to stay. He would have insisted that he and his family would stand by her and help her face whatever storm lay before her. She knew he would be right, which was why she had to leave.

A scandal like she would bring into the family would ruin them— ruin Elizabeth and Kate's chances of making a suitable match during their Seasons and cause stress and potential harm to Mary's pregnancy. The duke and duchess's titles would have been shamed, ridiculed, and bandied about the town. And then there was Carver. Her wonderful loving Carver who deserved every chance of happiness he could find. Not to be tied to a woman as shameful as her. No. Her week was up. It was time to go.

Tears burned her eyes as she took one last look at Carver. His piercing grey eyes were looking around the ballroom for her. She took a step back. And then another. And another until she bumped into a wall. Rose pressed her fingers to her mouth to stifle the sob growing within her and began to run down the hallway.

Chapter Thirty-Two

"My lord, there is a gentleman in the parlor requesting to see you," said Henley, pulling Carver to the side of the loud ballroom.

"Did he give his name?" asked Carver.

"Yes, my lord. Mr. Fenton is his name."

Carver's brows pulled together as he eyed Henley. "To see me? Are you certain he didn't wish to see His Grace?" He didn't recall ever having met a Mr. Fenton.

Henley nodded. "Yes, my lord. He specifically asked for Lord Kensworth." Odd. What the devil could be so urgent that a man would request an audience with him during his father's ball? And where was Rose? He hadn't seen her once since he left her in the hallway.

Even as he threaded his way through the crowded ballroom, his thoughts remained on that incredible kiss. He hadn't been able to take his mind off it or the beautiful woman he had shared it with. He hadn't intended to kiss her. But when he found her alone and crying in the hallway, it had felt like the right thing to do. The woman had been stealing his breath all evening. Kissing her felt like coming home. He loved her and could not make her his wife soon enough.

Henley preceded him into the yellow parlor that the family reserved for private audiences. "Lord Kensworth to see you, sir." Carver stepped into the room and Henley left, closing the door behind him.

Carver eyed the damp, short man before him. Henley had obviously taken his coat and hat already but his snug jacket looked soaked through as well. Apparently, this man had just arrived and was not an invited guest.

"Ah, Kensworth!" said the man. "Seems you and I have some business to discuss. Where is she? No sense trying to pull the wool over my eyes. I know you've got her here, so you might as well make a clean breast of it and I promise I won't be too harsh with you."

Carver tried to hide the astonishment he felt at the impertinent words that flew out of this little round man's mouth. Who the devil was he, anyway? And what authority did he have to be harsh with him?

Carver kept his voice level and raised a brow. "It would appear you have the advantage of me, sir. I don't believe I have ever had the pleasure of making your acquaintance before."

The man chuckled making his round belly bounce under his brown wet jacket. "Those are some mighty flowery words you've got there m'lord, but I'd rather put the civil whiskers away if you don't mind." Carver could barely keep his shock from showing on his mouth any longer "I'm Miss Daphney Bellows' uncle, you see. And as such I demand to know what it is you've done with m'niece."

Carver froze. His first thought was that Rose didn't have any living family. But then he realized that the man had claimed to be *Daphney's* uncle not *Rose's* uncle. Realization shot through him.

He advanced toward the man, towering over him and speaking low. Low enough so that if any servants were lurking behind the door, they would not be able to hear his words. "Is it possible, sir, that you are in fact her *Uncle Felix?*"

The man's eyes narrowed, making the deep lines around his eyes even more pronounced and his expression skeptical. "How is it you learned that name?"

Carver smiled. "Rose has told me all about you."

Now it was Felix's turn to look shocked. The man spoke, this time with a thick Scottish brogue that had conveniently been missing before. "Rosie girl? Told ya her name, did she? Does that mean you found her out?"

Carver nodded and did not try to hide the affection he felt for Rose. "She told me everything. How long did it take you to find out that you sent her to the wrong earl's house?"

"No more than a day. When the lass didn't show up to our meeting place, I knew something went wrong. But I was already a day's journey outside of London and then those tight lipped servants of yours wouldn't tell me a blasted thing about where you'd gone. And by the time I finally discovered where you'd taken her, I learned something else as well."

"And what's that?"

"I'm assuming I can trust you since Rosie told you everything?"

"You can. And I...Well, the truth is, I love Rose very much."

Felix eyed him thoughtfully for a moment before he looked around the room and said, "Then you should know she's in danger here."

Carver felt his body stiffen. "Why? What's happened?" He felt a surge of protective energy shoot through his veins.

"I have reason to believe that a Bow Street runner left London yesterday with the purpose of coming to Dalton Park."

"How do you know that?"

Felix rocked back and forth on his heels one time as if he were too proud of what he was going to say next to contain it. "This particular runner has been chasing her for years. Rosie doesn't know it, but I've been having the man watched by a few of my own friends, keeping me apprised of his movements."

"And you think he's coming after Rose?"

"I know he is," said Felix. "Someone must've grown suspicious of our girl and tipped him off." The man's gaze grew hard. "If he finds her, m'lord, there's no doubt about it—she'll be clapped up or hung. The girl's got too good of a heart to be thrown away like that."

Carver would never let that happen to her. Surely, even if the runner found her, there was something that could be done? Or, that his father could do.

Carver turned on his heels and headed for the door. "We need to find Rose." Having this new information made him feel increasingly uneasy about the fact that he hadn't seen Rose since their time in the hallway. He needed to find her immediately.

"Henley," he said as soon as he stepped out into the corridor. "Have you seen, R—Daphney?"

The nervous look that Henley gave him only added to his unease. "Yes, my lord. Well...not personally, my lord—that is, Daniel, a footman came to me while you were in with Mr. Fenton and said that he saw Miss Bellows leave out of the servant's entrance earlier wearing her cloak." The butler's lips pressed into a tight line before adding, "And...I believe she also had her valise on her person, my lord."

"She must have seen the runner," said Felix.

Carver's stomach sunk to his feet. Did that mean she was gone? She had left without telling him? "How long ago did she leave, Henley?"

"About an hour ago, my lord."

"An hour!" his hand scraped through his hair as he went over his options. "Henley, send for my horse to be saddled. If I go now, I can overtake her. She will not have gotten far by foot."

"Do you not keep a stocked stable, my lord?" asked Felix. "If I know my Rosie she would never have left by foot if there was a prancer nearby she could take." Blast. He was right.

Rose would have most definitely taken a horse. That was exactly what she had planned to do the night he had caught her in the stables. Dread settled in his stomach. What if...but before his mind had time to formulate any more thoughts, his legs were propelling him down the stairs, taking them two and three at a time. His boots thudded against the stone floor as he quickly moved through the servants hall. "Has anyone seen Miss Bellows since she left an hour ago?" he asked loudly to any servants who were nearby.

"No, my lord," several replied.

Carver threw open the old wooden door of the servant's entrance.

The hinges screeched with protest. As if things could not get worse, outside he found rain and sleet coming down in heavy sheets. A tense breath fell out of his mouth and formed a cloud in front of his face. The temperatures were freezing. Surely Rose had not gone out there? Maybe if he went upstairs, he would find her safely tucked into her bed. But deep down he knew that if he looked in her room, all he would find was an empty bedchamber and the pain that he never seemed to escape.

Behind him he could hear Felix's quick approaching footsteps. He, too, paused at the alarming sight beyond the door. "No one should be out in those temperatures," said Felix, voicing Carver's same thoughts. "I had a blasted time of it and it wasn't even sleeting then."

Henley came running down the stairs, out of breath, with Carver's great coat and hat. "My lord! You'll be needing these."

Carver threw on his coat and hat and ran out into the freezing rain toward the stables. He pushed open the door and commanded that his horse be saddled, and quickly. Only a moment later a stable boy came running out of a stall. "Right away, m'lord!"

Carver paced back and forth, considering his options. Where would Rose go? The nearest inn was at least ten miles away. She could never have made it that far in an hour. And definitely not at night, in this weather. He chose to hope for the best. Rose was a smart woman. Most likely, she had stopped and taken shelter as soon as the weather had taken a turn.

"My lord!" The stable boy came running back. "Thunder's not in his stall."

Rose. No. She promised.

Anger, fear, and helplessness all warred within him. She had taken his horse, and although she was a fine horsewoman, he knew that Thunder spooked too easily during storms. The sound of hooves outside of the stable interrupted his thoughts. He heard the familiar whinny of his horse.

Relief flooded him. She had come back. Carver ran to the door and out into the rain, but any hope he had was dashed to bits when he found Thunder standing alone in the stable yard with an empty, askew saddle. "No!" he yelled into the rain. Despair began to take its grip, but he refused to allow his mind to picture his worst fears.

Carver ran as fast as his legs would allow back into the servant's hall. Felix was in the process of pulling on his own coat and hat when Carver stepped into the room, his muddy boots sloshing onto the floor. "Her horse has returned without her." Carver saw the fear he felt mirrored in Felix's eyes.

"We'll find her," said Felix as he finished shoving his arm into his sleeve.

Carver turned his attention to his butler and the few gathered servants. "We need to send out a search party." He hoped he looked calm and assured, and that no one could tell he was trembling beneath his jacket. "It appears that Miss Bellows has been tossed from her horse and is lost somewhere on the grounds." He pointed in the direction of a footman, allowing his need to be useful to dominate rather than letting his fear cripple him. "You. Go fetch His Grace, Lord Hatley and Mr. Turner. Be quick about it, but whatever you do, appear calm and say nothing to anyone about the situation." The footman nodded and darted up the stairs. "You two," he said to the worried looking chambermaids, "have a fire lit in Miss Bellows' room, and ready plenty of blankets for when she returns." Because she would return. There was simply no other option.

Carver and Felix were discussing a strategy for searching the grounds when his father, Robert, and Oliver came running down the stairs.

"What's happened?" his father asked, concern surging through his words.

It was time his father knew the truth. This was certainly not how he had planned to tell his father, but it was imperative that he knew all of the details. He could no longer hide from his father's eyes. From the memories. From the pain he felt when he saw his father's empathy. He needed him.

As quickly and in as few words as possible, Carver explained the entire situation. When he had finished relaying the details, his father stepped in front of him and laid a hand on his shoulder. Carver really looked into his father's eyes for the first time in years. His father smiled and Carver felt a weight fall off of him. "Don't lose hope, son. We'll find her." He held his father's gaze for several moments. *We'll find her.* He wasn't alone anymore. He didn't have to face whatever was to come by himself.

Chapter Thirty-Three

"I'll take the north grounds," Carver called out over the loud rain, knowing that was the way Rose was most likely to ride since it led toward the main road.

"We'll cover the East and West!" Oliver shouted back. It was just Oliver, Robert, and himself who would be riding out to find Rose. They decided that Felix should stay at the servant's entrance in case Rose returned while they were gone, and his father planned to find the runner and do all that he could to clear Rose's name before she returned.

All three men nodded their understanding before Carver kicked Thunder, sending him running into the harsh storm.

It was nearly impossible to see through the dense wall of rain, but Carver did not stop his pursuit. He would not stop looking until he found Rose. He never should have left her alone in that hallway. He should have insisted that she stay by his side and come back into the ballroom. He remembered her tears. Was that why she had been crying? Had she heard about the runner and been planning on leaving even then? Why had he not asked her why she was crying? There was no way he would ever be able to forgive himself if something happened to Rose.

Thunder's hooves pounded the ground, mimicking the sounds of the roaring winter storm. As they approached the forest line, Carver began to yell for Rose, but he knew the chances of her hearing him above the rain and wind were slim.

Veering Thunder down the path that Rose would have taken to reach the main road, Carver continued to yell with everything his voice had. Trying to push away the horrifying possibilities of what could have befallen Rose became more difficult with each passing second. A panic started to settle deep within him as his eyes raked over the grounds with no signs of the woman he loved.

But something in him knew she was out there. She was in trouble, and she was slipping from him. Somehow he knew it. And he was going to lose her just like he had lost Claire.

He continued to raise his voice above the storm, slowing Thunder's pace to get a more steady look around him. A small cluster of trees caught his attention. He squinted through the rain, willing his eyes to see what they couldn't. He placed a hand at his brows, trying to aid his hat in shielding his eyes from the pelting rain. He spotted a shadowed object lying under a tree. He squinted harder. *Rose!*

Carver put his heel in Thunder's side and galloped to the tree. The horse had barely stopped before Carver jumped from the saddle and fell onto his knees beside Rose. She was lying on her back, motionless under the tree.

"Rose! Rose!" he said, pushing the freezing wet hair out of her face. She didn't move. Her cloak and dress were completely soaked and her skin was ice cold beneath his touch. He leaned his ear in close to her mouth but he couldn't make out whether she was breathing or not over the loud rain. He put his fingers to her neck, praying to feel a beating rhythm.

Thud, thud. Thud, thud.

It was slow and weak but she was alive. Carver took off his coat and wrapped it around Rose before pulling her into his arms. Her skin was ice, but she wasn't shivering. That was a bad sign.

"Rose, darling, wake up! Answer me!" he begged as he held her close trying to offer whatever warmth he could. She didn't answer. Didn't flinch. He needed to get her out of the cold.

The sound of hooves approaching drew his attention as Robert rode up and jumped down from his horse. Carver scooped Rose up in his arms and moved toward Thunder. "She's alive but unconscious," he yelled over the rain. "I need help getting her onto my horse."

Carver placed Rose in Robert's arms before mounting Thunder and then took her up with him. Riding double was hard enough when the other person was holding on, but with Rose unconscious and the relentless dumping rain, it felt nearly impossible. But he had no other choice. Rose was depending on him to make it work.

Resisting the urge to give Thunder his head, Carver held his horse to a slow trot, focusing all of his attentions on keeping Rose pressed to his chest and secured in the saddle.

"You're safe, Rose. I'm taking you home. You're going to be okay," Carver said the words out loud as much for Rose's benefit as his own. But he wasn't even sure if she could hear him. And he wasn't sure he believed them.

After what felt like an agonizing amount of time, Carver made it to the front lawns of the house where one stable hand immediately took Thunder's reins and another held onto Rose until Carver could dismount and pull her down to him.

Cradling her tightly in his arms, he jogged up the front steps where Henley stood holding the door. "Send for a doctor," he said, sweeping through the door.

His mother and sisters had been waiting and moved to his side. Thankfully, it looked as though no one from the ball had been alerted to the situation or else there would have been an unwanted crowd forming around them. He could hear the music from the ballroom playing as he looked down at Rose. The joyful sounds did not match the lifeless picture in his arms.

From the light of the candles, he could see that Rose's skin looked almost blue, and crystals covered her eyelashes. He had only been out the weather for half of an hour, and he was cold to his bones. Rose had been out much longer and was literally freezing to death because of it.

"Carver, take her to her room!" called out his mother, her own eyes wide from the shock of seeing Rose so motionless and pale. There was only one other time in his entire life he had seen such worry in his mother's eyes. This night was beginning to feel far too familiar.

He didn't hesitate, but flew up the stairs taking as many at a time as he could manage until he was outside of Rose's door. He suddenly remembered telling the maid to light the fire in her room. But wasn't there some kind of rule about warming a person slowly after they were freezing? He felt even more helpless. She needed a doctor, someone who knew what they were doing. Not him. He had no choice but to follow his instincts. He instructed a maid to open a window in her room before he carried her inside.

He crossed the room and gently laid her on the bed. He felt her pulse and noted that it was even slower than before. Her eyes were still closed and her wet hair clung to her face and arms.

Carver's fingers started fumbling over the buttons of Rose's cloak with the intent to remove the wet clothes from her fading body as fast as possible.

"Carver, go out!" said his mother as she ran into the room.

He didn't stop. Hands shaking he continued to release any button or fastener that he could find.

Mary, now at his side, caught his hands. His eyes shot to hers, ready to push his sister aside. But the softness in her voice stopped him. "You cannot be the one to do this, Carver. Let us help you." That brought him to his senses. He was not her husband. No matter how pure his intentions, he could not be the one to remove Rose's clothes. Not when his mother and sister were there to do it for him. He had to let them help. "Go change and collect yourself. We will tend to Rose and call you once you can return," said Mary.

Carver did not want to leave Rose's side for anything in the world, but Mary was right. He would be no help in his current state. With a clenched jaw and sodden hair, he nodded his agreement and left the room. Left the woman he loved there to die. Just like the last time.

Chapter Thirty-Four

"You are going to wear a hole in the floor if you keep pacing like that," said Robert. But Carver couldn't bring himself to care, so he continued his back-and-forth track outside of Rose's bedchamber.

"That blasted doctor has been in there a half hour," said Carver. The physician had arrived while Carver was away, changing out of his wet clothes. He had never been so thankful to have a doctor who neighbored the estate in his entire life. But right now, he hated him for closeting himself in that room without giving anyone outside an update.

"That blasted doctor is saving Rose's life," said Robert.

Carver wanted to believe that was true more than anything. But he hadn't seen or heard anything about Rose's condition since he had left her cold, wet, and unconscious on her bed. He never should have left.

"I'm going in," he said, losing his last bit of resolution and heading toward the door.

Robert stepped in front of the door, blocking his way. "No, you are not. She might be indecent."

"Frankly, I could give a dash, Robert. Move out of my way."

Robert didn't budge. "Carver, try to think rationally," he said, putting a firm hand on Carver's shoulder. "When Rose is recovered, how do you think she will feel knowing that you got an eye full while she was unconscious?"

Biting back all of his rebuttals, Carver released a breath. "You're right." It wouldn't be fair to her.

"I know I am," said Robert with a smile that didn't annoy Carver because it was more sympathetic than happy. "Why don't you go eat something?" But it was difficult to eat when he felt like vomiting.

Carver moved to the adjacent wall of Rose's room and sat down on the floor. He shook his head. "I'm not going anywhere until I hear if she's alright."

The minutes passed at a grueling pace. No one came or went out of Rose's door. Was that a good sign? Or bad? Elizabeth and Oliver had come to see if there had been any changes with Rose, and to inform them that the last few guests had finally left the ball. The duke had announced to the crowd that there was no need to be alarmed, but that a family member had suddenly taken ill, and because of that, they would need to end the ball early. Most were staying the night at Dalton Park in the guest wing but the few who lived nearby had departed as soon as the weather had let up.

By that time, the whole family had been informed about exactly who Rose was. None of them seemed angry. None of them peppered him with questions. Everyone was just as solemn and worried about Rose's health as he was. They had fallen in love with her as well.

Eventually, Elizabeth and Oliver left to see to the servants and help close up the ballroom. Felix took up their post in the hallway outside of Rose's room. The man looked every bit as distraught as Carver felt. No one could seem to find any words to say. The silence was thick and heavy and oppressive and felt as if it could swallow him up. Even though he was silent, his thoughts were loud and frantic.

Would she wake up? Had frost bite set in? Would she lose her fingers or toes? Would she ever be able to forgive him for not being there when she needed him?

Just then the door to Rose's room opened, and the doctor slipped out with Mary following closely behind. The doctor did not stop to talk to Carver, only gave a brief nod and then headed for the stairs. Carver watched the procession mutely. Did no one think he deserved to know whether the woman he loved was even alive?

He was just about to demand that the doctor stop and tell him exactly what he knew about Rose when Mary spoke up first. "He has another emergency to see to. I will fill you in," she said in a soft voice. "But first—Robert, please go ask a servant to bring a tea tray. We want to have one ready for when Rose awakens."

"She isn't awake yet?" Carver asked as Robert stepped past him to go find a servant.

Why hadn't she awoken? And at least a hundred other questions buzzed through his mind as he frantically searched for an answer hidden in his sister's obnoxiously calm face.

"No, she hasn't. But Dr. Barton is hopeful that she will soon."

"Does he know what is wrong with her? Is she hurt at all?" And if he shook Mary, would she answer his questions faster?

Mary gestured toward a window seat down the hall with a bench. "Can we sit a moment?" She rested a hand on her middle. "I need a rest while we talk."

"Of course." He followed his sister at a sedate pace that made him want to curse.

She turned to face him after they were seated but still he didn't see any revelations in her eyes. "Until Daphney wakes up, we won't be able to know exactly what happened. But the Doctor was able to assess that she has a sprained ankle and a few bruised ribs, most likely indicating that she was thrown from the horse." Mary was talking slowly as if English was not his first language. "That would explain why you found her on the ground. Dr. Barton suspects that once she was thrown, she had trouble walking from the pain and got trapped in the rain. The rain mixed with the frigid temperatures made her body temperature drop lower than what it should be, resulting in what is called hypothermia."

"I know what hypothermia is. But why is she unconscious?" His knee was bouncing. He felt the need to pace again but didn't give in to the urge.

"Apparently, that is the body's natural response when its temperature gets too low. Before that, she likely could not even think soundly and lost the use of her limbs." Mary paused, her eyes conveying the unspoken message he was looking for a moment ago. "You found her just in time." That was a polite way of saying the woman was half dead when he finally got to her.

Anger boiled inside him. He was not Rose's hero. A hero would have been there at the first sign of trouble. A hero would have asked her why she had been crying instead of selfishly kissing her in the hallway.

As if reading his thoughts, Mary took his hand in hers. "None of this is your fault, Carver."

His fists clenched and his words raced. "Yes—it is. I should have found her sooner. I should have noticed that she wasn't in the ball-room." His voice grew louder, more desperate with each word. "I should never have left her side. I should have been home when she came to see me—,"

"Who?"

"Claire!" he shouted and then felt the weight of her name settle into every inch of that hallway. His face fell blank, and he felt stunned from his own word.

A heavy pause filled the space between him and Mary. When had his thoughts turned back to Claire? But really—they never left her, did they? Not ever. He was a wreck.

He dropped his face in his hands. Mary placed a soft hand on his arm, not saying anything, just letting him process his own words. "I should have been there that day, Mary," Carver spoke into his hands.

He would never be able to forget that fact that if he had just been home when Claire had ridden her horse over to find him, she would not have ridden right back home. Her horse would never had stepped into that rabbit hole and she would have never fallen to her death. If only he had been there…she might be alive today. And if he had been watching out for Rose, she would not be fighting for her life in the next room.

Mary's voice was quiet. "You couldn't have known, Carver. Asking yourself *what if* will not bring her back. It will only continue to torment you. Things in life happen for reasons we will never be able to know. Give yourself the freedom to accept that it happened and know that Claire's decisions were out of your control."

"I can't, Mary. If I accept it...If I say it out loud—then it will be real. She will be gone." His voice shook with barely suppressed emotion. He felt like he was barely holding himself together. Ready to break.

"Carver," the tenderness of Mary's voice wrapped around him. "Claire *is* gone." She rested her hand on his back again. "She won't be coming back. But you do have a woman in the next room who is alive and who loves you."

He felt numb and weary, and couldn't bring himself to say anything. Life was moving around him but he felt trapped in the past. *Claire is gone. She's not coming back.* After a while, Mary patted his arm and then left him alone with his thoughts.

After the rain began to slow and the house settled into a quieter rhythm, Carver was told that he could finally go in to see Rose. He opened the door and found his mother quietly working on her needle-work in the corner of the room. It was a stark contrast to the frenzied chaos of earlier in the evening. Felix had been sitting by her bed holding her still hand, but when the man saw Carver enter he stood and crossed to him. He looked in Carver's eyes and nodded, offering his thanks and blessing. One that Carver did not feel at all worthy of receiving.

He reverently made his way to Rose's side and took the seat beside the bed. Other than the steady and comforting lift and fall of her chest, she did not move. Her golden brown waves cascaded over the pillow making her look more like a woman in a painting than his real-life Rose. Something in him needed reassurance that she was really there and alive. He reached out and gently stroked her blessedly warm fore-head all the way down her soft hair.

A slight pink had returned to her cheeks, removing the last bits of fear from his chest. She would wake up. And the doctor was fully confident that she would make a complete recovery. But would he? Carver wasn't sure he would ever be the same after that night. He felt as if he had lost Claire all over again. But he had been granted another chance with this woman in front of him who he loved very much.

Carver had learned enough about Rose to understand that she deserved and needed a man who could tenderly hold her heart and patiently put back together the pieces that life had torn apart. And for the first time, he could admit that he wasn't strong enough to be that for her. If he continued to pursue her as he was, he would only break her further.

He ran the back of his hand down her warm arm until his fingers clasped around hers. She looked peaceful and light in her sleep. The creases that often rested between her brows were cleared. She was beautiful. He took a deep breath, feeling a resolve settle in his chest. It was time to face the truth he had been avoiding. He leaned in and placed a kiss on her temple and let go of her hand.

Chapter Thirty-Five

T he first thing Rose noticed before opening her eyes was that her body was no longer on the hard cold ground. In fact, wherever she was, felt like heaven. Was this heaven? Had she died? That question was quickly answered by the sudden and massive ache in her head, ankle, and ribs, as well as a general overall discomfort that one might have after being forcefully thrown from a horse.

With a jolt, all of Rose's memory rushed back. Her eyes flew open and she propelled herself up in bed. The pain in her rib came sharp and strong. She winced and caught her hands around her abdomen. Pain coupled with a rush of emotions when she realized that she was no longer out in the cold, freezing to death, but alive and safe in the house. Tears burned her eyes.

"It's alright, Rose. You're safe now," said a comforting voice. But not Carver's voice. And also one that knew her real name. "Lie back down, dear." The duchess's sweet, motherly words went a long way to soothe Rose's nerves. But not as far as Carver's would have gone.

With a hint of nervousness, she looked around the room. *Her room.* The fire was lit, mounds of blankets were lying on top of her, and a man's cravat sat crumpled on a chair by the fire.

"What happened? How did I get back here?" Rose asked.

"Carver found you." That was the Duke's voice. Rose turned her head to the other side of the bed where she found the Duke sitting, poised, with a teacup. He leaned forward and gestured for her to take a sip. The warm liquid burned and soothed her dry, scratchy throat. It felt as if she had not had anything to drink in years.

"A footman notified Henley that you had left during the ball with your valise. Carver went after you immediately, and when Thunder returned without you, he sent a search party out to find you." Rose's eyes flashed to the linen in the chair. It was Carver's cravat. He had saved her. But where was he now?

How stupid and reckless she had been to leave during the night— and in the rain, at that. Rose had been so used to doing everything alone her whole life, that at the time it felt like her only option. But while lying half dead on the ground as cold had seeped into her bones, Rose had decided that she didn't want to do things alone anymore. And if she somehow made it out of that situation alive, she would give others the choice to walk with her through life if they chose to.

She decided to start making good on that promise to herself now. "I'm so sorry. I've lied to all of you. I'm not Daphney Bellows and I'm certainly not a lady." A warm tear slipped down her cheek. "I am nothing but a crook. I steal and I scam and I lie, and although I haven't stolen from you, I have lied about almost everything." She couldn't bear to look them in the eyes. Perhaps she was a coward, but the hurt and disappointment she would find was too much to handle, so instead she looked down to her fidgeting fingers.

"I've been doing it nearly all my life. It's how I first met Carver—I thought he was Lord Newburry and…well, none of that matters right now. All you need to know is that I'm not who you thought I was— who I led you to believe I was. And for that, I'm terribly sorry. I hope that you can forgive me, but if you cannot, I don't blame you."

She paused for a moment and then remembered one important thing. "And at the ball, I saw a Bow Street runner who has been searching for me for years. That's why I left…to get out before he found me. But then Thunder spooked at a bolt of lightening and I lost my seat and it hurt too badly to walk on my ankle." She was getting away from what mattered again.

"But I won't ask you to hide me," she said. "If you see fit to tell him where I am, I will willingly hand myself over to him." There. That was all of it. There was a good chance that Rose was going to be arrested for the declaration, but for some reason, she didn't mind. She wasn't hiding anymore, and, finally, being able to admit the truth felt like an odd sort of freedom. To confess it meant that she didn't have to be that person anymore. She was done with that life.

Rose felt the duchess's hand press on top of hers. She willed herself to meet the woman's eyes. The sight stole her breath. The duchess was smiling—tender and warm. Almost unable to believe what she was seeing was real, she looked over to the duke. He too was smiling.

He picked up her other hand and clasped it in his own. "We know all of that, Rose." He squeezed her hand gently just as Papa used to. "And we also know that you lost your father when you were only a child and were forced to face a harsh world all on your own. We know that you have seen more hardship and pain in your early years than most people see in a lifetime," he said. "We know that you do not own a warm pair of gloves because you are always giving yours away to children who need them." How could he know that? She hadn't even told Carver that she had done that. "Sometimes you go for days without eating because you feel that people around you need the food more than you do. And where most people would keep every penny they stole to ensure their own wellbeing, you give all of yours to the upkeep of an orphanage you opened several years ago."

Rose pursed her lips and tasted the salt of her tears. "How do you know all of this?"

"Cause I told them." Rose snapped her head to the door. Her round, jolly Uncle Felix stood framed in the doorway, smiling like an idiot. A joyful chuckle broke free of her mouth. "Turns out when a duke keeps you closeted in his study for an hour, a man tends to spill his whole budget."

"Uncle Felix!" She let go of the Duke's hand to stretch it out toward her uncle. He took her hand and pressed it firmly with a kiss. "I was so afraid that I was going to die without getting to tell you how much you mean to me. I'm sorry for trying to push you away for so long. I was scared of losing you like I lost Papa." She looked down and squeezed his weathered hand. "You're a good man and a blasted good uncle. And...I love you."

Uncle Felix's eyes welled up but his eyebrows shot up to his hair line. "Well lass, you sure know how to put an old man to the blush. But I'm glad to hear you say it because the truth is, I love you like my own girl. Always have."

She smiled, feeling light and happy and whole for the first time since she was a girl. She looked around the room and her gaze caught the clock on the mantle. She squinted at the time and realized that it was three o'clock in the morning. How long had she been unconscious? And where was that Bow Street runner? She had so many questions and no idea where to start.

But then she thought of someone and a panic rose up within her, "Mary," she said. "Does she know about all of this?" Carver hadn't wanted any stress to fall on his sister. Had Rose's emergency put her pregnancy in danger?

The duchess patted her hand. "She knows. And she said that she thanks you and Carver for trying to spare her the worry, but next time to not be such ninnys as to listen to Robert." The woman chuckled adorably, helping Rose's stiff body relax against the pillow. "Apparently, she knew something was amiss from the first moment you arrived and decided to look into who you really were," said the duchess. "She sent a letter into Bow Street, thinking to hire a man to investigate who you were. But instead she found out there was a con woman by the name of Rose Wakefield who perfectly fit your description.

"At first, she thought about having you arrested. But the more she watched you and Carver together, she realized you both really did love each other. She sent a request for the runner to attend the ball so that she and Robert could talk to him and convince them to burn your records."

Rose's mind was spinning. Mary was the one who had tipped off the runner? And it was all so that she could clear her name?

"And imagine her surprise," the duke added, "when she found out that I, too, had already invited our obliging runner to attend the ball and have a private meeting with me after the festivities had ended."

Rose blinked at the duke, almost unable to believe the family had gone through so much trouble to help her. "Do you mean Miss Gardener hadn't sent for him to have me arrested?"

"No, my dear," the duke laughed. "I doubt that Miss Gardener has enough brains to even know how to go about contacting Bow Street."

"But...I saw them talking," said Rose.

"Yes," said the duchess. "I believe our dear Miss Gardener took a bit of a fancy to the handsome young runner who showed up to talk with Charles."

Rose pushed out a breath and sunk further back into her pillows. There had been absolutely no reason for her to run. These people were not trying to trap her, they were trying to free her. To give her a new start. Rose bit her lip, unwilling to cry anymore.

"And Rose," said the duke. "I was able to convince the runner to drop his pursuit and burn your records. You don't have to hide anymore."

A relief like Rose had never known before swept over her. She tried to hide her eyes with her hands but she could still feel her tears slipping under them. Rose was free. After she had somewhat recovered her embarrassing sob, she said, "I don't know how to thank you. I don't deserve any of this. Or any of you."

The duke smiled and leaned in close as if to share a secret. "Someone once told me that the world is often more gray than black and white. And as such, a person ought to be treated with compassion before justice." He winked. "I think she was right. And I'm happy to be able to give you a second chance at life, Rose. I hope that this time you will know that you are loved and do not have to go it alone anymore."

Rose's smile felt stupid and over-indulgent but she didn't care. Despite her exhaustion, bruises and near death experience, she felt light. Accepted. Loved. And it was all because of Carver and his family. They had given her hope again.

As Rose looked around the room, she remembered that the most important person in the world to her was missing. "Where is Carver?"

Chapter Thirty-Six

An entire week had passed since the night of the accident, and Carver had only been to visit her once. One blasted time. He hadn't stayed long or said particularly much during his time at her bedside, but it was long enough for Rose to notice the dark circles that pressed under his eyes and the sadness that clung to him. She barely knew what to think of it. He was so closed off. So distant and unapproachable. Had he changed his mind? Did he no longer love her? Perhaps he had finally realized how moronic it would be to take her as his wife.

The past week had wrung every drop of emotion out of Rose's heart. Never before had she allowed herself to feel so exposed and aware of her own emotions. In Carver's absence—and mainly because she had been confined to her bed from her various injuries—she had spent the majority of the week in his sisters' company. Rose was touched at the amount of time each sister wanted to spend with her. And it was *her* they wished to spend time with. Not Daphney.

Rose had finally been able to share the details of her life she had kept secret for so long. It was equal parts freeing and exhausting.

"Has Carver ever told you about Claire?" said Oliver, interrupting her conversation with Elizabeth about London parks during one of his and Elizabeth's usual afternoon visits.

She died, were the only words that came to mind. "Not really," she said. Actually, Carver had never even told Rose the woman's name before. But instinctively she knew it was the same woman. "Only that she died three years ago."

"He didn't tell you how?" No. And Rose could never bring herself to ask.

She shook her head and forced her gaze out of the bright sunny window. Everyday had been nothing but glorious beautiful sunlight since that stormy night a week ago. If only Carver had come around to enjoy it with her.

Out of the corner of her eye, Rose noticed Oliver and Elizabeth share a look. Elizabeth nodded as if giving Oliver unspoken permission. "Claire was Carver's very best friend," said Oliver. "Her family's estate shares a boundary line with Dalton Park. They grew up together and loved each other nearly their whole lives. Carver finally proposed to Claire a little over three years ago and she of course accepted." Tension increased with each word. Rose could feel her body stiffening with dread.

"A week after their engagement, she rode her horse over to visit him, but he wasn't home." Oliver swallowed and Rose watched as Elizabeth began fidgeting with her skirt between her fingers. "She returned home instead of waiting for him. Claire always rode neck or nothing, and on the way home, her horse stepped into a rabbit hole and broke its leg." He paused and swallowed. "She was tossed from the saddle and broke her neck. She died instantly. A servant found her first and brought her back here." He paused again and took a breath. "Carver returned from a hunting excursion to find his betrothed dead in his home."

Rose's heart crumbled for him as all of the pieces to his puzzle fell into place. It was why he hadn't wanted to come home. He couldn't face the memory of his loss. It was why he hadn't wanted her to ride his horse. He was afraid she would fall to the same fate. That's when she realized that she *had* almost fallen to the same fate.

What must Carver be going through? Is that why he was avoiding her?

"Thank you for telling me," were the weak words she managed to spit out. Why had he told her all of this?

Oliver nodded and leaned forward in his seat, as if he hadn't even told her the most important part yet. "Carver has been hiding from Claire's death these past few years. I think your accident last week finally made him face it. And when he almost lost you, it nearly broke him." His look only grew. "I—I only tell you this because I hope that by you knowing…you'll be less inclined to give up on him." Give up on him?

It would seem everyone had noticed Carver's distance over the week. As much as Rose wanted to believe that she and Carver did have a future together, and as much as she had grown to love his family as her own, she did have doubts. Not doubts that she loved him and wanted to be his wife, but doubts that he still wanted her.

"I have no doubt that Kenny loves you, Rose." She stiffened. Had she voiced her thoughts out loud? "But I think he's working through the healing that he's needed for a long time. He's pushing all of us away because of it. Carver excels in taking care of others, but he absolutely has no idea how to let others take care of him. I'm confident that once he has some time alone with his feelings, he'll come back to us." His gaze became pointed. "All of us."

∾

Rose had tried to hold on to Oliver's words the past three days. She really had. But when Carver never came to visit her—and then seemed to never leave his room when she was once again able to walk around the house—she had to face the fact that their relationship might truly be over.

She snatched the last dress from her wardrobe and shoved it a bit too forcefully into her valise. All of her emotions were hovering just below the surface and it was getting harder and harder to keep them from showing. She felt anger. Disbelief. And mostly…sadness.

Carver clearly needed the time to heal and Rose was happy to give it to him. But would it have killed him to convey that to her? Did he have to be so entirely inattentive? One smile. One word of hope. One reassuring look was all she needed for her to stay and remain content with his distance.

Even more so, she wished that he would just come to her and let her help him shoulder his grief. She had plenty of experience in that area. But maybe...he just didn't love her enough for that.

She punched a shawl into her valise and felt somewhat better. Finally, she moved to her vanity and opened the bottom drawer. Underneath a handkerchief she found her pistol. She hiked up her skirt and placed it in its familiar holster. She wasn't going to thieve anymore, but that didn't mean she had to completely give up her old way of life. It was nice to know she could protect herself if the need arose.

A small knock at the door made Rose drop her skirt. Her heart raced. Was it him? But then Elizabeth's familiar blonde curls dashed that hope. But still, she was happy to see the girl. They had grown particularly close over the week.

"Can I come in?" asked Elizabeth.

Rose smiled. "Always," and settled on her bed, signaling for Elizabeth to join her.

Elizabeth crossed the room and sat on the bed next to her, tucking her knees up to her chest. That was different. More and more over the course of the week Rose had been able to see a different side of Elizabeth. The girl seemed to constantly be trying to convince everyone as well as herself that she was a woman—no longer the wild, adventurous child. But just now, she seemed to be giving up the fight. Her normally bright face wore a forlorn expression.

"Is something wrong?" asked Rose, reaching out to take Elizabeth's hand. The gesture surprised herself. When had she become so affectionate and soft?

Elizabeth attempted a smile that didn't reach her eyes. "He'll never see me as anything besides his little Lizzie who was constantly stepping in the mud or tearing her dress climbing apple trees." Rose knew exactly who *he* was even though Elizabeth had never spoken of him before. It had become plainly obvious to Rose over the course of the week that Elizabeth was deeply in love with Oliver. It seemed ridiculous that Oliver didn't seem to notice. But then again, it was hard for someone to notice a look that was only cast to the back of one's head.

"You love him," Rose said quietly and with a smile she hoped looked sympathetic.

Elizabeth's eyes rolled away from Rose while blinking back tears. "Yes. But it doesn't matter," she said. "He'll never fall in love with me as he does all of those London dashers. I'll never not be ten years old to him."

Rose pressed her lips together, searching her mind frantically for adequate words. This sister role was completely new for her. Saying the wrong thing seemed like too great a possibility. And yet...Elizabeth had come to her. That said something, didn't it?

"Have you told him how you feel?"

Elizabeth's eyes snapped to hers, wide and frantic. "No! It would change everything." She shook her head in quick movements, her blonde curls bouncing against her face. "No. He must be the one to declare himself if he wishes for our relationship to change. I've no desire to profess my affection, only for him to pat my hand and say, 'oh, my little Lizzie,'" said Elizabeth. "I attend to my pride too willingly to place myself in that position."

Rose could relate. But she also didn't see how a man would know to declare himself if not given at least a small measure of encouragement. She took a minute letting the silence rest comfortably between them as she searched for an answer to the problem.

Finally Rose said, "London!" Elizabeth just blinked her long lashes and Rose decided to expound. "You are having your come out this season in London, are you not?"

"Yes...and I'm dreading it. I get terribly nervous meeting new people," said Elizabeth. "It will be awful. Not only will I have to watch and second-guess my every movement in front of the prying eyes of society, but I will have to watch Oliver dance and flirt his way across every ballroom, all the while returning to my side only to confide in me which debutante he finds the prettiest."

"Well, then I suggest you not be so available for his confidences," said Rose letting her grin twist into something more mischievous.

Elizabeth looked at her from the corner of her eyes. "What do you mean?"

Rose felt like finally her years of studying the art of flirting to effectively con gentleman would serve a purpose—a more noble one. "If you want Oliver to see you as the eligible woman you are, he will need to see that reflected in the eyes of every other gentleman in London."

The creases that formed between Elizabeth's eyes told Rose that the girl...no, *woman*, was contemplating the idea. "So," her words were slow and contemplative, "I need to get other men to wish to marry me so that Oliver will realize that I'm not a little girl anymore?"

"Exactly." Or something like that. "Sometimes, men can be utterly daft. They don't often know what it is they want until it's out of their reach."

"I'm to play with Oliver's emotions, then?"

"No. You are to go to London and enjoy your first season. Don't spend your evenings as a wallflower pining over Oliver. Go on a ride through Hyde Park during the fashionable hour and visit the opera. Flirt. Dance. Socialize."

"And if no one wants to dance with me?"

Rose couldn't hold back her laughter. "Elizabeth, if you are not the most courted woman in all of London this season I will undoubtedly die of shock." Apparently, Kate's drama was wearing off on Rose.

Elizabeth smiled with amusement, but then it turned nervous. "And if it doesn't work? If Oliver doesn't love me after all?" Rose couldn't help but feel that there was a very slim chance of that. But still, Elizabeth should be prepared for such an event. Just as Rose was preparing herself for the very real possibility that she would never see Carver again. But she couldn't think of that just then. Mainly because the thought made her feel sick to her stomach.

"If he doesn't...then it means he wasn't the man for you. And hopefully, you will have found someone who deserves your love." Rose said the words as much for Elizabeth as for herself. Did Elizabeth believe them? Did Rose? She doubted that there was anyone else in the world who she could love as much as Carver.

Elizabeth's eyes moved their focus from Rose to the packed valise behind her. Her eyes snapped back to Rose and her sadness was almost too much to bear. "You're leaving?" Her dark blonde brows pulls together. "You've given up on him, then?"

Rose stood from the bed and smoothed her skirt. "I'll never give up on him, Elizabeth. But I can't continue to stay here if…if he doesn't want me to." It was painful to admit. Especially after she had felt so cherished, wanted and loved by him the week before. "I need to move on and live my new life."

Once again, she was leaving after a job, but this time it was different. She wasn't running away or closing herself off to anyone. Well… she was running a little. Every day that Carver did not visit only brought her more pain. There was a moment where she wondered if it had been worth it, opening herself up to love only to feel the familiar ache of loss, but it didn't take long to answer her question with a yes. It was worth it. Carver was worth it. His family was worth it.

Rose was leaving Dalton Park a stronger and healthier person for having loved and lost. She now had an entire family who she knew she could turn to in need, and that was something she would never regret. And as heartbroken as she was to leave the man she loved behind, Rose felt eager to begin a new phase in her life. And she knew just where to do it.

Chapter Thirty-Seven

C arver stood in front of Claire's grave for the first time since her burial. There was no denying it anymore. She was gone. Yes, she had died three years ago, but for him, it felt like she had died all over again that week. After Rose's accident, Carver had barely left his room. Couldn't leave his room. He felt weary and exhausted. Crying no longer became something that belonged to the gentler sex, but rather something he was fearful would become his constant affliction.

He swallowed and stepped forward to place the bouquet of Claire's favorite yellow flowers at the base of the headstone. He laid it down quickly and stepped back as if the stone might lunge out and bite him. It didn't. All around him birds chirped, the sun smiled over the grass, a subtle warmth that hinted at spring swept over his face, and the day felt exactly opposite of his mood.

The past week, though painful, had finally given him the closure he had been avoiding for so long. It wasn't easy for him to focus his attention on how he felt. Every bit of him wanted to push it all down and run to Rose's side. But he knew he needed that time alone with his thoughts and memories of Claire to finally mourn what had happened so long ago. He had pulled out the box of letters he and Claire had exchanged over the years and allowed the ghosts of memories to haunt him.

He had cried, smiled, laughed, and thrown his fist into his pillow once or twice. It had been an intense week full of emotion that had all lead up to this moment.

This very unemotional moment.

Was it supposed to feel like that? Nothingness? As embarrassing as it was to admit, perhaps he had just cried all of his emotions out already. Maybe if he talked to her, he would feel that high release he had been expecting. That connection and current that he had seen other's feel when they wept at their loved one's graves.

He clenched his jaws and cleared his throat. "Hello, love." He bit his lip. "Have you missed me as much as I've missed you?" The ugly gravestone stared at him. "I'm sorry I haven't been here to visit you yet. I—I've been scared and—," he cut himself off, frustration from his lack of feelings rising in his chest. He kicked a rock and sent it soaring into someone else's grave stone. Hopefully no one saw that. "Blast, this feels uncomfortable." He was no longer talking to the headstone, but himself. "Why do people do this? It's not as if she's going to talk back to me."

"Wouldn't that be frightening if she did?"

Carver's shoulders jumped at the male voice behind him and he whirled around. "Mr. Brighton," he said and offered a quick polite bow to none other than Claire's father. A man who he hadn't seen since the day of the funeral. For how long had Carver had an audience? And had he seen the rock incident?

A sad, empathetic smile tugged at the man's kind face. Carver remembered Mr. Brighton looking old even when he and Claire were young adults. Now, deep wrinkles sat around his eyes and mouth and snow white hair covered his head. Carver felt a strong wave of guilt. He should have gone to visit Claire's family after her death. He should have been stronger. He should have…

"Is this your first time visiting her grave?" The man asked as he came to stand shoulder to shoulder with Carver.

Tension gripped him. "I'm ashamed to admit it, but yes."

"No need to feel ashamed. We all grieve on different timelines. You're here now and that's all that matters," said Mr. Brighton.

Carver glanced at him from the corner of his eye. The silence hung heavy for a minute as the two men stood with hands clasped behind their backs and eyes fixed on the motionless stone. But after several minutes he couldn't take it anymore. His thoughts were nagging at him to say what he felt. So he said, "It—feels…different than I imagined it would." And then paused and tried to figure out exactly what it was that felt so odd about visiting.

"Do you mean that you feel more apathetic than you were expecting?"

"Yes!" Carver said with a measure of relief at being understood. He turned to face Mr. Brighton. "I had expected to feel her here. But I don't…"

"Of course you don't." The man shrugged. "Because she's not here." What did he mean? Was he somehow at the wrong grave site? No. It clearly stated her name right there. Mr. Brighton smiled, clearly seeing his confusion. "What I mean is, her spirit is not here. It lives in heaven now with her Creator and we all know that. She will live on in our memories but she's not confined to this stone and oppressive cemetery." Mr. Brighton's eyebrows lifted as he surveyed the bleak surroundings. "And that gives me great comfort."

Carver looked back at the grey, lifeless headstone. "Claire was certainly the opposite of this place. She was joy itself."

Mr. Brighton chuckled softly. "That she was. The girl never sat still. Her mother gave up on Claire ever learning to accomplish a pretty stitch before she was even out of the schoolroom."

Carver found himself smiling and even chuckling. He realized that this was the first time since her death that he had been able to talk about Claire with a smile. To enjoy the memory of who she had been without the overwhelming regret of who she would never be.

"Mr. Brighton." He turned to face the man who at one time was like a second father to him. "I'm so sorry that I went to London after Claire died. And I'm sorry that I haven't been by to visit you or Mrs. Brighton since then," said Carver. "Truth be told, I—haven't been able to truly come to terms with her death until recently. I've…had a difficult time of it." But he felt stupid and like the worst sort of person admitting that to Claire's father. The man likely struggled with Claire's loss even more than he did.

Mr. Brighton turned and put his hand on Carver's shoulder. "Like I said before, there's no need to apologize. We understand. We all heal in our own time and our own way. I'm just sorry to hear that you've been struggling." He took a breath. "You and Claire loved each other deeply. Those wounds don't heal overnight."

"Are yours healed?" Was that too personal to ask? Likely the man hadn't come to Claire's grave so that he could be prodded with questions. But when standing there next to the only other man in the world who had been so affected by Claire's loss, he felt that he had to ask.

Mr. Brighton's arm slid from Carver's shoulder as he turned to thoughtfully gaze back at his daughter's headstone. "I think so—yes." He paused a moment and then added, "But that doesn't mean I don't miss my girl every single day. At first, I thought the pain of losing her would swallow me up. But over time, I learned to take great comfort in the fact that she's where her soul has always longed to be." He paused and his brows pulled together. "Coming to terms with her death looked different than I thought it would. It's not that I've ever become comfortable with her death—and I don't think I ever will—but Mrs. Brighton and I have learned that *we* will be well even though Claire is not with us anymore." The man turned his weathered eyes to Carver and pierced him with his gaze. "And, you're going to be well, too."

"Sometimes it doesn't feel like it." The honest answer left his mouth before he had time to consider it.

"I know. But you will. Let yourself hurt when you feel pain, and smile when you feel like smiling. Little by little, you'll find that the smiles eclipse the tears. And," his voice was thick with sincerity, "if ever the day comes that you find a woman who makes your heart feel alive again, don't push her away. Claire wouldn't have wanted that." How did he know? Carver swallowed down the lump in his throat. Something about those words gave him the permission he hadn't realized he needed.

"And if I have found her already?" Carver asked, desperate for approval from the only connection to Claire he still had.

A warm smile pulled at Mr. Brighton's mouth. "Marry her. If you are waiting for the day that you no longer feel broken to marry, you'll die a single man. Unfortunately, life gives us more pain than we can carry sometimes. But thankfully we're given other people to help carry it. Let her help you. And I'm sure she's got plenty of burdens for you to shoulder too."

Mr. Brighton stepped away from Carver to kiss his fingers and then place them on Claire's headstone. He turned back to Carver with a mischievous smirk that didn't exactly fit the setting. "Never thought I'd kiss a rock, but here we are." He winked and then slapped Carver on the back. "It was good to see you, Carver. Come by anytime you want to talk."

"Thank you, Mr. Brighton. It was good to see you too." And exactly what he had needed.

Carver remained at Claire's grave for several minutes after Mr. Brighton had left. The man's words continued to swirl around and around his head until he felt like he understood them. And slowly, his mood felt as if it matched the day around him.

Claire was really gone, but he was going to be okay without her. He was *allowed* to be okay without her.

He mimicked Mr. Brighton's gesture and placed a kiss on Claire's headstone. He allowed himself to imagine her smiling at him and remembered the way her infectious laugh bubbled out of her. She was gone, but he could hold on to the joy they had shared together.

"Goodbye, love." His voice broke as he said the words but they still felt right. They felt like closure.

~

Carver flung open the door of his father's study and stormed inside.

The duke looked up from behind his desk and noticed Carver's determined strides. "Carver," he said, jumping up from his chair behind the desk. "What's happened?" Every muscle in his father's body looked poised for battle.

"Rose is gone," Carver said loudly as if he were announcing the start of another war. In some ways, he felt like he was.

His father's shoulders relaxed. "Oh, that." He put his hand over his chest as if to still his heart while retaking his seat. What was he thinking? Now was not the time to sit down!

"What do you mean, *Oh, that?* The love of my life has left and I have not a clue in the world where she has gone."

His father just obnoxiously settled his spectacles back on the bridge of his nose and looked down at whatever unimportant thing he had been reading before. "Take a damper, son."

"Take a damper?" And now he could add repeating everything someone said to the list of unfortunate traits he had collected that week. "Why should I do that?" Did his Father not wish for him to marry Rose after all? Did he think she wasn't eligible enough?

"Because I'm afraid you are going to feel like a fool when I tell you that *the woman you love* left three days ago." A leveling glare found its way over his father's spectacles.

"Oh." Carver sunk down in a chair, feeling all of the momentum and energy from a moment ago leave him. Rose was gone. He looked up and didn't like the way that deuced wolf was mocking him so he stood up again and started pacing the room. "I suppose I haven't been the most aware of Rose's movements this past week."

His father tipped his brows. "That's one way of putting it." And then put down the paper. He focused all of his attention on Carver and for the first time in three years, Carver felt as if his father was unafraid to tell him what he thought. "None of us begrudged you the time you needed this past week, Carver. But neither did we begrudge Rose her decision to leave when she felt unwanted by the man who had supposedly loved her." Carver winced.

Unwanted. That couldn't be further from the truth. He wanted her with every fiber of his being. And it made him feel sick to think that she felt in any way undesired by him. "I didn't mean to push her away," he said, his voice low and heavy with the remorse he felt. "I only hoped to put myself back together before I married her."

His father smiled and Carver felt relieved that the barrier he had placed between himself and his father was gone now. He had missed him. Needed his honesty. "I appreciate you trying to be honorable. But in this case, that was a stupid decision." The duke had never been one to mince matters. He stood up and leaned against his desk, folding his arms across his chest, fully leaning back into his role of protector, teacher, and father. "What do you intend to do when you experience hardship and trials during marriage? Leave her until you can sort out your pain on your own? If you're going to marry her, you need to be able to talk to her about what you're going through. She deserves your honesty and vulnerability."

"I know she does," said Carver, rubbing a hand over his face. "I'm afraid it's too late." He pushed his hand through his hair and began to pace again. "I need to find her, but I have no idea where to start looking. I suppose London would be a good place." He froze. "But what if she took a position in service? She wasn't going to go back to her old life. She could be anywhere in England by now." His newfound hopes were sinking with every word. "Perhaps I could hire another runner to seek her out. But that comes with the risk of opening back up her old crimes and I doubt she would be too pleased if I did that." But what other choice did he have? She felt lost to him.

"Or..." His father's voice cut through his despair. He lazily held up a small piece of paper between two fingers. "You could just follow the direction she wrote down for us before she left."

Chapter Thirty-Eight

I t had been almost two weeks since Rose had left Dalton Park. Her heart still ached at the thought of never seeing Carver again, and her stomach fluttered with hope every time there was a knock on the door. But it was never him.

Despite missing Carver, Rose had truly begun enjoying her new life. She and Uncle Felix had left Dalton Park and ridden straight to Hopewood Orphanage. And with the Duke of Dalton's recent patronage, Rose and Uncle Felix were able to see to the needs of the children and staff without having to steal a single penny. The Duke had even provided enough funds to have major repairs made to the small orphanage as well as purchasing a neighboring estate so that they could begin expanding the number of children they were able to take in.

They were even gifted enough funds to be able to take on a new staff member. After having Uncle Felix's brother send word that a position as a nursemaid in a small orphanage was being offered to her, Daphney Bellows had written to accept the position and was due to arrive any day.

For the first time in her adult life, Rose had a home and a life she could be proud of. She finally allowed herself the freedom of getting to know each of the children in the orphanage and letting them know her.

All of the children had been rescued from similar situations to the one she had lived as a child. Having understood their hurts, fears, and even nightmares, she had bonded quickly with the children. She loved them.

Rose was really living and no longer pretending or hiding from anyone. Except for just then. Rose actually *was* hiding in a coat closet.

"I found you's, Miss Rosie!" said little John as he flung open the door to the closet, allowing light to spill over her. Laugher fled from her chest as she wrapped her arms around the proud little boy. "Very good, John! That took you no time at all."

Two more children fluttered up behind John, congratulating him on his victory, bouncing and squealing with excitement. The joy she felt was real and tangible and presented itself in the form of dimpled little urchins squealing in an entryway.

The only way she could be any happier was if…

Knock knock knock.

No. It couldn't be. Rose swallowed and forced the flutters in her stomach to still. *It's not him.* Would she ever be able to hear a knock on the door without silently hoping she would find Carver on the other side?

"Run along and wash up for dinner, now," she said, shooing the children up the stairs. "Uncle Felix will be back from town any minute and he will expect to see thirty clean and smiling children!" That last bit she had to yell up the stairs after the children running away from her.

Rose turned back toward the door and took a deep breath. She crossed the creaky floor, smoothed her apron, and braced herself for the disappoint she would feel after she opened the door.

Disappointment never found her.

"Carver," she said in little more than a whisper when she opened the door to the handsome mountain of a man she loved. Was it really him? Or was she just going mad and conjuring him up in her mind? "What are you doing here?"

The warm afternoon sunlight glistened over his wavy hair and kissed the tops of strong shoulders, only highlighting the man's handsome form.

He smiled rakishly, crossed his arms and leaned against the threshold of the open door. Rose's heart felt like it would burst from her chest. "You never answered my question." His carefree attitude felt completely opposite to Rose's frenzied nerves.

"What question?" Her words came out breathless and broken. Probably because she was actually holding her breath.

"Will you marry me?"

She released her breath and her worries and her fears. But words. She needed to say words. Unfortunately, she couldn't pick any out of the endless swirling stream of them flowing around in her mind. And her legs felt weak. She had hoped and dreamed of this moment over and over again, and now it felt almost unreal.

Carver stepped through the door and took her hands, proving that he was really there and not just her imagination. "Rose, my love." The aching tenderness she heard in his voice wrenched at her. Tears began streaming from her eyes. "I'm so sorry for my inattentiveness the week after your accident." But he was there now and somehow, that's all that mattered to her.

She shook her head to protest, knowing that he had an excellent excuse for being inattentive, but he stopped her. "No, please, let me say this." He paused to take a breath, and she shut her mouth. "After your accident, I was forced to see just how much pain and grief I had not yet faced concerning Claire." He looked as if he had just realized that Rose might not know who Claire was. "Claire was my fiancé who died three years ago. And although I did need to finally seek the closure, I shouldn't have pushed you or my family away while I found it. Part of me was scared that if you saw how weak and vulnerable I was, you wouldn't think I was strong enough to love you like you deserve. And also, that you would think, by my still loving Claire, that somehow meant I didn't truly and deeply love you."

Rose stepped forward, closing the gap between them emotionally and physically. "Carver, I know all about Claire. You can thank Oliver for that." She smiled a little, hoping to ease some of his tension. "I never need you to pretend you do not still love her. I know that your love for her does not take away from the feelings you have for me now." She reached up and touched his jaw feeling a bit of stubble beneath her fingers. "I don't want a husband who is flawless and free of hurts. What a dead bore you would be," she smirked and then let it fall away. "I want a husband who will love me enough to let me walk with him through the hard times as well as the good. Who will need and want me just as much as I need and want him."

He smiled and took her face in his hands. His grey eyes burned into hers and the warmth of his hands sent a tingle through her entire body. "Rose Amelia Wakefield, I need you. I want you. I want you when we are laughing and when we are crying. I want to hold you every day for the rest of my life. I want to love you like you deserve to be loved. And I want to be honest and true with you always and forever. Will you be my wife?"

Rose was smiling up at him like a fool. Like someone who had just found a stream after days in a desert. Tears stung her eyes and her emotions kept her from speaking. She pursed her lips together and nodded her acceptance.

Carver's arms were around her waist as he lifted her into the air. He twirled her around and then set her down. Before she had time to catch her breath, he was pulling her up close and kissing her. This one was completely different from the last. It was breathless and urgent. Her arms clasped around his neck and everything slowed. The world spun on end. Sounds all faded. It was just her and Carver as he kissed her with a flame that only the promise of forever could produce.

Finally, Carver broke away and pressed his forehead to hers. He smiled with his eyes in that way that only he could, and Rose fell for him all over again. She raised on her tip toes and gave him one more chaste kiss. He lowered his brows and eyed her as if he held a wonderful secret. "Tell me, my love, do you keep a vicar around here anywhere?"

She laughed a little skeptically. "What? Why?"

He smiled both joyfully and mischievously as he ran his calloused thumb over her bottom lip. "What? Did you really think I would make a romantic speech like that and not have the forethought to procure a special license first? Really, darling, I'm ashamed at how much you underestimate me."

Was he joking? Her heart begun racing and in that very moment, Uncle Felix decided to step into the room.

"Kensworth! Devilish glad to see you!"

Carver did not release her or even look away so she didn't either. But out of the corner of her eye she could see Uncle Felix rock back and forth on he heels.

"Felix. Always a pleasure," said Carver still not taking his eyes off of her. "You wouldn't happen to have a vicar in the area we could send for, would you?"

Rose's mouth fell open. "You are serious. You mean to marry me tonight?"

He smiled bigger and then raised her hand to kiss her palm. "Now, in fact."

"Do we?" Uncle Felix's voice boomed. "The good vicar lives just a few houses down the way! I'll go fetch him m'self. Do you mean to shackle yourself to my Rosie girl tonight?"

"I do."

"Well, I say it's a dashed good thing. The girl's been in the mops all week. This is just the thing to put her to rights, if you ask me." And then he was gone and Rose and Carver couldn't contain their laughter.

But then a thought struck her, and she pushed away from Carver. But he was unfairly strong and did not budge, only pulled her back to him. "Carver, we can't get married tonight."

"Why not?" His expression was too serious to be serious.

"Because...your family." Carver's family already felt like her own. She loved them and it would be wrong to not have them present at something as monumental as their wedding. "I don't want to get married without them. They..." she paused and bit her lip feeling it a little difficult to admit all of her feelings. She was still new to the concept. "They mean too much to me."

A warm, heart-melting smile spread over his face. "Well then it's lucky for you that I've brought them. Why do you think it took me so long to get to you? Mary and Robert had already returned to their estate, so I had to go retrieve them before coming here."

Her eyes widened and then snapped to the movement just beyond the door they had yet to shut. Sure enough, everyone, including Oliver, was making their way up the front stairs.

She gasped and looked back at Carver with a horrifying thought. "Have they been just outside that door the whole time?"

He winced apologetically. "Sorry about that. I sort of forgot they were waiting."

Oliver sprung through the door and slapped Carver on the back. "But there is no chance that we will ever forget *that*."

Rose's face burned with embarrassment but it quickly faded when everyone began giving their congratulations.

They were all buzzing with laughter and conversation, but Rose took a moment to slip back away from everyone. She paused in the entrance of the door and allowed herself a minute to imagine what it would be like if just maybe she stayed.

Sunlight poured into the room as her eyes lingered over the family, the orphanage, and the future that she could see with perfect clarity. She and Carver would live together in the orphanage, caring for the children and seeing to their futures. The family would come to visit often and Rose would always request that her new mother bring with them a bundle of flowers from Dalton Park's greenhouse. Rose would finally get the chance to make sure the vase was always filled with water. But most of all, they would be happy.

Carver caught her eye and smiled. What she saw was beautiful and exactly the life she wanted. Rose stepped back inside and shut the door.

THE END

Acknowledgments

This book is only in your hands today because of the tremendous amount of support and encouragement I received from the following people:

Thank you to my family for all of the days you cheered me on, watched my daughters so I could write, and encouraged me not to give up. Thanks, Mom and Dad, for always encouraging my dreams and buying me endless amounts of blank journals.

To all of my Sweet Regency Romance writing friends, thank you for your inspiring stories, advice, critiques, venting sessions, and pep talks (looking at you, Martha Keyes.) I couldn't write in a better genre!

Thank you to my amazing beta readers: Kari Kulak, Kadi Tingle, Casey Smith, and Ashtyn Newbold. You guys read my manuscript when it was riddled with typos, too many crazy historical phrases, and an inconsistent plot; and for some reason, didn't make me throw it away right then. Thank you for seeing through the mess and telling me to keep going!

To my editor, Emily Poole, you are the real star. Thank you for your attention to detail and for making my words better than I could have imagined.

Ember and Reese, I love you more than anything. And thank you for not giving up your naps yet so I could write this book.

And most importantly, my super good looking husband, Chris Adams. Thank you for all the sacrifices you made so that I could follow my dream. I decided I was going to marry you from the first day we met, and it was the best decision I've ever made—even though I know you will likely read this entire book in the voice of Mrs. Featherbottom.

And lastly, my amazing readers, thank you for taking a chance on this book! I hope I was able to give you a few enjoyable hours without thinking of laundry, dishes, or your child's homework.

-Sarah

Also by Sarah Adams

It Happened in Charleston Duology:

The Match: A Romantic Comedy (book 1)

The Enemy: A romantic Comedy (book 2)

It Happened in Nashville Duology:

The Off Limits Rule (book 1)

The Temporary Roomie (book 2)

Standalone Romcoms:

The Cheat Sheet

Regency Romances:

To Con A Gentleman

To Catch A Suitor

About the Author

Born and raised in Nashville TN, Sarah Adams loves her family, warm days, and making people smile.

Sarah has dreamed of being a writer since she was a girl, but finally wrote her first novel when her daughters were napping and she no longer had any excuses to put it off.

Sarah is a coffee addict, a British history nerd, a mom of two daughters, married to her best friend, and an indecisive introvert. Her hope is to always write stories that make you laugh, maybe even cry; but always leave you happier than when you started reading.

Made in the USA
Middletown, DE
19 August 2024

59413325R00170